'Heart breaking and then heart mending. *Bradington Bay* is a story of family legacy and the minefield that is adolescence as a gay man in a largely homophobic world. This is the type of redemptive story needed today more than ever.'

Carlos Dews, author of *Hush: A Fiction*

'A wry, humane, expansive and searching debut exploring home, yearning and loss through a cast of unforgettable characters.'

James McDermott

'The love-child of Cheever and Updike. Its godparents are Edmund White and Alice Hoffman."

Stephen Dunn, author of *The Light of the Body*

Bradington Bay

Alaric Mark Lewis

**Story
Machine**

Print ISBN: 9781912665167
Ebook ISBN: 9781912665174
Published by Story Machine
130 Silver Road, Norwich, NR3 4TG;
www.storymachines.co.uk

Set in Garamond.

Printed and bound in the UK by Seacourt Ltd.

Story Machine is committed to planet positive publishing. Our world is better off for every single book we print.

Story Machine is committed to the environment.
This book is printed using processes that are:

100% carbon positive | 100% EMAS | 100% renewable energy | 100% ISO14001 | 100% eco-friendly simltri® toner | 100% recycled FSC® stock | Zer0% waste in landfill

Printed by **seacourt** – proud to be counted amongst the top environmental printers in the world

Bradington Bay

Alaric Mark Lewis

For Kathy

Prologue

In January of 1983, Edward James Allerton Bradington IV hatched a conspiracy to commit academic fraud. As conspiracies go it was rather simple: Edward would approach a stuttering-but-brilliant scholarship student from Winston-Salem, North Carolina and offer him money to write a paper on *The Odyssey*. But as is often the case with conspiracies, straightforward simplicity gave way to a series of twists and turns that would involve not only the two boys but also Edward's cousin Annabel, credit card fraud, and Krispy Kreme doughnuts.

It should probably be noted that Edward was not a substandard student – on the contrary he was in the top quarter of his class. He reached out to his co-conspirator because he just couldn't be bothered to do the work, couldn't even feign an interest in the comings and goings of Odysseus. Edward's mind and heart were elsewhere, and his privilege instilled in him the confidence that he could sit this exercise out without really having to face any consequences. Even if he were caught, he surmised, nothing would come of this infraction, his wealth protecting him like the veil of the sea nymph Ino (about whom Edward knew next to nothing).

An agreement was made: the paper would be delivered for the not-insignificant price of $150 plus a dozen warm Krispy Kreme doughnuts. Edward agreed to pay half of the money up front, and the other half and the doughnuts upon completion of the paper.

The paper was a triumph, truly capturing Edward's own style, and he happily forked over the remaining $75. The unforeseen problem was the delivery of the warm doughnuts. Unfortunately, at the time Krispy Kreme doughnuts were only available in the southeast, some eight hundred miles away. That was challenge enough, but the stipulation that the doughnuts had to be *warm* significantly elevated the complexity.

Edward immediately called his cousin Annabel, who was overjoyed to be of some seedy service to her seemingly perfect cousin. She loved the idea that she would have something to hang over his head, stole her mother's credit card, and booked two round-trip tickets from Boston to Winston-Salem.

On a free weekend, a car was arranged to pick up the two academic fraudsters and drive them to Logan Airport. At first feeling churlish that he been played, Edward soon gave into the nerdy charm of his travel companion. As they had very little in common, their conversation revolved mainly around – of all things – *The Odyssey*, and their discourse was so stimulating that Edward almost wished he had read it.

But more than any grand insight into hexameter, what Edward discovered on that trip was simply how enjoyable life could be if he paid attention to the journey and – most importantly – to the people who could crop up like a pack of pleasant Phaeacians along the way. Sitting with his rather improbable new friend whose enthusiastic, pimply face was bathed in the red glow of the "hot doughnuts now" sign, Edward realized that they were out there – these experiences, these improbable friends, this courage. And he learned that journeys could begin whenever he allowed himself to be gently moved by fate's hand.

So it was that fate began to stir in the fall of 2012 in a

hurricane's violent winds and Edward stepping in to help his father. Sea terrors and a father's rescue? Had Edward actually read *The Odyssey* he might have suspected that his life was about to become positively Homeric.

Chapter One: 2012

The rains at first seemed almost gentle. Sitting in a small but well-lit conference room with his anxious client, Edward remarked that the water which ran down the windows in sheets didn't seem too bad; he'd seen worse. His client – Julie? Judy? He'd have to look at her file – didn't appear to take much comfort in his words. He didn't care, really. He was there to make both her and her soon-to-be-ex-husband pay through the teeth.

Edward had never planned on becoming a divorce attorney. It had always been assumed that he would do corporate, working for a few years in some prestigious firm before getting involved in the running of the assortment of his family's enterprises as an only son and heir should. But just as he was finishing law school a CFO of one of his father's businesses embarked upon a rather contentious divorce and hearing the details of it piqued his interest. Edward had always loved a good story (especially if it was about other people's drama and not his own) and he ended up in family law, specializing in divorce. Even if he had now been working in that field for twenty years, his father still seemed to regard it as a phase and, since Edward was making ridiculous amounts of money, tolerated his choice.

But no one – including Edward – had counted on him *liking* divorce law so much. Maybe because he didn't really need the money or maybe because wading into the brambles of other people's lives meant he could avoid the thornier parts of his own, he viewed his professional life much like a game. He treated the women who hired him – his clients were almost all women – much like pieces on a game board: after rolling the dice he would gently move them where they needed to be. "You're heartless," Ben, his romantic partner of three years, once said to Edward when he was discussing the details of a particularly salacious case; he was visibly horrified when Edward responded with "Thank you."

"They're late," Julie or Judy said, looking at her Cartier watch.

Edward smiled and placed his hand on her arm like a parent dismissing the anxiety of a child. The opposing lawyer was playing the game in much the same way that they all did – according to time-honored rules that Edward, personally, found ridiculous. *Meet in a neutral place so that no one has the upper hand.* Edward chose to meet at the offices of opposing counsel as their confidence in the home-court advantage made them sloppy. *Women should wear business casual in muted colors.* Edward advised his clients to wear cocktail dresses and expensive jewelry as it frequently produced an unbalancing impact on the husband. *If possible, avoid any emotional displays.* Edward actually tried to wind his clients up, as emotional displays frequently brought an embarrassed surrender from the other side.

Although he knew what he did was almost always horribly sad and quite frequently downright sordid, the game thrilled him so much that he was able to ignore the sordid sadness, was able to get to the point where he saw the institution of marriage itself as little more than part of the game.

He himself had never married, having grown up in a time and environment when such things weren't even considered for gay men. There had been boys, of course. Lots and lots of boys. But Edward had never seriously considered anything permanent with them. Ben was the only one with whom he had ever shared a home. Although Edward had been forthright about the fact that he didn't ever want to settle into anything more permanent (and Ben had said he accepted that), in the past few month cracks had been appearing. Edward believed – not in some religiously dogmatic way, but rather in that way that *things just were* – that only married couples had children. And since Edward would never marry, the syllogistic conclusion was quite evident.

Evident to Edward, of course. Over time Ben seemed to become less tolerant of Edward's philosophy. A silence had grown between them, the not-mentioning of something becoming a clashing cymbal that, when combined with the cacophonous din of shattered expectations, was leaving little peace in their home.

His phone buzzed in his pocket. It would be Ben. "I need to take this," he said to Julie or Judy before stepping out into the hallway. "Hello."

"Where are you? We need to leave for the luncheon in fifteen minutes."

"I think you're going to have to go to this one without me. We're still waiting for the other side to show up."

The silence that Edward had grown so accustomed to was ringing once again. Seconds went by before Ben spoke. "This was really important to me."

Edward hoped that he could detect some sadness skittling like a water spider on the surface of Ben's words, misguided but harmless. Instead, there was only coldness, the water had turned to ice.

"I know it was, and I'm really sorry, but there's not a lot I can do about it. It's just one of those things that comes with my job. Please don't be angry. I'll make it up to you, I promise. You go without me, and I'll see you at home later tonight. We can have a late supper at Angelica's and talk about vacation. Just think, Benny: two whole months of lying on our asses in the sun somewhere."

More silence.

"Don't bother with supper reservations," Ben replied, "I'm going to go out with Michelle and Larry tonight. Don't wait up."

"OK," Edward replied, trying to sound cheery, as if everything was fine and no one was unhappy.

"Later," said Ben before the click that brought another different, though equally troubling, silence.

Edward turned around to see his client's husband and lawyer walking down the hall. He couldn't play the game if his head wasn't in it, so he banished any thoughts of his own disintegrating relationship and turned his attention back to the matter at hand. "Fuck him," he said under his breath, and he was already so into the game that even he didn't know who he was talking about.

Later, back at the office so as to avoid Ben, Edward's phone buzzed in his pocket again. High from the afternoon's meeting – he had fucking *slayed* it – he was sure his winning streak was continuing and that it was a penitent Ben on the other end but was surprised to see that his father was calling.

"Dad?"

"Did I catch you at a bad time?"

"Not really. What's up?"

"Well, I've had a little spill."

"A little spill? What the hell does that mean?"

"Calm down – Jesus, you love the drama. I was getting out of the Jacuzzi earlier tonight and I slipped and fell. It's nothing serious, but I've got a hairline fracture in my hip. I'm at the hospital now. It's not a big deal, but I do have to rest up for a while."

"Where was your wife?"

"She's right here."

"No, where *was* she when you fell?"

"At bridge. What the hell does that matter?"

"Well, Dad, you're not thirty years old anymore. And don't tell me that you still work twelve-hour days – I know you do. It's just … well … what's the use of having a wife who is so much younger than you if she can't look after you?"

"I don't need looking after, you goddamned know-it-all. These things happen. You never fall?"

"Yes, of course I fall. But I don't break a hip when I do."

"It's a small fracture – you can barely see it on an X-ray. It was bad luck – I just happened to land the wrong way, that's all. Don't be an ass."

"Right. Anyway, do you need something? Do you want me to fly out?"

"Of course not – I'm fine. The only problem is that I'm not going to be able to make it to Bradington for Founders Day. There's never been a Bradington Founders Day without a Bradington family member present to do our part. Never – not even during *both* of the World Wars. I don't want this year to be the first. I'll need you to go."

"You mean, like, go do all those silly rituals and all that? Are you serious?"

"Don't be an ass, Eddie. Pardon me if I sound like a curmudgeon, but there are such things as tradition and honor left in the world. It's important to the people of Bradington. It's important to me."

His voice cracked, and images of his father as a young man washed over Edward, memories of a man who was once caring and light-hearted, but now a man whom life seemed to have hardened more than most. Hearing his father's voice like that momentarily instilled a strange kind of hope in Edward that the father of his childhood was still in there somehow, even if he had been difficult to see for many years.

"Yes, Dad, of course I'll go. Is it still Thanksgiving weekend?"

"Yes."

"OK. I've been needing a vacation, so I'll probably go somewhere else first – Antibes or someplace sunny – but I'll make sure I get there by then."

"OK. Thank you. It means a lot to me. I'll give Leo Koester your phone number – he'll be in touch with the details. Talk to you later, son."

"OK Dad. Bye."

Edward hung up, feeling like he maybe should have told his father he loved him.

He didn't end up leaving the office until after midnight but was surprised to see the streets so deserted; people must have really been worrying about the hurricane. Walking up Broadway he was stopped by a young woman with a baby in her arms, big eyes looking around calmly while its mother's signaled fear and panic with every blink.

"Excuse me," she said, on the point of tears, "I'm not from this neighborhood, but I heard there was a Duane Reade in these parts that still had flashlights. You don't know where it is, do you?"

"No, I'm sorry, I don't." Edward walked the same street twice a day every day, but, outside of the café where he got his morning coffee, rarely noticed anything. He liked walking and not seeing, thinking himself a part of the city somehow without feeling bound to it. "Is it really supposed to be that bad? The hurricane, I mean?"

The woman gave him an incredulous stare. "Haven't you seen the news? They're *evacuating* parts of the city!" She stretched out the word *evacuating* so that each syllable was equal, like a third grader sounding out a big word.

And then, looking up and holding her free hand out, palm up, she said, "Great. It's beginning to rain again."

She ran off without another word, her baby bouncing up and down like a kid playing on a trampoline.

He was completely soaked by the time he arrived home. Knowing that Ben would not be pleased if he dripped water all over the new parquet, he stripped naked in the hallway. Rummaging around for his keys he thought how funny it would be if Mrs. Dawson in 14B – a sour-faced old woman who smelled of cinnamon but made it seem like disappointment's perfume itself – happened to come out at that moment and find him, totally nude, in the hallway. But he entered the apartment without being seen.

"Ben? You here?" The apartment was dark and silent. Relieved, he grabbed a beer from the fridge, went into the bathroom and stepped into the shower. He drank the beer slowly, relishing the sensation of its coolness sliding down his throat while the hot water cascaded down his body.

He finished, wrapped a towel around his waist, and went into the living room to watch CNN. The hurricane was, indeed, due to hit New York later that morning. The woman on Broadway had apparently not been overdramatic. He looked at the clock on the wall: 12:51. Where was Ben? Edward wasn't really worried, but he did wonder if he *should* have been worried.

His phone rang and he saw Ben's familiar smiling face appear on the screen.

"Hey you. I was beginning to get worried. The wind is really picking up outside. Where are you?"

Silence.

"Hello? Ben? Everything OK?"

Silence.

"Listen, I think we've got a bad connection – god-damned AT&T. Hang up and I'll call you back."

"No, I'm here." Ben's voice was soft, distant. "I'm staying with Larry and Michelle."

"If this thing is as bad as they say it's going to be, that's probably a good idea."

Silence.

"The worst is supposed to happen tonight – early this morning, actually – so we'll make plans when you get home tomorrow. There might be some trouble at the airports, but we'll figure it out."

Silence.

"Listen, Ben, is everything OK? You're not saying much."

"I'm staying with Larry and Michelle," Ben repeated.

"I know."

"Let me finish. I'm staying with Larry and Michelle for a while. I'm not going on vacation with you. We've got some serious problems, Edward, and I need some time away from you to sort them out."

"Wow," was all Edward managed to say.

"It's just that I don't feel like we're moving forward. We're just sort of stuck. It's something I've felt for quite some time."

"OK," Edward said. He looked at his feet crossed on the coffee table in front of him and noticed that he needed to trim his toenails.

"So, you take off. Go on vacation. I'm going out to Southampton with Michelle. When you get back, we'll see where we are."

"OK, if that's what you want."

"Well, obviously, Edward, it's not what I *want*, but it's

the way it's got to be."

Edward sat up straight as if talking to a client, getting back in the game. "Listen," he said, "if all of this is just a way to break up with me in stages, I guess I'd prefer you just did it now, you know? If you think that the probability is that when we get back from vacation, you're just going to pack up your things and leave, then you may as well let me know now. If you're sincere about this whole time away and thinking thing – fine. We'll do that."

"*I'm* always sincere," Ben countered.

"And I'm not?"

"I didn't say that."

"No, but your stress suggested that, didn't it? I've always been honest with you."

"Whatever."

"Whatever my ass. Tell me! Tell me when I haven't been honest with you!" Edward's voice raised with the indignation of a liar caught in a lie.

"Look, Edward, it's late and there's a hurricane. I don't want to discuss this now."

"Well maybe I do."

"I don't care, Edward. I'm going to hang up now. We'll talk when you get back."

"Yeah, we'll see."

"Goodbye, Edward."

"Goodbye, Ben."

Silence.

He opened another beer and turned his attention back to the television. A reporter somewhere in Delaware was standing screaming into a microphone while rain pelted him in the face. Onlookers were waving and mugging for the camera; what kind of idiots chased after disasters just to get on TV?

He watched television and drank beer until the power

went out. Ben was mad for candles – Edward teased him that the number of candles and pillows they had spoke more about the gayness of the apartment than the fact that two men were having sex in it – so Edward lit several of them and just sat, staring into space, able to enjoy the sound of the wind outside even if he knew that it could well be causing harm to someone. On top of the piano across the room, photographs of family and friends seemed to dance in the flickering light. One photograph of his mother's parents stood out.

It would have been taken in 1971 or 1972 and it was certainly taken at the Bay, because he recognized the pattern on the wallpaper from the kitchen: rows and rows of old-fashioned percolator coffee pots sitting on tables with checked tablecloths. How many times, sitting at the table, being tutted over by Grams, had he imagined how many cups of coffee could be poured from all of those pots, how many hours of conversation and laughter and dirty jokes and occasional quarrels they would fuel? Enough coffee, surely, to fill the bay that lapped up against the grand house's stilted wrap-around porch.

In the photo Gramps and Grams are sitting in the kitchen, chairs facing away from the table, bodies blocking what is surely a coffee pot not unlike the hundreds on the wallpaper around them. Gramps' mouth is open in a big talk-smile, as if he were in the midst of a story, or teasing Grams, or some combination of both.

Gramps' arm is draped around Grams, who is looking straight-on into the camera, annoyed, lips pursed as if she has just accidentally drunk a coffee without putting her customary three spoons of sugar in it or, more probably, as if she is registering disapproval at whatever it is her husband has just said. She is wearing what she described as her "best house dress," which is a step down from her

Sunday dress but a step above all the others. Her hair sits imperiously upon her head, rows and rows of hair tiaras piled high and shellacked into place by the Aqua Net Hair Spray she bought by the case. It must have been a Saturday, because the hair is so perfect that she most certainly has just come from the Klip and Kurl. And if she has, indeed, just come from the Klip and Kurl, it means that Gramps has dropped her off there and gone to meet his buddies at Buck's Tavern, which accounts for the big-mouthed story-joke pose on Gramps. Grams said she could never shut him up when he was "in his cups." (To which Gramps would reply, "Woman, I'm not in my cups, I'm drunk. Giving it a fancy name don't make it more genteel!")

Those were the good times. And though he didn't relish the thought that, at age forty-six, his best times were perhaps behind him, sitting there alone in the midst of a hurricane Edward had to admit that it just might be the case. How many summers had it been that the Bay had remained closed? How many summers had it been since the kitchen had hosted laughter and stories and fried chicken and oceans of black coffee and the occasional drunken polka?

He continued to stare at the faces.

The next morning he woke up in the same place on the sofa. He looked at the photograph and Gramps seemed to be saying, "You really knocked back the brewskies last night, Spark Plug!" Grams was silent, judgmental. Edward reached for his phone.

"Hey Dad, it's me," he said, still looking at the disapproving face of his grandmother.

"Hello Eddie. I was just talking about you. I guess you survived the hurricane?"

"To be honest, Dad, I slept through the whole thing."

He got up and looked down to the street below. "Seems quiet now. How's the hip?"

"Fine, but I'll have to do some physical therapy. I'll work from home, of course."

Edward felt a tenderness that surprised him. "Hey, listen, Dad, I was wondering if it would be alright if I came out there early. I'm sure the airports are a mess here, but as soon as I can find a flight, I was thinking about taking off and spending a couple months in Illinois."

There was a pause on the other end followed by some shuffling noise.

"Listen, son," his father said quietly like he was trying not to be heard, "you know you can't really stay here. I'd love to have you, but your stepmother ... well you know how she feels. And we may not agree with her beliefs, but we have to respect them."

"*You* have to, Dad, not me. At any rate I wasn't planning on staying with you. I want to open up the Bay and stay there."

Silence.

"Dad? Did you hear me? I want to open up the Bay. Do you have any objections?"

"I heard you. Gosh, Eddie, I don't know. It hasn't been open in years and I'm not sure it's worth bothering Leo to get it all ready. The old boarding house in town is lovely – really luxurious now that they've renovated. Why don't you just stay there? I know you've got some good memories at that house, but Ben's not going to want to spend his vacation in a musty old mansion."

"Ben's not coming."

"Don't tell me there are problems between the two of you. Oh, Eddie, I hate to hear that. I really hoped you two would last."

"It's not the end of the world, Dad, I just want some

time alone. Anyway. The Bay?"

"Why the sudden interest in the Bay?"

"I spent a good chunk of my life there, Dad, and some of my happiest memories are connected to that place. Is it so strange that I would want to go back there?"

"I just think it's odd, that's all."

"Correct me if I'm wrong – it *is* already technically mine."

"That it is, son. Yeah, well, OK. Sure. I'll call Leo today and tell him to get the place ready. Will you want Alice to come in and cook for you?"

"No, that's alright – I'll fend for myself. I'll let you know when I can get a flight out so Leo can know when the house needs to be ready."

"OK. Eddie?"

"Yeah, Dad?"

"Eddie, they say you can't go home again and there's a reason they say it. It never works. People *think* they can go back, but they can't. I just don't want you to be disappointed if you don't find whatever it is you're looking for at the Bay." His voice cracked again.

Edward permitted himself a moment of silent imagination. "Well maybe I'm not going back. Maybe I'm moving forward.".

"Dad?"

"Yes, son?"

He found he couldn't bring himself to say the words that he wanted to. "Never mind, Dad."

"Eddie?"

"Yes, Dad?"

"Never mind too."

Every airline he called had the same story: due to the hurricane and the cancelled flights there would be nothing available for at least five days. The post-hurricane air felt heavy, constricting, and Edward thought he would be able to breathe more easily if he escaped for a while.

Was a classic road trip still classic if one took it alone? It seemed that the fates were pointing him in that direction. Maybe driving halfway across the country would help him put his life in order.

He threw a few things in a duffel bag that he found under the bed in the guest bedroom, and which hadn't been used in years. (Ben preferred more "dignified" luggage.) Tying the string of the old bag Edward thought how it seemed so much more beautiful than the expensive luggage that was resting in the hall closet waiting to be summoned like an imperious concubine. Before leaving the apartment, he walked to the piano and grabbed the photograph of Grams and Gramps. He wouldn't be alone; *they* would be his companions on the journey.

He got his car from the garage. The photograph fit perfectly in a compartment on the dashboard, and, after placing it there with a kind of solemn reverence, he drove out into the wounded streets of Manhattan. Maybe, just maybe, you really *could* go back. Maybe people *said* you couldn't because they were too afraid or weak to actually do it, to make the journey.

"I am neither weak nor afraid," he said, looking at the photograph front of him.

Grams, through ever-pursed lips, seems to say, "Of course you're not, dear," while Gramps is laughing and bellowing, "Give 'em hell, Spark Plug!"

Chapter Two: 1970

I'm blowing spit bubbles. Stretched out in the back of the car which is so big that there's room for me and Snickers too, curled up at my head purring like a cat even though he's a dog – a mutt dog Daddy says. Tree leaves are dancing and waving as the car goes by and I'm trying to count the leaves but there are too many because the car just keeps going and there's not enough time to count. I count to one – sometimes two – and they're already gone. I'm not too sad about not being able to count the leaves, though, because I'm lying in the back seat and Snickers is purring and smells kind of good and yucky at the same time and it's a smell that I like.

I like the way the spit feels on my lips, like the little plop plop sound the bubbles make when they break. I wish they would get bigger, wish they would grow and grow until the whole back seat was one giant bubble and me and Snickers could just float up to those treetops and real slow-like count the leaves. But they never get that big.

"Eddie, stop it."

OK, Mommy has seen me, and she hates it when she sees me blowing spit bubbles. I'm not so sure why she hates it so much. Maybe it's because she never even chews bubble gum – let alone make spit bubbles. She just smokes, which I think is really cool and I would like to do as well but I can't even *pick up* a lighter so how can I light a cigarette if I can't even touch the lighter? Plop. Plop.

"Eddie! Stop it. It's gross."

I don't know what gross is. I think it's connected to the market where I go sometimes with Grams but I'm not sure so maybe I got it wrong. I get things wrong sometimes and sometimes they all laugh like when I said to Mr. Jenks that I had done adultery because I was sassing back to Dina my nanny and she said "There's no need for you to sass back to me, you're just a little boy and you're trying to act like an adult!" so I thought I had done adultery. Sometimes I get it wrong and they don't laugh, or they try not to, like when Reverend Finney asked me at the drug store what I wanted to be when I grew up and I said hell if I know, man. Plop. Plop.

"Edward James Allerton Bradington! Stop that right now!"

When Mommy uses all of my names I know it's best to either stop doing what I'm doing, or do what she wants me to, because the next thing is ONE TWO THREE and if I haven't stopped doing something, or haven't done something that she wants me to at THREE I can get paddled. Sometimes I like to play a game where I keep on, just to test Mommy. But today, since we're going to see Daddy's Daddy and we don't visit him very often I decide not to risk getting in trouble because I almost always cry when I do and I don't want to show up at Grandfather Bradington's house with a runny nose because Grandfather Bradington scares me a little bit and I'm always afraid I'm going to do something wrong like tip over a spittoon (which I did do, but on accident) or let Snickers in the house (which I did on purpose).

"Will Grams and Gramps be there?"

"No, son. Grams and Gramps are *Mommy's* parents and we're going to see *my* father."

"But if you and Mommy live together why don't Gramps and Grandfather Bradington live together? And

Grams, naturally." I like saying "naturally" because it always makes Daddy smile.

"It doesn't work that way, sport." And I can see Daddy's eyes in the rearview mirror and they're twinkling like he's happy. "Naturally" always makes Daddy happy.

Snickers wakes up and yawns really really big and licks my face and Snickers' breath kind of stinks when he licks but I sort of like it anyway. Snickers wants to play now but even though there's like a mile in the back seat of Daddy's car there really isn't enough space to play with Snickers. So I give Snickers a little push towards the door just to let him know we're not going to play and Snickers gives a little squeak which makes Mommy turn around to see what's going on. But by then Snickers is sitting calmly and so Mommy turns back around and I love Snickers even more and feel a little bad that we can't play in the back seat. But we can't.

"How much longer?"

"One and a half *General Hospitals*," says Mommy and I understand because both Grams and Dina make me watch their stories with them and it's a long time to sit still and I hate it but at the same time I love it because all the doctors are handsome like Daddy and all the nurses are pretty like Mommy. I also like when Grams gets so mad at the people on the screen that she shouts at them and when I giggle at her she says "I'm gonna' tie a knot in your tail, you little imp!" and then I say "Grams you're a dear without antlers" and sometimes she laughs so hard that she starts coughing so much that I wonder if she's choking like that time I did on a piece of chicken and Mommy squeezed me until it came out.

But a *General Hospital* and a half is a really really long time, so I ask Mommy if we can we read.

"OK darlink," she says. (She always calls me "darlink"

or "sweet pea" and Daddy calls me "EJ" or "sport" or "little man" and Grams calls me "my baby" which I don't like so much and Gramps calls me "Spark Plug" which is my favorite.)

I climb over the front seat, careful not to kick Daddy while he's driving (it's happened, but always on accident) and Snickers whines a little but he can't come up to the front seat so he just has to lie back down and he looks sad and a little mad. I scooch next to Mommy and give a little sniff because Mommy always smells so good. She is wearing a white shirt without sleeves and her arms are tan and thin and I like them a lot better than Grams' arms which jiggle like Jell-o. Mommy's wearing shorts and her legs are tan and thin too.

"What do you want to read?" Mommy asks as she puts a tote bag on her lap and looks inside like she's all excited, like there's a treasure in there (which there kind of is).

The problem is that I have already been reading almost a year and most of the books that I have are boring now because they're so easy and even if in other books I don't know what all the words mean I like sounding out big words like "carpeted" or "murmuring" or – my favorite – "studiously." So most of the books that Mommy has for me in her magic bag don't really interest me that much because the biggest word in any of them is "yellow" and "yellow" isn't even a hard word.

"Let's read from your green book," I say to Mommy and she looks at me like she knew I was going to say that. Mommy has a big green book with lots of different poems and stories and things, and I love reading them, sounding out the words and trying to figure out what they mean.

So Mommy pulls out the green book, "Hmmm … what can we read, my darlink" and I say "What can *I* read" and she laughs and says, "Of course, what can _you_ read" and Daddy shakes his head and smiles.

And so Mommy flips through the pages and stops at one and says, "Here's a good one" and sets the book on my lap and then sets me and the book together on her lap, like she's reading me and I'm reading the book.

And I look at the book and there's no trouble reading the title and I understand it all and that's a sign that it's going to be a good poem: _Casey at the Bat_. Daddy smiles because he really likes that poem (and I think that Mommy may have chosen it more for Daddy than for me) and tells me it's about baseball, which is something Daddy loves, even if the goddamned Cubs always let him down.

And I begin reading and it's going pretty well until I come across the word "wonderment" and have to stop, even if I've probably read it right. I look up at Mommy and she says "You know what wonder means" and I do because I learned it in a song in Sunday school once. And she says "Well it's pretty much the same thing."

"If it's the same thing why don't they just say 'wonder' instead of 'wonderment'?" I ask and I'm proud of my question because Daddy says, "Excellent question, EJ!"

And Mommy says, "Because there's a rhythm to this poem like drums with music. Listen." And Mommy begins to read and taps her finger on the book: "But Flynn let drive a single to the wonderment of all / And the much despiséd Blakey tore the cover off the ball."

I say, "But I thought the word was 'despised' not 'despiséd' I mean, that's the way they say it in Grams' stories."

And Daddy says, "Touché, EJ!"

"Well," says Mommy, looking at Daddy like she does sometimes when Snickers chews on one of her shoes, "you can't say it without adding the _ed_ because the rhythm would be off. It's got to be DUH duh DUH duh DUH" and again she taps her finger, "MUCH de-SPIS-ed BLAK-ey. Do you get it? The rhythm?"

"I guess so," I say but I'm still not sure if it's a good thing because it sounds funny and also I have never seen a little line over the *e* before and even if Mommy says it's an accent mark so that you know how to read it I still think it's kind of silly.

"Let's move on," says Mommy but I'm not ready yet because I'm thinking about something real hard and I can't think and read at the same time.

"Wait," I say to Mommy, "why can't it be 'very hated'?" And when Mommy doesn't answer and just crinkles up her nose a bit I go on and say: "And the VE-ry HA-ted BLAK-ey TORE the COV-er OFF the BALL."

Daddy swerves onto the shoulder of the road he's laughing so hard and Mommy grabs me and squeezes me tight and says, "Where did I find you, my little darlink?" and I say "In the cabbage patch!" because it's a little game we play and then she squeezes me a little more and I let out a little fart and Daddy almost drives into the ditch that time and Snickers barks in the back seat and everybody laughs really hard.

And then we move on with the poem and I learn lots and lots of new words like doffed, sneer, sphere, unheeded, tumult, scornful and vengeance, and Mommy explains them to me and takes my notebook out and makes me write them down so I'll remember them and that takes more time than reading the poem. It always does.

And then before you know it we're just outside the town where Grandfather Bradington has his house and Daddy is rolling down the window like he always does and says, "Smell that air EJ – it's the sweetest on earth!" And I breathe in real deep like he always does and even if I don't smell the difference between that air and any other air I act like I do because I know that it's important to Daddy. And then Daddy points at the green sign and asks me, "What's that sign say?" and I answer "Bradington!" and then Daddy says, "What's your name?" and I answer, "Edward James Allerton Bradington the Fourth!" and Daddy says, "Welcome to your town, my boy!"

I jump into the back seat and roll down the window and hang my head outside like Snickers does and I look in wonderment at the little houses that we pass with green yards and flowers and some with basketball hoops in their driveways. I live in a big city where people have apartments and don't really have yards just parks which are open to everybody so are less special. But here every family has its own house and I think they must be rich because they don't have to live on top of or underneath other people and can do what they want with their yards. And they do. There are flowers and fences and gardens and one house even has a car without wheels in the front yard.

And we drive by the post office, the tavern and the United Methodist Church and turn right and drive through a gate and down a long road which just has rocks on it and has big trees on either side with so many leaves that you can't count them even if the car is going very very slow. And soon I can see the house and the bay and think that if the people in the town are rich with all their space then Grandfather Bradington is super rich because he has this huge house and an entire bay that is attached to a channel that is attached to the Illinois River itself. I'm not sure if Grandfather Bradington owns the whole river or not, but I think he must own part of it because he owns the bay and the channel and they go out into the river so it kind of makes sense that he owns at least some of the river if not all of it.

And Daddy stops the car in the big circular driveway

out front (which is really the back since the front sits on the bay) and we all get out of the car and Snickers pees on the flagpole and Daddy yells "Snickers!" but just because he's always nervous around Grandfather Bradington, not because he thinks Snickers shouldn't pee on the flagpole. And Grandfather Bradington's maid Elsie comes out and she tries to smile but doesn't try very hard. I drag Snickers towards me on the grass because I know that Elsie hates Snickers and I want to keep Snickers kind of close, just in case Elsie tries anything.

"He upstairs," Elsie says, "he not doin' so well today. Doctor say it about time." Elsie talks funny and once I sort of made fun of her and Mommy didn't even say "Edward James Allerton Bradington" or "ONE TWO THREE" she just paddled me right there on the spot. So now I barely open my mouth in front of Elsie but I still think that she talks funny and she smells funny too – like medicine – and she chews tobacco and spits it into Grandfather Bradington's spittoons and her teeth are small and black like black Chiclets even though everyone knows that Chiclets don't come in black.

Daddy carries the suitcases in. Snickers can't come in, so while Daddy is taking care of the luggage Mommy gets a little Scooby snack from a plastic bag in her purse and gives it to Snickers. Snickers eats it but also looks at Mommy kind of sad, like he knows he can't come in the house, which he can't because Grandfather Bradington won't have it.

And I'm sad like I always am when I have to leave Snickers outside and I'm trying not to cry because I know that crying is another thing that Grandfather Bradington won't have. And in concentrating so hard on not crying and trying to make Snickers not-so-sad and keeping away from Elsie I kind of forget that I have to pee. And I can't worry about not crying and Snickers and Elsie and hold in my pee all at the same time and all of a sudden I feel this warm feeling spreading through my underwear and it's too late to do anything about it at that point.

Elsie spits, points at me and says, "Boy done wet his trousers!" and this time she tries to smile and does and I can see all the black Chiclets teeth in her mouth. Now I have to worry about the fact that I peed my pants, I can't cry, I have to make Snickers not-so-sad, and try and keep Snickers away from Elsie. But I can't do all those things at the same time so I start crying, trying to stop myself, but tears are a little like pee and once they start you can't really stop them until they're done.

Mommy picks me up and says, "Shhh don't worry my little darlink, these things happen. I should have got you in the bathroom as soon as we arrived – it's my fault." She carries me in the house and runs up the stairs two at a time to the third floor and runs a bath. She strips my wet clothes off of me and I get in the bath but I'm really tired and I don't want to play or splash or really do anything but get washed and take a nap. I never want to take a nap but right then I really need a nap because I'm afraid if I think about everything that's happened I'll start crying again. And Grandfather Bradington won't have that.

So Mommy washes me up good and puts me in a pair of shorts and my favorite Spiderman t-shirt and puts me down on the bed that smells kind of old but not bad and says "Close your eyes for a little while, my darlink, and later we'll take the paddleboat out on the bay. OK? Now give me squeezins!" says Mommy and I do and already feel a little bit better, like I'm not going to cry, but I think that I better just stay in bed anyway, better not risk it.

"I love you, my little darlink," says Mommy and kisses the tip of my nose and I respond "I love you too" and close my eyes and try not to think about Snickers running around outside on his own scared and mean old Elsie and the fact that I peed my pants.

I wake up and I want to go outside to check on Snickers but I'm not allowed outside on my own so I go down the stairs, walking like a ghost on the second floor so I don't bother Grandfather Bradington. I go down to the first floor past the big sitting room with the piano I'm not allowed to touch past the dining room. I tiptoe down the hallway past the kitchen where I can hear Elsie coughing and cooking, past the family room to the screened-in porch where I'm pretty sure I'll find Mommy and Daddy.

And I hear them talking out there but they don't hear me so I stand by the door between the family room and the screened-in porch and listen to them, although I think it might be wrong. But I'm feeling good again after my nap and I feel strong in my Spiderman t-shirt, so I just decide to do it, to stand there and listen to Mommy and Daddy talking.

"Elsie's called Reverend Finney," Daddy is saying. Daddy's rubbing his eyes like he has been crying, like he peed his pants or is afraid of mean old Elsie, but I know that Daddy never cries so it must be the light off the water that is making me see things funny. "He thinks the church is too small and that we should have the funeral here."

I know about funerals because Mr. Fletcher who lives in our building died and we went to the funeral in a big church with lots of smoke and a man in a pointy hat. And I know what death is because Mommy explained it to me, that Mr. Fletcher went to sleep and the spirit inside him went up to heaven and they put his body in the ground until the day when his spirit will come back to his body and Mr. Fletcher will wake up again and fly kites on Oak Street

Beach like always.

"It will be huge," says Mommy, rubbing the back of Daddy's neck like she sometimes does to me too. "We could set up a big tent on the side lawn, have it overlooking the bay. He'd like that, I bet. Elsie won't be in a state to do anything, so I'll take care of it myself."

"What're we going to do with Elsie?" Daddy asks. "She's not well herself. She can't stay here alone."

"Good luck trying to move her," says Mommy and Daddy laughs so maybe he isn't crying after all.

"I guess I'll have to hire a caretaker. I couldn't sell the place even if I wanted to."

"You wouldn't want to!" Mommy says. "This place is filled with too much history. And love."

"Lots of history – that's true – but not much love. My mother hated it here, you know." Daddy's mother would be Grandmother Bradington, I think, and I know that Grandmother Bradington died a long time ago because we go to the cemetery and put flowers at this big stone house where her sleeping body is waiting for her spirit to come down and wake it up.

"I guess I didn't know that," Mommy says.

"Our place in the city … it was more Mother that bought it than Dad, I think. The last few years before she died, I think she lived there, and he lived here."

"How do you know?"

"I'd hear the servants talking about it when I would come home from school. There were other rumors, of course, lovers on both sides. Who knows? I suspect Elsie knows the whole story but she's not talking."

Mommy and Daddy sit in silence for a while and look out over the bay.

"I'd better get back up there," Daddy says. "Dr. Anderson says he won't last the night, but he probably will just to spite us all. Hell, he could be up at Founders Day this year, playing the Lord of the Manor. I wouldn't put it past him. Anyway, I think EJ should see him. Will you go wake him?"

"Of course," Mommy says. And when they get up to leave the screened-in porch they see me standing there.

I think I might be in trouble but Mommy just smiles and says "Here's our little eavesdropper now!"

I don't know what an eavesdropper is but I don't think that this is the time to ask.

"Did Grandfather Bradington die like Mr. Fletcher?" I ask.

"No, Little Man," answers Daddy, "but the doctor says he is going to really soon. Will you come with me to say goodbye to him before he goes to sleep?"

I don't really want to, but Daddy called me Little Man which is what Daddy calls me whenever things get real serious, so I think I have to go say goodbye to Grandfather Bradington even if I don't want to.

Together we go to Grandfather Bradington's rooms. Daddy opens the door and we go into the sitting room but just keep walking and go into another room where I have never been before which is naturally Grandfather Bradington's bedroom. Grandfather Bradington is in bed and his eyes are closed and there is a potty chair next to the bed like I had when I was really really little, only for grownups. The grownup potty chair seems kind of funny but I know I can't laugh so I stare at the picture on the wall above it, a bunch of ducks on some water that is kind of like Grandfather Bradington's bay but a little different from it too.

"Father?" Daddy says and that sounds funny too, almost like Daddy is talking to himself. But then I think about it a little and realize that Grandfather Bradington is Daddy's father so it's not so funny anymore. But that grownup potty chair still is so I keep my eyes on the ducks.

Grandfather Bradington is breathing funny, like he swallowed a rattle. His eyes are closed but his eyelids are moving really fast like he's faking being asleep.

"Father?" Daddy repeats and this time gives Grandfather Bradington a little nudge on his shoulder which causes him to open his eyes.

"Father, I've brought Edward in to see you."

Daddy lifts me up to the side of the bed and I look into Grandfather Bradington's eyes, which are yellow and red but not like Mr. Fletcher's kites or Chiclets but different, like a dirty yellow and red.

"Hello Grandfather Bradington," I say and because I don't know what else to say I turn around to look at Daddy who nods back towards Grandfather Bradington. And then, because I know I have to say something, I say, "I learned a bunch of new words in the car on the way here but the only ones I can remember right now are tumult, scornful and vengeance. But I still don't know exactly what they all mean. I'll have to study them more and let you know."

Grandfather Bradington nods like he knows what the words mean but he doesn't say anything so maybe he doesn't. Then Grandfather Bradington reaches up and touches my face and his hands are cold like Grams' are when she's been snapping peas.

Daddy sets me back on the floor next to Grandfather Bradington's bed and says, "OK we'll let you rest. I'll run him down to Jean and be right back."

When they get back downstairs Daddy says to me, "It's OK to cry, you know. It's sad for us when someone we love dies, so it's OK to cry."

But I look up and see that Daddy isn't crying even if Grandfather Bradington is *his* Daddy. And since Daddy isn't crying I won't cry either, because Grandfather Bradington probably won't have it, whether he's dead or not.

The funeral is nothing like Mr. Fletcher's and I am a little disappointed because I wanted to see the man with the pointy hat make smoke again. Instead there is just Reverend Finney who talks on and on and on and at one point I'm afraid I'm going to pee my pants again because Reverend Finney is talking so long. But I manage to squeeze my thingy a bit so that I won't have to pee. Mommy sees me and gives me a hard look and grabs me and takes me past the rows and rows of people in chairs on the lawn to go inside the house and pee. And I'm glad that I peed but then also embarrassed when I have to walk past the rows and rows of people in chairs on the lawn again and I am sure that they're all thinking that that boy just went to pee right in the middle of Reverend Finney's speech.

After Reverend Finney's speech a tall man gets up and says more words about Grandfather Bradington and I lean over to Daddy and say "Who's he?" and Daddy says "It's a former Governor of the State of Illinois, the lousy crook," and Mommy and some of the people sitting around chuckle a bit, but real soft like so that the Governor and Reverend Finney probably don't hear them.

And then just Mommy, Daddy, Daddy's sister Aunt Margaret, Elsie, Reverend Finney and me follow the big station wagon where they put Grandfather Bradington's coffin into the stone house where Grandmother Bradington is already asleep. Reverend Finney says a few more words and we go back to the house where everyone else is eating and drinking and tables have been set up. Daddy goes around and talks to everybody.

Even before everyone leaves Mommy tells me it's my

bedtime and this time I don't mind going to bed because I am getting tired of people I don't know pinching my cheek and rubbing my head.

Mommy helps me into my pajamas and tucks me in, but she doesn't say "I love you" or kiss the tip of my nose, she just holds up a finger like wait a second and leaves. Then from out in the hallway she says, "Hey, my darlink, I've got a surprise for you." Then she walks in carrying Snickers in her arms and puts Snickers in bed with me and Snickers snorts and licks my face and it stinks but I'm so happy I don't care. Then Mommy says "I love you" and kisses the tip of my nose and goes out of the room, leaving the door open just a crack.

And I think that there's no way I'll be able to sleep with the excitement of Snickers who maybe peed a little in the bed – or maybe it was slobber – I can't tell which and I don't really want to check too closely. But after a little bit Snickers settles down and starts purring like a cat even though he's a dog and before I know it I'm sleepy too.

Life at Grandfather Bradington's house sure is different without Grandfather Bradington. First of all, Elsie decides to leave and go back to North Carolina to be with her people and so she isn't skulking around anymore. Mommy has all of the spittoons cleaned and put back where they were and they don't stink anymore. Daddy goes out and buys a television and puts it right in the middle of the family room and even though it's got one of those rabbit ear antennas it still gets three channels, two OK and one kind of fuzzy. And Mommy says to me, "Go ahead and play," when she sees me in one of the big rooms eying that piano. And I discover that I can listen to songs on the big old-fashioned radio in the room and play the same tunes on the piano and Mommy says, "Look he's playing by ear!" and I say, "No

I'm not I'm using my fingers!" and Daddy has tears coming out of his eyes he's laughing so hard and Mommy spits iced tea right out of her nose. And I don't exactly understand what's so funny about it but I repeat it and they still laugh but a little less.

But the best change is when Grams and Gramps come to stay and Daddy explains that they're going to live and work there as caretakers of the house, in addition to Gramps' work digging coal out of the ground. And so I begin helping Gramps fix things around the house and I watch Grams' stories with her on the fuzzy channel and it's like a new place. Daddy works during the week but comes back every weekend and we all sit and eat and tell stories and lots of my aunts and uncles come to visit as well because Grams and Gramps live there now and my aunts and uncles are their children and loads of fun, probably because they're not Bradingtons or Allertons but McColloughs and the McColloughs get to act differently than the Bradingtons and Allertons do.

But there are strange things going on as well, things that sometimes Grams and Gramps are talking about and stop when I come into the room. And then when Mommy has to start going away a lot and then comes back pale and with bruises and sometimes can't lift me anymore even though I haven't grown that much and Grams cries more easily than usual I know I have to do something that I'm not supposed to do and that's eavesdrop. And in my note-book of words to learn I write down things I've been eavesdropping: cancer and chemotherapy and metastasis. And I find cancer in the big dictionary in Grandfather's Bradington study (which is now Daddy's study) and it can either be a sickness or a horoscope sign or a constellation which has something to do with stars, I know, and so I hope that it's *that* cancer they're talking about when they think I'm not listening. And probably because I'm not sure how to spell chemotherapy and metastasis I can't find either in the big dictionary, so I think they must be stars too.

And so I decide that Mommy is going away so much because she's a secret astronaut and they're flying her to the stars and of course she's going to lose weight and be weak because it's not easy being shot into space like that. And when she's gone for some days and I eavesdrop chemotherapy, I knows that she's on a mission and so I go out on the balcony off my bedroom and look up at the twinkling lights which are shining from a zillion miles away and try to see if I can find the one that Mommy is going to.

And I can always find it, I always know which star is hers. And sitting there with Snickers I know that if I can see her then she can see me too and so I wave and make Snickers' paw wave too and the star – Mommy's star – always twinkles back.

Chapter Three: 2012

Somewhere in Pennsylvania the voice of one radio evangelist began to fade, as if he were no longer sure of his message, and Edward searched for another voice, for another companion. Around 1040 he found it, a new voice promising salvation, but soothing and soft, not like the bombastic brimstone of the last guy. Pastor Earl was talking about the passage "Man does not live by bread alone, but by every word that comes from the Father's mouth" in such a way that it almost seemed like a song.

"The world offers us the bread of possessions and power, violence and hatred, jealousy and greed, and it smells so warm and buttery cooling on our windowsill that we know, we just know, we'll only be happy if we sit down at the world's table, tuck our napkin in our shirts and taste of its sweetness, even if we discover that it's not sweet and it doesn't fill us up. But we keep eating simply because we don't know how to push ourselves away from the table. But I'm here to tell you, brothers and sisters, that you *can* push yourselves away from that table of possessions and power, violence and hatred, jealousy and greed. And, when you pray for the strength to get up from that cursed worm-eaten table, and when you hold out your hand in supplication for a piece of the *true* Bread of Life, the sweet word that falls from the Father's mouth like raindrops made of apple cider, you will know a fullness in your belly and a love in your heart. Pray with me now, brothers and sisters! Pray with me that God almighty will give you the strength to push yourselves away from that demonic table. Push push push yourselves away; it's the only way. Push push push yourselves away; it's the only way."

That's what New York is, thought Edward: Satan's table. And he was push push pushing himself away from that table. "Push push push" he said over and over again in the same singsong way that Pastor Earl was. "Push push push."

Further on in Pennsylvania, not long after the sky had gone from the fatigue of light blue through the languor of orange to the danger of black, all of Pastor Earl's talk about tables and buttery bread was making him hungry, and he realized that he hadn't eaten anything. He looked up to see a big yellow sign, flashing in the distance, with "Traveler's" and "Plaza" intersecting in a way that made it look like a giant cross. If he couldn't find Pastor Earl's bread of life here, he most certainly would find something that would tide him over until he could.

He entered the big glass doors of the wayfarers' neon chapel and turned right at the velvet pictures of Elvis and Jesus and slid into a booth, brown and synthetic, comfortable as an old armchair. Before he had even had a chance to look at the menu that was wedged into the metal holder on the side of the table, a waitress came by, offering coffee. Her green-field-white-picket-fence name tag said she was Laverne.

He looked around at the brightly lit truck stop. There were truckers, of course, gruff men whose minds were probably somewhere else, soothed to be at least for a while in a place like home. There was a family, two young, harried parents drinking black coffee, their three kids running from the table, past the merchandise area to the alcove with video games and back again when their money ran out. There was an old couple, sitting quietly, not speaking, but in a way that didn't suggest rancor or even boredom but that sweet acceptance of another that comes with time, if it comes at all.

Edward was in America, this garish world of pleather and pancakes and coffee and darlin' and sweetie and Jesus and Elvis. And he found it overwhelming, almost like a child at a fair.

He marveled at how little of his country he really knew. Grams and Gramps knew America, of course. *Were* America, to a large degree. Had it not been for them he probably wouldn't have known anything at all about the wondrous country that surrounded him like an old quilt. They, not bound by the Bradington family code of conduct, were free to speak how they wanted, to listen to country music and square dance and go to Mann's IGA and the Klip and Kurl and Buck's Tavern and the VFW Hall freely. And they would bring bits of that outside world back to him, teach him the language and customs of a people vastly different than the stern Bradingtons and the pinched-nosed Allertons. And Edward drank it all in like lemonade at a summer picnic.

The lovely waitress Laverne returned. "Hey Mr. Deep Thinker," she said with a genuine smile. "You're sitting here staring off into space! Do you want to order or just be left alone?"

"How about I order? Let me see. I'll take chicken fried steak with mashed potatoes and gravy."

"Sides?"

"Oh, right. How about green beans? And corn. Can I get both?"

"Honey, you can get whatever we got – as long as it's on the menu. Bread or biscuits?"

"Biscuits. With gravy."

"It's always you fit ones that eat all these things you're not supposed to," she said, shaking her head, and, when

Edward blushed, "Oh don't worry honey, I'm not flirting with you. You're half my age!"

"Well, ma'am, unless you're ninety, I'm not half your age."

"I'll be damned! You don't look a day over thirty. Maybe I *will* start flirting with you!"

He drove another three hours on the interstate and began feeling a little sleepy, so he thought it might be better to take a smaller road, where having to pay closer attention to things would make him more alert. Pastor Earl had been replaced by Delilah, calling out to lovers everywhere, dedicating songs to soldiers in Afghanistan, an unjustly-imprisoned boyfriend, a wife of thirty-five years and – slightly out of the lover category (at least Edward hoped) – "the best daddy a little girl ever had." Delilah's voice was soothing like a warm breath on his neck and, though it didn't really make him sleepier, it relaxed him so that he found driving suddenly burdensome. In a small town in what he assumed to be central Ohio (he had seen signs for Columbus) he came across a hotel called the Tomahawk Lodge, an L-shaped ranch-style building with fake log cabin siding and a small pool on the side of it, empty rusted chairs surrounding it which seemed to suggest it didn't get a lot of use. On the other side, carrying on the questionable Native American theme, sat The Redskin Inn, Michelob and Bud Light signs shining like jewels in the windows.

At the Lodge's small reception office sat a boy ignoring the high school geometry book in front of him and watching *The Breakfast Club* on a small television above a coffee bar stacked with leaning towers of Styrofoam cups.

"Good evening. Are there any rooms available?"

"Are there?" laughed the boy. "Only all of them."

"Well, I don't need all of them, but I will take one."

"ID?" asked the boy, looking up at the screen. Molly Ringwald was smoking pot, pouty lips gingerly approaching the joint. Edward gave his driver's license and credit card, feeling old; this boy most certainly hadn't even been born when Edward went to see that film.

Business concluded, the boy handed him a key with a green tag giving postal directions should someone come across it. When was the last time that Edward had stayed in a hotel with an actual key? It seemed heavy and foreign in his hand.

"What do you think?" Edward asked nodding towards the television. "Do you like it?"

"I've seen parts of it before," said the boy matter-of-factly. "It's OK. A little dated, you know, but OK."

Edward finished watching the film in his room, a surprisingly clean place that seemed as dated to him as *The Breakfast Club* had to the boy. Relaxed but not tired, he decided to check out The Redskin Inn. With the possible exception of arriving first to meet friends, he had probably never been in a tavern by himself. The night air which should have been cool seemed still and warm; it stuck to him like a sweaty t-shirt.

There were more people in the tavern than the number of cars outside suggested. Edward was worried that he was going to have to stand, until he heard "See you tomorrow Hank!" and saw a rather large man in an out-of-place suit and tie vacate a seat at the bar. He grabbed it immediately.

The bartender approached him. He was wearing a tight t-shirt. The man wiped down the bar in front of him, displaying a tattoo on his forearm that read "Stella" and said, "What can I get you?"

"What have you got on tap?"

"Bud Bud Light Michelob Miller Light Blue Moon and

Sam Adams," he said so quickly that all the words seemed like one giant beer with a really long name.

"Blue Moon, please."

"Sure thing."

Edward watched him walk away. There was something boyish about him, but the way he moved was slightly feminine. He could, he thought, be anywhere from thirty to fifty.

"Can I get a slice of orange in that?" Edward asked when he set the beer down in front of him.

"Orange?"

"Yeah. I used to drink this a lot and where I went they always served it with an orange slice." He smiled, trying to appear charming.

"The customer's always right," the bartender responded, reaching into the relish tray and dropping a piece of orange in the beer unceremoniously. (Edward noted that it was a wedge and not a slice but said nothing.) "That'll be four dollars".

"Are you serious?" responded Edward incredulously.

"Well, it's not on special. A Budweiser'll cost you three. Of course, Buds usually don't come with oranges." He smiled to show small white teeth neatly in a row with the exception of one of his canines, which slightly jutted out defiantly, as if it didn't want to play by the rules established by the others.

"No, it's not that it's too much," Edward said smiling, reaching for his wallet, "it's just where I come from it would cost you double that – if not more."

"Where you from?" he asked.

"New York."

"Oh, I get it," the bartender said brusquely. "Anyway, four dollars please."

Edward was confused by the change in his tone. He

opened his wallet and discovered that he only had two dollars. "Get what?".

"City people who come in here and say 'Wow – can you believe these bumpkins only charge four dollars for a beer?' and laugh in that 'Ain't that cute!' kind of way."

Edward began to say "condescending" but stopped himself before it was too late. "Listen, I didn't mean any disrespect. I spent a large part of my life growing up in a town in Illinois that had fewer than nine hundred inhabitants. Trust me: I wasn't being rude."

"Sorry. It's just that it happens from time to time and it really chaps my ass." The smile returned.

"Listen," Edward said, "I don't have any cash. Can I start a tab and pay for it with a card at the end of the night?"

"Sure," replied the bartender. "But I'll need the card now. There's no way of knowing that you're not a big city crook out to bamboozle simple country boys like myself."

"Of course," said Edward, handing over his American Express.

"Wow – black," the bartender said, holding it up to the light like it was a fine wine or a precious gem. "First time I've seen one of those."

"Yeah, well, it's for business, you know," Edward said dismissively. He wasn't sure why, but he really wanted this man to like him. "By the way: I'm Edward. Are you Stella?" he asked, indicating the tattoo.

"Ha ha. No, Stella was my Grandma. She's dead, by the way: now don't you feel like a dick? The tattoo's for her. My name's Hank."

"Hank. I like that." Edward smiled his half smile, suggestive, sly, usually irresistible.

"Well, it's a name, isn't it?" Hank asked, leaning on the bar. "Got a cousin named Ida Gay Titzer – no lie – and she gets by just as fine with that as I do with Hank Robert Drummond. You got any other names?"

"What, like nicknames? Not really. Not anymore."

"No, not nicknames, actual names," he said. "I think you can tell a lot about a person by their name. Like Ida Gay Titzer. You just know she's going to be sweet but tough, you know?"

"And Hank Robert Drummond?" asked Edward, not really wanting to lay his whole name down.

"Definitely a person who doesn't take no shit," Hank said, smiling, crooked tooth poking out like a shy child waving. "And loyal. Hanks are always loyal. And you?"

Edward sighed. "Edward James Allerton Bradington the Fourth. What the hell does *that* say about me?"

"Jesus H. Christ! Are you shitting me? That's really your name?"

"Afraid so. What does it say about me?"

Hank scrunched up his nose and rubbed the back of his neck. "Wow," he said smiling, "we don't *even* got enough time to go into that one!"

Edward liked watching him. At first, he told himself that it wasn't a sexual thing, that the strange combination of the way he moved like an old house cat and that crooked tooth and that "Stella" curling through the veins on his forearm was interesting, fascinating even. It wasn't a sexual thing, because Edward and Ben hadn't broken up, and he had technically never cheated on Ben.

But by the time Hank brought him his fourth Blue Moon and joined him in two kamikaze shots on the house, Edward no longer had the clarity (nor the desire) to negate the possible sex part of it all. He liked watching Hank because he wanted to taste him, run his hands over that chest, lick that wayward tooth with his tongue.

The beers seemed to be making things much clearer in his mind. He wasn't the type who cheated, but as one beer followed another, he had to acknowledge that he wouldn't even be questioning any of this, wouldn't be allowing his gaze to rest on Hank for far longer than was necessary, if he and Ben were, indeed, still together. What had Ben said? Something about moving forward, that they weren't moving forward, that he'd felt it for a long time. How long, exactly? And what the fuck did that mean, that they weren't moving forward? And Ben hadn't said "We'll talk later" but rather "Goodbye," two short syllables surely chosen because they could bear the weight of three years, were strong enough to break something that was pretty flimsy to begin with.

Edward was a single man now. This seemed certain, and he chastised himself that he had even thought otherwise.

And so, he liked watching the bartender, and that was OK. And it seemed increasingly clear to him that Hank liked being watched as he allowed his gaze to float continually in Edward's direction. And though he looked in a way that suggested that he just wanted to know if Edward was still watching him (and he always was) it was nonetheless a look that offered no resistance and made no demands but was there and open somehow.

"I'm closing out my till," Hank said after bringing Edward his fifth beer, "Do you mind settling up?" And then, perhaps responding to the near-panic Edward felt he must be trumpeting with his eyes he reached out his Stella arm and placed his hand on Edward's, "Don't worry! The bar's not closing. I'm just getting off, that's all."

"Sure," Edward answered. "Any rules against joining me for a drink now, or have you got somewhere to go?"

"No rules and nowhere to go," Hank replied. "No

rules and nowhere to go. If I were smarter I could write me a kick-ass song with that title."

Their knees touched as they sat next to each other, and that touch, such a small thing, excited Edward more than anything had in years. At first, they said little, both pretending to be more interested in the television above them and its motocross racing than either was.

"So," Hank said after several minutes of this silent communication had strengthened and bonded them. "What's a guy from New York with a shit load of names and a Roman numeral after them doing here in Bumfuck?" He played with the neck of his Budweiser. The veins on his hands reminded Edward of the vines on a medieval tapestry.

"Well, eventually I have to go to this small town in Illinois and since I couldn't fly because of the hurricane and since I don't really have to be there right away, I thought I'd just drive. The interstate was getting boring, so … I don't know … I just sort of ended up here."

"What's with this small town in Illinois? Does it have a name?"

"Yes," Edward said sheepishly. "It's Bradington."

"As in Edward Something Something Bradington the Fourth? Fuck me!"

"Yes," Edward replied. "It's a long story."

Hank picked up his beer, sending the cardboard coaster beneath it falling to the floor. Edward bent over to pick it up, suddenly eye-level with the crotch of Hank's worn khakis. He froze, staring at the contours and lines for far longer than was necessary. He looked up and saw that Hank was looking. Edward felt a wave of heat go to his face. "Nailed," he said.

"Nailed," repeated Hank, grabbing the coaster and

putting it back under his beer. "I'm not going anywhere, and you certainly can't get behind the wheel of a car. So I'd say we got time. So, let's hear about it, Mr. Bradington of the Bradington Bradingtons. Or I won't ever let you stare at my dick again."

Edward, of all people, knew a lot about human communication – his entire professional life was spent picking among the ruins of crumbled communication. At the beginning, back when he thought he could go beyond just practicing law and really *help* the people who came to see him, he looked for keys to how a couple who were so completely and irrationally in love that they would commit to spend the rest of their lives together could end up with nothing but lawyers and impotent hatred. He tried to pinpoint exactly at what point it was that whatever had been living before died, what exactly caused the two people involved to cease communicating.

In the end the only explanation he could come up with – and he knew it was banal – was that most couples had never really communicated at all. They shared palely, they talked, they enjoyed life, they moved from one thing to another like members of a tour group walking through an old Roman ruin, *thinking* they could see the full-fledged buildings that had once risen from the crumbling stones, but too embarrassed to admit that they could not. (And, certainly, never thinking for a moment that their partners were also unable to put it all into context, to see the bigger picture.)

Hank was asking him to communicate something profound, the story of a family and a town and a heritage that went back centuries and that – for better or worse – in large part went into making Edward who he was, helped him see live buildings where only ruins had existed. What could he possibly say? Better not even to try, to make up some bullshit, get it out of the way so that he could get this man to come next door with him, to give himself to Edward on top of the brown and yellow-patterned bed-spread while stale musty air blew over them.

But then Hank said, "Listen it's not that big of a deal. Jesus – chill!" and laughed in an open-mouthed way that was strikingly similar to a man in a photograph that was at that moment resting in Edward's car next door. And *that* man was one of the exceptions to Edward's observations about communication; *that* man could look right at you with his steel-blue eyes and let you see a piece of his soul and know and understand yours as well. And so, inspired by the coincidence of the presence of two laughs, Edward decided to give it a shot.

"Well," he began hesitantly. "Do you want the long story or the short story?"

"I'm afraid my attention span ain't what it used to be. Better give me the short story."

"Right," he said, unsure if the story really *could* be short. "Well, my father's family have been in the States for a long time. His mother's family – the Allertons – actually came on the Mayflower, but his father's family – the Brad-ingtons, naturally – a few years later. And – long story short – the Bradingtons made a shitload of money and had lots of land. Skip ahead to the 1850s and one James Bradington, my great-great grandfather. He was kind of kooky by stand-ards back in Boston – there was a rumor that he was nearly kicked out of Harvard for advocating something really close to 'free love' – and he decided that he wanted to live in a different kind of society than he was living in. So he bought pretty much an entire county in the wilds of Illinois and had the idea to start his own kind of society there."

"Like a cult?" Hank seemed interested.

"I don't know," Edward said. "Maybe like a cult. Anyway, it was pretty shocking at the time, but strangely enough he found a woman who was interested in his plan, a certain Alice Allerton, who – another shocking thing for the time – was ten years older than he."

"Wait a second," didn't you say your father's mother's name was Allerton?" He cracked open a peanut from a bowl that had appeared without Edward noticing.

"Yeah. Same family," he said smiling. "We're more inbred than the worst hill-dwellers of West Virginia. Anyway, the two of them moved all the way out to Illinois with a handful of servants and James built this big house called the Bay and – God, this is way too complicated to do a short version after a zillion beers – they sort of founded this town where no one actually owned their property but rented it on a ninety-nine-year lease for one dollar a year. He thought that life would be more peaceful if men didn't own land."

"But he owned the land, right?" Hank asked, eyebrows raised in accusation.

"Yeah, well let's say there was a hole in his logic. Anyway, the town grew – never big, and James and Alice had a son – Edward James Allerton Bradington, my great-grandfather. James dies and then James' brother dies so young Eddie I inherits all the family holdings back east and has to move back to Boston and that was pretty much the end of life in the town that is now called Bradington and sits on Bradington Bay."

"This sounds like something out of *Dynasty*."

"And I'm leaving *a lot* out!" responded Edward.

"Anyway, skip ahead again. My grandfather Eddie II comes back from World War I a bit fragile and it's pretty much decided that he can't be trusted with the family fortune, so Eddie I gets the idea to buy him a coal mine in

Illinois and send him off to Bradington with his bride, my grandmother Lucinda – yes – Allerton. He tears down the old house, builds a ridiculously massive new one, and moves pretty much full-time to the Bay. But fragile Eddie II sort of has the last laugh on the financial front, because he manages to make a lot more money in Illinois than the family ever had back in Boston. Anyway, my grandparents are pretty happy there, by all accounts, although they spend a lot of their time in Chicago and out east as well. My father, Eddie III, is born in 1935 and a sister, Margaret a couple years later. Grandmother dies in 1959. My father marries my mother – *not* an Allerton, but the penniless daughter of a Scotch-Irish coal miner whom he met when she was working as a waitress in a café – in 1960 and my Aunt Margaret marries – get this – a motherfucking Allerton and moves back east permanently. My parents live out there for the most part as well, but after suffering two miscarriages in Boston, my mother decides that life can't grow in her if she's not near her family, so she and my father move to Chicago where I'm born. Grandfather Bradington dies when I'm four and my mother dies when I'm seven and my father's second wife doesn't like the place so Bradingtons stop living full time at the Bay when I'm just a little tyke. My father hires my *mother's* parents to be the caretakers, so I spend most of my summers there until I'm seventeen. And I've never really been back since then. Now there's a caretaker named Leo and there's always talk about turning the place into a museum or hotel or something, but it never gets done. That's the short version."

"Interesting," said Hank. "But why are you going back now?"

"Jesus, this is really embarrassing," said Edward, reaching for his beer. "There's this celebration every year on

Thanksgiving weekend called Founders Day. And at that celebration the head of the Bradington family takes part since – technically – the Bradingtons still own Bradington."

"What do they – you – do?" He signaled to his replacement, a skinny, fragile-looking woman, to bring another round.

"Well, on the Wednesday evening before Thanksgiving we go around to certain houses that are chosen by the Bradington Historical Society and we 'inspect' the tenants' houses, make sure everything is OK, and hear from them if there's something we can do. But it's all kind of just symbol and tradition – they don't really ask us to *do* anything. Usually – if I remember correctly – they just give us a drink or a cup of coffee and – if they're old-timers – share stories about Eddie II. Then, on Friday, Saturday, and Sunday there's a big festival in the town square, culminating in what's called The Collection on Sunday afternoon."

"The Collection? Sounds kind of mafia-ish."

"Well, you know, they have to pay their 'rent' every year, and so, once again the Historical Society picks ten families to officially do this at Founders Day. They usually get dressed up in clothes from the 1800s and bring their dollar – yes, it's still a dollar – to the Bradington who is sitting on a stage and he collects the money and says a few words. My father is usually that Bradington, but he can't do it this year, so he's asked me."

"And what does he do with the money?"

"Well, my father started this tradition sometime in the late seventies where he took the money and went over to the beer garden and gave it to them and then bought the beer for the town until the end of the festival. Which, of course, costs a lot more than the ten bucks he just collected from a bunch of people dressed up like Mary Todd Lincoln."

"Your Dad sounds like my kind of guy," said Hank.

"Yeah. He's cool. Or I guess he used to be," said Edward with a sadness in his voice. "I don't know. People change."

"Well it's a kick-ass story. And it obviously means a lot to you." He reached over and placed his hand on Edward's arm.

Edward looked into his beer. "It's really not that big a deal."

"Dude," said Hank, squeezing his arm, "you said you'd give me the short version. If I'm not mistaken, the short version would be 'I've got to go do this family thing in Illinois at Thanksgiving.' You're proud of it. You *should* be proud of it."

"I don't know. Maybe. I guess I haven't thought much about it really."

"I don't believe you," said Hank before suddenly but gently standing up. He nodded towards the door and started walking out and Edward James Allerton Bradington IV followed him, leaving their beers untouched. Later, as he slept, Hank's naked body pressed next to his, Edward closed his eyes and imagined crumbling ruins becoming shining temples once again.

Chapter Four: 1973

It's my birthday and we're going to Springfield. I've been to Springfield before, of course, because it's the place closest to the Bay where Mommy can find doctors who will help her. But I never really see much of Springfield, even though I know it's important and President Abraham Lincoln worked as a lawyer there before he was president. And they even brought his body back there after he got shot by John Wilkes Booth and it's buried under like a zillion pounds of concrete because someone might want to steal it.

But I never really see Mr. Lincoln or anything of Springfield because I always go to the hospital where Mommy is and where usually I can't even go in to see her and I have to sit downstairs while Daddy and Grams and Gramps go. Sometimes Mommy is strong enough to come down and see me and sometimes she's not. And when she's not there's a nice woman there who everyone calls Sister even if I know she can't be *everybody's* sister but she's Catholic and Gramps always says those folks have their own special way of looking at things and so I just accept it and call her Sister too. And now I know she's not as scary as I thought she was when I met her for the first time, dressed up like the Bride of Dracula that I saw once late at night on TV when everyone thought I was in bed. The first time I saw her I cried because I didn't know any better and she *did* seem scary all in black with that tablecloth on her head. But Gramps told me she was a lovely lady and since Catholics had their own special way of looking at things it was really

OK that she dressed like that.

And so Sister would come down and talk to me when Mommy wasn't strong and only Daddy and Grams and Gramps could go upstairs to see her. At first I didn't really know what to say to her and so I was quiet but then when Gramps heard that I hadn't said much he said "Spark Plug, we usually can't get you to shut up and now you're a mute!" and it was clear that Gramps wanted me to talk to Sister, so the next time I did. I talked to Sister about reading, mainly, because by then I had read maybe hundreds if not thousands (but surely not millions yet) of books and I could remember them all because Mommy made me write everything down. And Sister smiled and always said "Wowzy wow!" which I had never heard before and thought sounded funny coming from this lady wearing a tablecloth on her head but then maybe anything would sound funny from a lady wearing a tablecloth on her head.

So it's my birthday and I'm going to Springfield with Daddy and Grams and Gramps and Daddy and Gramps are in the front seat and I'm in the back seat with Grams and she's wearing her best dress and smells like lavender and is wearing gloves even though it's warm outside. And I'm asking Daddy how long it is until we get to Springfield and Grams says "Stop pestering him, you little imp!" like she's mad but she's really not because she smiles at me and then pinches my cheek.

And so I say to Daddy "Quiz me!" which always makes the time fly and at first Daddy doesn't want to, but then maybe he decides that since it's my birthday he should just go ahead and quiz me.

"Who said 'Give me liberty or give me death?'" asks Daddy and I shout out "Patrick Henry!" because it's always the first question and it's easy.

"What is two plus eight plus four divided by two?"

Daddy asks next and I shout out "Seven!" and look at Grams who is smiling at me because I'm so smart.

"What year was Bradington, Illinois founded?" Daddy asks next and that one is real easy too because I don't have to do any math I just has to remember a date and so I answer "eighteen fifty-seven" like it's no big deal, which it kind of isn't.

Then Daddy says to Gramps "Dad he's too damn smart for me; you better ask him one." I like it when Daddy calls Gramps "Dad" and Grams "Mom" even if they're not really his mom and dad. Maybe that's why I like it so much, specifically because they're *not* his mom and dad.

And Gramps looks up in the air like he's thinking and asks, "What happens if you're out fishing for channel cat and you catch a gar?"

And I think real hard because I want to get the words exactly right like Gramps would and I finally answer "Drown the son of a bitch because there's too many of the ugly bastards in the river already!"

And Gramps and Daddy both laugh but Grams doesn't. She just says "Charlie McCullough!" to Gramps like he's in trouble and then she says, "Don't listen to a thing your grandfather tells you and don't ever talk like he talks!"

And then I get a little bored with the quiz because Daddy never thinks of hard questions when he's driving so I ask Gramps if we can play the key ring game and Gramps says "Certainly" but pronounces it in his funny voice so that it sounds like "Soitenly" which is always funny, no matter how many times he does it.

Gramps pulls out his big key ring that has like dozens of keys on it. Since Gramps works in the ground in a coal mine, he's always saying that one of his keys is the key to the earth and so the game is I pick a key and ask if that key is the key to the earth and Gramps says "No, that's the key to something-or-other" and then later Gramps asks me what each key is to see if I was paying attention.

"Is this the key to the earth?" I ask Gramps and Gramps answers, "No, that's to the tractor shed."

"Is this the key to the earth?" I ask holding up another key and Gramps answers, "No, that's to the old Buick."

"Is this the key to the earth?" I ask holding up one that looks kind of silvery-blue and Gramps says, "No, that's to my girlfriend's house but don't tell your grandmother!"

And Daddy and Gramps laugh but Grams doesn't laugh and says "As if anyone would have you, you old fool!" and she looks out the window and crosses her hands with the white gloves on her lap.

"Is this the key to the earth?" I ask holding up the biggest key and Gramps says, "No, that's the key to my heart, which belongs to your grandmother," and he turns around and looks at Grams and he's smiling with his mouth wide open like he does and kind of plays with his hair because she says he knows it makes him look adorable.

And Grams says "You're so full of it it's a wonder your eyes aren't brown!"

And finally Daddy says, "What do you want your last birthday present to be?" Because every year I get one present each day before my birthday – one for each year. And I've already got the Game of Life, a pair of binoculars, a remote-control crane that builds things, a giant Tonka truck, an antique pocket watch that belonged to Grandfather Bradington and a brand-new bike that looks like it's more for a grown up than a kid. And I think real hard because I know there's only one present left and I don't want to waste my last wish on something little like a G.I. Joe or Lincoln Logs.

"Well?" says Gramps because I haven't answered. And

I feel like I have to answer them right then and there and so I say the first thing that comes to my mind, even if it's not really a present. I say, "I just want to see Mommy."

And Grams makes this choking sound and looks out her window again and starts crying and Gramps says "Now, Lucille" like she shouldn't be crying but I look in the rearview mirror and see that Daddy's eyes are getting wet too. And I'm sad because everything was real fun before that and I wonder if I've spoiled things by asking for a present that really isn't a present. But Gramps reaches back and tickles my knee and winks at me and says, "Sounds like a good gift to me, Spark Plug."

And Grams grabs me and presses my face in her chest so I almost can't breathe and she says, "O my baby," and rocks back and forth and Gramps says, "Now, Lucille" again and this time I'm kind of glad that Gramps said it for two reasons: one is that I don't like being called "baby" and the other is that Grams let loose of me a little bit and I can breathe better.

We get to the hospital and Daddy and Gramps let me and Grams out under the big canopy so that me and Grams can go pee. Grams has to pee a lot and Gramps is always teasing her about having a bladder the size of a pea. And Grams always says to him, "You try giving birth to eight kids and see how you get along afterwards," and then when Gramps doesn't answer she says "That always shuts him up." And I wish Gramps had given birth to eight kids so that he would have to pee more because every time Grams takes me I have to go in the ladies room and I don't like that because everything happens in stalls and I like being able to look at the men at the urinals.

After, we meet up in the big room where I always sit when I can't see Mommy, and Daddy walks off and comes back with Sister. She smiles and says, "Good morning, Einstein!" She always calls me Einstein and Daddy says it's a compliment because Einstein is the smartest man who ever lived (even if Grams thinks it was Solomon and even if I think it just may be Gramps). I don't answer right away because even though Sister is nice it always takes me a few minutes to get used to the tablecloth on her head and I need to get what Gramps calls warmed up.

Daddy says, "We're going to check in on Mommy and you sit here with Sister and we'll be back lickety split." Grams touches my cheek with her white-gloved hand and Gramps winks at me and messes up my hair and Daddy kisses his finger and touches it on the tip of my nose like Mommy does but now Daddy is doing it more and more, which I like, but it's also kind of sad because it reminds me that Mommy isn't around as much as she used to be.

And then Sister starts talking to me but I'm having a hard time listening because there are a bunch of ladies in high heels walking through the big room and their feet are making clip clop sounds really loud and this – along with the fact that I haven't got warmed up yet – is making it hard to listen to Sister because I'm imagining the women are horses and I wonder who let horses into a hospital.

And sister says, "Hey Einstein I don't think you're listening to me," but she's smiling and she doesn't say it like she's mad but more like a joke. "What are you thinking about?"

And because I suddenly feel I've got warmed up I decide that I can tell Sister exactly what it is that I'm thinking and so I tell her about the clip clop and the horses in the hospital.

And Sister laughs really loud and it echoes throughout the big room and she covers her mouth like she's embarrassed but I don't think she really is because she's smiling the whole time. So I smile too.

So sister says "Let's play our game: let's come up with some stories why horses might be in the hospital. I'll go first. The horses are here because many of the hospital workers have got the flu and are off sick and since there aren't enough hospital workers to deliver things to the doctors they've trained horses to do it. How's that?"

I say that it's pretty good. But then I say that I think there has been an explosion at the veterinarian because some Gook has got a hold of napalm and burned it down like happened in Viet Nam where Uncle Tom was. And so since there isn't an animal hospital they have to bring the animals to the people hospital and they're up on those floors where you have to be ten years old to go and the horses are more than ten years old and they're going up to visit their family members. But, since they're horses and can't fit in the elevator (which is called a lift in England) they have to take the stairs which are at the far end of the big room and so they walk through – clip clop – to get to the stairs.

And Sister claps her hands together and says "Wowzy wow – what an imagination!" But then she turns all serious and says "You really shouldn't say 'Gook,' Einstein," but I think maybe she's just saying it because she knows my story is better than hers and grown ups don't like it when you act smarter than they do.

Sister then looks like she's thinking real hard, trying to come up with a better story that doesn't have Gooks in it. And she begins saying something about flowers and I'm not getting the connection and suddenly she stops speaking and starts smiling a huge smile that goes from ear to ear (if you could see her ears underneath the tablecloth). And I'm thinking that she must have come up with a humdinger of a story to smile so big like that when I hear a voice say,

"Happy birthday, my little darlink."

And I turn away from Sister and there's Mommy in a wheelchair with Daddy pushing it and Grams and Gramps walking behind. And all of them are smiling smiles as big as Sister's, except maybe Mommy, whose smile seems different from the others.

And she says "Come here so I can squeeze you to pieces!" and I run to her and although she's not really hugging me that hard I feel like she's hugging me hard because I know she wants to hug me hard. And that's certainly enough for me. I really don't need any more.

But then she says that her doctor has agreed that turning seven is such a big deal that she should be able to spend the day with me outside the hospital, even if she can't come back to the Bay just yet. And even if at first I'm a little disappointed that she won't get to be with me for the evening party where I know that Uncle Jerry is going to shoot off fireworks I then change my mind and think that this, too, is certainly enough for me. I really don't need more.

Grams and Gramps say they're going to walk over to Eleventh Street and visit an old mine buddy of Gramps who lives there so they take off, Grams crying and Gramps saying, "Now, Lucille" as he puts his arm around her shoulder. And then Sister says that she has work to do and says "Talk to you again soon, Einstein" to me and "I'm really happy for you, Jean" to Mommy as she swishes away with a little gallop that makes me laugh because I'm really happy and I've definitely got warmed up to Sister at that point. And Daddy says he's going to get the car and so for the first time in a really long time I am alone with Mommy, if you don't count all the people walking through the big room on their way to the elevators and stairs, which I don't.

Mommy gets out of the wheelchair and we sit in two

regular chairs and she says, "So my little darlink, I've got a great day planned for us. And you know how I'm always telling you that you can't be selfish and you have to share your toys with your cousins because they're not as fortunate as we are? Well, today I'm going to break my own rule and I'm going to be selfish and not share you with anyone – not even Daddy. He's going to be our chauffeur but for the most part it'll just be me and my little darlink. How does that sound?"

"It sounds great, Mommy."

"Another word for 'great?'"

"Fantastic!"

"Another word for 'fantastic?'"

"Fabulous!"

"Another word for 'fabulous?'"

I think real hard and try to see the page of my notebook where I've written my words and I'm just about to say "You win, Mommy," when it comes to me: "Superlative!"

"That's my little genius!" she says hugging me again in a way that feels like it's hard even though it really isn't. "Where did I find you, my little darlink?"

"In the cabbage patch," I answer, even if it's a game we played more when I was really little. But Mommy still likes playing it so I like playing it too, even if it is kind of just for really little kids and I *am* already seven.

First of all Daddy drives us out to Mr. Lincoln's tomb which is in a big cemetery with lots of trees. We walk all around the tomb, which is the biggest tomb I have ever seen, even bigger than Grandfather and Grandmother Bradington's, which is pretty darn big. There's a really big statue of Mr. Lincoln's head out front of the tomb and I reach up and rub his nose because everyone does that and that nose is all shiny even though the rest of it is dull. I think Mr. Lincoln looks a little bit like Gramps and Mommy says she never thought of that but she thinks it's true even if Gramps is more handsome than Mr. Lincoln. And I agree that Gramps *is* more handsome than Mr. Lincoln.

And then we sit on a bench under a big tree a little way off and she pulls out her big green book and says that we should read something together. She tells me that there was a man who lived right there in Springfield and is buried in that same cemetery (but she doesn't remember where and doesn't really feel up to going in search of his grave) who wrote some nice poems and he wrote one about Mr. Lincoln's ghost.

I think it must be pretty exciting – like a real ghost story – but am a little disappointed. There are some great new words for my notebook like portentous and dreadnaughts and travail, but the story doesn't really make Mr. Lincoln seem scary, just sad.

"That's the point of it, my little darlink. Mr. Lincoln *is* sad because he tried to bring a country together and was sad that there had to be a war to do it. And when Vachel Lindsay wrote this poem there was another war starting up and he was sad so he wrote about that sadness putting it like Mr. Lincoln's sadness. Get it?"

I think I get it, but I also still think the poem is so sad that it's not fun and I'm supposed to be having fun on my birthday. And Mommy laughs and hugs me and says I'm absolutely right and she has another poem to read by that same Vachel Lindsay that is still a little sad but also a little scary and fun. And she turns the pages of her big green book to something called "The Congo."

And I begin reading and discover Mommy is certainly right about the scary and fun part. It's scary because there are witch doctors and warriors screaming "Blood!" and men being killed and some poor guy named Leopold whose ghost is burning in hell and there's this Mumbo Jumbo guy who you have to be careful what you do or he will hoo-doo you. And even if I don't know exactly what hoo-dooing is I know it can't be good, especially when it's put with witch doctors and warriors screaming "Blood!" and men being killed and poor Leopold's ghost burning in hell.

But it's fun, too, because the rhythm – always Mommy's favorite thing – is like a drum and it's beat beat beating faster and faster and then slower and then faster again. And when we read it again – this time Mommy reading to me which is OK in this case – she pounds my chest where the drums go and says, "Can you feel it, Eddie? Can you feel it?" And of course I can feel it because Mommy's fist is beat beat beating on my chest with the mumbo-jumbos and the hoo-doos and the boomlay boomlay boomlay BOOMS!

And I say to her, "Yes, Mommy, I can feel it."

And Mommy asks, "Will you be able to feel it if I'm not here?"

And I think that's strange because I obviously won't be able to feel it if she's not there but then I think that maybe I *could* read the words and still feel her pounding and so I say "I think so" because I'm not really sure what the right answer is and I hate getting things wrong.

And Mommy takes me and squeezes me tight and her body is shaking and I feel it just like the pounding of her fists and I knows that she's sad because she's crying but I don't really understand why she's sad and I don't know what to do to make her happy. So I just let her squeeze me like that and with my own fists I start pounding a little on her back with the same rhythm as in the poem because I know she's crazy about the rhythm.

And we just sit like that for a long time and finally Daddy comes up and says "Come on Jean we have to go," and me and Mommy follow Daddy back to the car. And even though it's way past lunchtime, Daddy drives us to Bob's Big Boy and even though Mommy had said that it was just going to be me and her, Daddy comes in with us to Bob's Big Boy and we all sit down together in a booth – Daddy on one side and me and Mommy on the other. And Mommy's not hungry but I get a cheeseburger and French fries and a Coke and then a hot fudge sundae and Daddy gets a bowl of chili but doesn't really eat much of it.

And then Mommy says she's tired and has to get back to the hospital and she seems sad but a little mad too which is confusing. So they go back to the hospital and Grams and Gramps are in that big room and Grams is knitting and Gramps is just watching the people and whistling. And someone brings a wheelchair back and Mommy sits in it and says to me, "Come here my little darlink."

And I walk over to the chair and she gives me squeezins again but they're not as strong as they were earlier. "Happy birthday, my beautiful, beautiful boy," she says and then gives me her big green book. "Mommy loves you very very much. Don't ever forget that." And she starts crying again and Daddy says "Now, Jean" just like Gramps says "Now, Lucille" to Grams.

And I say, "I love you too Mommy," and then Daddy turns the chair around and we go off in the direction of the elevators.

I'm holding the big green book and it's heavy but when Grams says, "Here, let me put that in my knitting bag," I jerk it away and say "No!" really sassy-like and I think I'm probably going to get in trouble for sassing Grams like that but I don't care.

*

Daddy and Grams and Gramps have been gone for two days and even though it's the summer there aren't any cousins at the Bay it's just me and my nanny Dina and the cook Lorraine. When I ask Dina where everybody is she tells me that they're with Mommy and when I ask Lorraine she just shakes her head and doesn't answer, which makes me kind of mad. And so without anyone to play with I just sit in Mommy and Daddy's sitting room and read from Mommy's big green book or I play with Snickers or sometimes I play the piano but it's not the same if no one is there to listen to me.

And then Snickers starts barking which means that someone is pulling up in the driveway and I run down the stairs and open the door and see Daddy and Grams and Gramps pulling up in Daddy's car. And Gramps is driving, which is really strange because Daddy always drives and what's even stranger is that Grams is sitting in the front seat with Gramps and she always sits in the back seat but this time Daddy's in the back seat. They get out of the car and Daddy comes up to me and gets down on one knee like people sometimes do on TV. He has whiskers and sometimes when he has whiskers Daddy will lift my shirt up and rub his whiskers on my belly and that makes me laugh and scream. But Daddy doesn't do that, he just hugs me really tight for a long time.

And then Daddy says "Your angel mother has gone to heaven," and Grams starts wailing like that cat who got its tail caught in the tree the summer before and Gramps grabs her and holds her as tight as Daddy is holding me.

But I don't cry like Grams and – now, I see – Daddy are crying. I don't cry because I'm thinking that going to heaven is what happened to Grandfather Bradington and

Mrs. Fletcher's husband. And although I can't really remember them a hundred percent, I know they were both really old and only really old people go to heaven. And Mommy is young and beautiful and so she can't go to heaven. And I figure that even grown ups can get things wrong sometime and Daddy has got this wrong. So I don't cry because it's all going to be OK and I'm going to read from the big green book with Mommy again and everyone will laugh about how Daddy got it wrong.

Lots of people are coming to the Bay and bringing ham and deviled eggs and casseroles but not very many cakes or pies. And many of the women are looking at me and shaking their heads and going "tch tch tch" and they sound like the pigeons that Daddy sometimes has to shoo away at the pool on our terrace in Chicago. And I want to shoo these women away too but know I'd get in trouble if I even tried. But I think about it.

But with all the people coming there aren't any aunts and uncles or cousins and that seems weird because they're always there in the summer. And I ask Daddy about it and Daddy says it wouldn't be right for the aunts and uncles and cousins to stay because Aunt Margaret is coming from Boston and it's really her house and not other aunts and uncles and cousins' so it wouldn't be right for her to arrive and find them all there camped out like Gypsies. Daddy's never talked about my aunts and uncles and cousins like Gypsies but he's mad a lot these days so maybe that's why he does it. When I ask Grams and Gramps why Daddy called my aunts and uncles and cousins Gypsies Grams gets all huffy and says, "We'll just leave if we're not good enough for his family!" but Gramps just says, "Now, Lucille," and she shuts up. But she still looks huffy.

And then finally Aunt Margaret comes and she hugs

me when she arrives but it's not really like a normal hug because Aunt Margaret is all stiff. One time when I was eavesdropping I heard Mommy's brother Uncle Jerry say that Aunt Margaret had something shoved up her ass and even if I'm pretty sure that Uncle Jerry was joking like he always does Aunt Margaret *did* kind of move like there was something up there.

And Aunt Margaret says to me that I must be strong, that I'm a Bradington and an Allerton and we are bold and fierce people. And she says that Daddy has to worry about a lot of things right now and he doesn't need to be worrying about me as well, so I need to be strong like a Bradington and fierce like an Allerton and not cry. "Be strong for Daddy," she says.

And then Dina comes and gets me and says that I need to get in the bath and I say I want to take a shower and she says don't sass me. So I take a bath and then Dina lays out my best suit for me and then Aunt Margaret comes in to help because Dina doesn't know how to tie a tie and I have a real tie and not one of those clip-ons like Uncle Tom has. And Aunt Margaret is tying my tie and telling me that I need to be strong for Daddy and not cry and I say OK but what I really want to say is that I can smell the whiskey on Aunt Margaret's breath and she might want to get a winter-green Lifesaver out of the jar in the family room or else people will think she's a drunk.

And I come downstairs and there's Daddy and Grams and Gramps standing there like they're waiting for me. And Daddy takes my hand and says, "Come on, little man" and I follow Daddy to the car and Grams starts crying really loud again and Aunt Margaret looks at her like she's done something bad.

We make the short drive down to the town and Daddy pulls the car under the canopy of Moynihan Funeral

Home and Mrs. Moynihan meets us at the door and shakes Daddy's hand and touches my cheek while saying, "You poor little thing!"

Me and Daddy walk into a room and there's a coffin there – not like the coffin in *The Bride of Dracula*, but one like Grandfather Bradington's, all shiny like a new penny or like Mr. Lincoln's nose. And Daddy takes my hand and we walk up to the coffin and Daddy lifts me up and I see Mommy inside, but she looks funny, and I'm starting to think that maybe she really did die and I don't exactly know what to do about it.

And Daddy looks at me and says, "This is just Mommy's shell – it's not Mommy. Everything that made her who she was has gone to heaven and this is left behind and it looks like Mommy but it's not Mommy because Mommy is in heaven. Do you understand?"

And I nod, even if I don't quite understand everything. I want to cry but I keep hearing Aunt Margaret's voice in my head saying I can't cry so I don't.

And then Daddy says, "Give me your hand" and I do and Daddy takes my hand and puts it on top of Mommy's hand. And it's cold and hard and scary and I want to pull away, but Daddy keeps pressing my hand down there and making me touch that cold hand.

Daddy says, "See? See how cold and hard this is? This isn't your Mommy. When you think of your Mommy you need to think of the part that lives in heaven, who called you her little darlink and read to you and taught you words and who is still with you in all of those things even if you can't see her. *That's* your Mommy, not this. Remember *those* things and remember that this is just a cold hard shell and that it's no more Mommy than that lamp there is."

And I nod because it seems pretty clear that Mommy *couldn't* feel like this and so maybe it can't be her, even if it looks an awful lot like her. I want to cry but I keep hearing Aunt Margaret's voice in my head saying I can't cry so I don't.

And then Grams and Gramps walk in and Gramps is wearing a suit and tie and I have never seen Gramps in a suit and tie and it looks funny, so funny that even though I am very sad I can't help but smile looking at Gramps. And Gramps winks at me and then rolls his eyes like he knows he looks funny in a suit and tie. Daddy takes me aside and tells me to sit down in a chair and I do and I watch Grams and Gramps come up to the coffin with Daddy. Grams starts wailing like that cat who got its tail caught in the tree the summer before and Gramps grabs her and holds her tight.

And then Aunt Margaret comes and sits next to me and all the aunts and uncles start coming in and most of them wail like Grams when they get to the coffin. And I'm sad not only because I know now that my mother is dead, but also because it hurts to see people like Uncle Jerry and Aunt Melinda and Uncle Tom and Aunt Louise so sad. I want to cry but I know I'm sitting next to Aunt Margaret who told me I can't cry so I don't. But I want to.

And after a while I lean over to Aunt Margaret and say, "I gotta pee" and she says, "One doesn't say 'I gotta pee,' Edward, one says 'Excuse me, I need to go to the restroom.'" And I say "Excuse me, I need to go to the restroom" even though everyone knows that you go to the restroom to pee or poop, but I would never tell anyone I had to poop. And then Gramps comes over from where he's standing and says, "I'll take him, Margaret," and we go off to the restroom.

Afterwards Gramps takes me to a little area where there are some chairs and sets me down on his lap. He says, "Spark Plug, it's a terrible thing that's happened. You don't know how much I hurt for you – and for me too."

I nod.

"And you're being such a brave little boy and being so quiet when usually you talk up a blue streak."

I nod.

"And I reckon that's because your Aunt Margaret is telling you to keep quiet."

I nod.

"Well listen to me, Spark Plug. Your Mommy's gone and that's just unfair and rotten, and there's not a whole hell of a lot any of us can do about it. And I'm so sorry."

"I'm sorry too, Gramps. Mommy was your daughter."

"Exactly. Why if you ain't the smartest little shit I've ever laid eyes on. Your Mommy *was* my daughter. And it ain't natural that a man should have to bury his child. It ain't natural, Spark Plug."

I nod.

"Now I know your Aunt Margaret is a really smart and important woman, and I know she means well, but I just can't help but think that she's a little off the mark here, and I don't mind sayin' so."

I nod.

"And so, Spark Plug, I don't know about you, but I know what I need to do is cry, because my little girl is gone. Do you want to cry too?"

I nod.

"Well then, to hell with em' all, Spark Plug. Let it out."

And then Gramps starts shaking and holds me tight. And Gramps cries, and I hold on to Gramps' big arm and cry too. The two of us just sit in that little area with the chairs and cry and rock back and forth and cry and hug until it just seems like it's time to quit. Then Gramps pulls out his handkerchief that isn't white like Daddy's but dark blue with white squigglies all over it that probably hides the snot better anyway. And we dry our eyes and wipe our noses and then we go back out into the room with Mommy's coffin and I sit back down next to Aunt Margaret, who doesn't say anything about the crying even though she probably knows but that's OK because I know that Aunt Margaret has had another swig of something because I can smell it on her breath.

It's five days after the funeral and everyone has gone away except for Aunt Margaret and of course Grams and Gramps. And without anyone to play with I just sit in Mommy and Daddy's sitting room and read from Mommy's big green book or I play with Snickers or sometimes I play the piano but it's not the same if no one is there to listen to me. So I go back to Mommy and Daddy's sitting room and I open Mommy's big green book and find that poem by Mr. Vachel Lindsay about the Congo with the mumbo-jumbos and the hoo-doos and the boomlay boomlay boomlay BOOMS!

And I remember what Mommy asked me: "Will you be able to feel it if I'm not here?"

And I can. I really can.

Chapter Five: 2012

The sun was shining through a gap in the curtains, a beam of light tentatively reaching the bed that was probably filled with dust motes, but that seemed more like sparkles. The air conditioner had been turned off and the air was still and warm.

Hank was lying on his back, having kicked the sheets to a clump at his feet. His mouth was open, and his head tilted as if he was considering what to do next. His naked body was whiter than Edward recalled from their rapid undressing of the night before.

Earlier, when a sliver of light was prying its way through his eyes and he was at that place where memory of the night before is also battling to come in, Edward feared he would be embarrassed or ashamed or even regretful. But he was none of these things. He was at ease.

His memory of the night was dented but intact. They had left the tavern and Edward got the idea to go for a swim in the pool, enticing in its desire to be used so late in the season. Hank wouldn't – he couldn't swim very well, it was too cold – but agreed to sit on the steps at the shallow end. They stripped and Edward saw Hank's body for the first time in the moonlight. The water swirled around them as if happy to be disturbed and Edward grabbed and kissed him, tasting his beery-breath mixed with the pool's chlorine. And he remembered Hank saying something about getting caught, that he worked next door, and someone might see them, that he was the secretary of the Chamber of Commerce, so Edward jumped out of the water, gathered up their clothes and ran to his room, not even telling Hank to follow.

Perhaps running across the parking lot naked had calmed them both, for when they were finally alone in his room the urgency of tongues and water, was subdued. And in its place came tenderness and an awareness of something, something just under the surface that Edward couldn't put a name to but that was present in them, between them.

Had they made love? Of course, Edward remembered the mechanics of it all; but had they made love? He felt, inexplicably, that they had, that it hadn't been about just getting off but about communicating. He shook his head, embarrassing even himself. Jesus, EJ, he thought, get a grip.

But then Hank looked at him, squinting a bit, and smiled. And Edward was certain it was not an awkward smile or – thank God – a regretful smile, but it was rather a smile that said he was glad to be there in that stuffy room, naked, while a beam of sparkles illuminated a corner of the bed.

"Good morning," Edward said, leaning over and kissing him on the shoulder.

"Good morning," he said. "What time is it?"

"I haven't got a clue," said Edward. He fished around on the night table and found his phone. "It's still kind of early – 6:43."

Hank reached up and ran his fingers through Edward's hair. "Jesus, that's basically dawn's crack."

"Do you want to sleep more?"

"What I want to do right now is piss," he said, hopping up and going into the bathroom, leaving the door open. "I'd say since we're up," he continued after the flush, "that we should get some breakfast. There's a little diner not far from here where I go almost every day. How's that sound?"

He plopped down next to on the bed, and Edward thought again how different he was from Ben, who was constantly covering himself and closing doors, who would really only allow Edward to see him naked when they were having sex – if he permitted the light to be left on.

"Sounds good," said Edward.

Hank lay back and closed his eyes. Edward studied his face and reached over and traced a line from Hank's forehead to his neck. Edward was shocked at how calm he felt, how the drama that always seemed to be just around the corner didn't seem to be arriving. There was a slight voice in his head, as harmless as a child's whisper, that told him what was happening was nothing more than a rebound, a physical response to the ending of his relationship with Ben. But the voice was so slight, so unconvincing, that he didn't give it any heed. Instead, another voice which he had not heard for years was saying that endings were always followed by beginnings, and that this man lying next to him gently rocking his head back and forth could well be a new beginning. That it all seemed too good to be true and didn't entirely make sense would ordinarily cause Edward to pause, if not flee completely. But he had the sensation that the gods of his journey were bidding him to move forward, not with his customary caution, but with a surrender to possibility that had been absent in his life for decades.

Hank opened his eyes. "Deep thoughts or just sex?" he asked.

"Yes," replied Edward, thinking that the two were not mutually exclusive.

When was the last time Edward didn't have to be somewhere, didn't have something that he had to do? In college, perhaps, if not earlier. The feeling of complete freedom that he was experiencing sitting across a booth from Hank, steaming coffee and the smell of bacon filling the air between them took him back to boyhood summers at the Bay. Even vacations hadn't offered this sense of freedom, as there was always a party to go to or an excursion, or dinner reservations or a tuxedo to be donned. Here there was just Hank, a big breakfast, faded khakis and an old Columbia t-shirt that Ben said was ragged and needed to be pitched, but that Edward had kept underneath his work t-shirts, feeling that throwing it away would be admitting some kind of defeat in a battle whose purpose he wasn't sure about.

He had to make it to the Bay, of course, but he had more than a month to get there. And as in all great voyage tales the destination more often than not paled in comparison to the trip itself, to the people who cropped up like magic mushrooms and changed established ways of looking at reality.

"Hello?" Hank was waving his hand in front of Edward's face. "You still with me?"

"Yes, of course," Edward said with a laugh. "Just thinking."

"I would say a penny for your thoughts," said Hank, "But I think you got a few more pennies than I do. What can I give you for your thoughts?"

Edward leaned over and tried to give his best leer.

"Woah! Keep your pants on. I'm sure everyone in here already thinks I'm a big himbo because I showed up at breakfast with this good-looking stranger and – although *he* looks like he just stepped out of some college catalogue – they probably all can't help but notice that I'm wearing the same clothes I wore to work last night. So let's just say I won't give you a hand job under the table for your thoughts, if that's what you're thinking." He crunched a piece of bacon.

"How about I tell you what I'm thinking, and you tell me what you're thinking? No hand jobs required."

"Sounds good. You go first." Hank leaned across the table, watching him closely.

"Well," Edward said, not sure exactly what it was he had been thinking, "I was thinking about how funny life is. I know it sounds banal, but two days ago I was in New York City thinking about where in the hell my boyfriend and I should go on vacation and the next thing I know I'm sitting in some small town in Ohio, single, on the way to some even smaller town in Illinois, eating a western omelet and talking to a smoking hot guy. You just never know what life is going to throw you, that's all. Especially when you veer out of your comfort zone. So that's me. What are you thinking?"

"Me? I'm thinking you're too good to be true, that you'll end up being an axe murderer or a rapist or in a boy band or something awful like that. I'm thinking that in all the years I've been working behind that bar I've never once hooked up with someone from there – not once – until last night. I'm thinking it's probably a good thing you're taking off because I want to remember everything just like this, you and me talking and laughing and not all the sadness that would come if we were together longer."

Edward grabbed his hand, a public gesture of affection he had never made with anyone before. "Why would it have to be sad? Jesus, anyone ever tell you you're a party pooper?"

Hank pulled his hand away. "You ever see *An Officer and a Gentleman*?"

"The movie? Yeah. A long time ago. Why?"

"Well even if we don't want to admit it, we all love that

movie, because we want to believe that anything is possible, and love conquers all and all that horseshit. And I know it's a story about a man and a woman but it's so gay in some ways - mainly in the way that we homos seem to wallow in our tragedies but love a happy ending when we can find one. But there's a reason why about half of your family is married to the same family. The reality is that it's a great fantasy because we all wonder how the other half lives. Am I right, or am I right?"

"Probably so," Edward said sadly.

"One night is the perfect time to forget the real world and get lost in a fantasy. But much more than that and things go sour – it's just common sense. So I'm glad you're just moving through because I'd be a big enough dumb-ass to try and stretch it out."

"I don't buy it," Edward said leaning back. "It's not always a fantasy, sometimes it actually works. My blue-blooded father married the eighth child of a poor-as-dirt coal miner and part-time handyman and farmer. A daughter – mind you – who also managed to work her way through college and get not only a bachelor's but a master's as well. Now you talk to me about fantasy, but for me it's not a fantasy; it's just the way things sometimes are.

"And another thing," Edward continued, spitting a piece of omelet on his coffee cup, "I think people talk like that because they're afraid of moving out of their nice safe world and going to places where they've never been. It's not common sense, it's what my Gramps used to call being yellow, though he pronounced it 'yeller.' I've been so fuck-ing afraid my whole life and I'm sick to death of it."

"My God who wound you up? So what's going to hap-pen now? You gonna' strip off that college shirt and wrap my head in it and pick me up and carry me out of the Red-bird Café while everyone stands and cheers and cries?"

"Why would I wrap your head in a shirt?" Edward asked, laughing.

Hank started laughing too, big snorts that drew the gaze of the booth-dwellers surrounding them. "That *was* pretty silly," he said, shaking his head. "It's just that in the movie he has a hat, you know, and he gives her his hat. I guess it don't make much sense to wrap my head in your shirt, but I said it, so there! You gotta better version?"

"Yes, I do," said Edward, leaning forward, smiling still, but seeming more serious, nonetheless. "We can walk out of here normal – I'm not thinking the whole head-wrapped -in-a-t-shirt scenario works quite as well – and you can get in my car and come with me to Illinois."

"You're serious?"

"I'm serious."

"You're full of shit."

"I've been told that before. But it doesn't change the offer on the table."

Hank studied him suspiciously. "So you're telling me that you would pick up some random dude that you just met and invite him to drive across two states with you?"

"You're not some random dude," he said, "You're Hank Robert Drummond, grandson of Stella, cousin of Ida May Titzer. You like old country music and hate boy bands, don't wear underwear, stopped smoking six years ago, have never been married, and you like *An Officer and a Gentleman*. You have a television but won't get cable because all you want to see is the local news anyway. The first time you voted was for Obama."

"Jesus, I sure do run my mouth when I get my drink on. I can't believe I told you all of that."

"You? I told you the story of nearly every one of my inbred relatives from the Mayflower on. Who cares?"

Hank studied him, seemingly trying to find a catch.

"Look," Edward continued, "I know this sounds crazy – it does to me too. And I understand if it's not possible to get the time off work or whatever. But if that's not a problem – if the only reason you wouldn't consider it is because it sounds crazy – then I say 'Fuck it!' and just come. I'm not an axe murderer and, though I went through a brief Back Street Boys period and still, to this day, admit an extreme like for 'I Want It That Way' and you *will* find it on my iPhone I, personally, have never been in a boy band. You can come for a few days and then I'll fly you back home, or you can stay as long as I'm staying. It's all up to you. I just know that I'm not ready to leave the first person who's made me feel happy in a long time. I'm just not ready to do that." His voice wavered.

"Jesus, alright! I'll come. Stop talking before you say 'You complete me!'"

"For someone who doesn't have cable you sure seem to reference a lot of movies. And they're all romantic comedies … hmmm … I bet if I dug deeper I'd find some NSYNC CDs somewhere in your past!"

"Fuck you," Hank said. "I said I'd come with you," fluttering his eyelashes for effect, "but a gal has her limits."

Edward liked that he said "gal," loved the campy unpretentiousness of it. At first he felt somewhat guilty about it, worried that he was acting like some aristocrat who found the patois of the peasant charming. But the more he listened to Hank talk – and he could talk up a blue streak, as Gramps would say – he realized that it was not condescending, this love of his speech, but rather exalting. Because listening to Hank speak, getting lost in his nasal tones and rolling patterns it dawned on Edward: this is how people *should* talk, not the rarified speech of his circle who, in constantly trying to be clever and fashionable and exclusive didn't really *say* anything at all.

Hank *said* things. Riding next to him, sipping his Coca Cola (which Hank actually called "Coca-Cola" and not "Coke") Edward learned more in their first two hours on the road than he had ever known about Ben. Hank wasn't from Ohio; he was from Louisville, Kentucky. He did a year of junior college there – had wanted to be a nurse – before he hooked up with an asshole named Chuck. Chuck's people were from Ohio, and so they settled there, but Hank never went back to college, as Chuck's lack of dependability and constant gambling problem necessitated that at least one of them had a steady job. And work he did and continued to do so long after Chuck had run off with a second cousin of his.

"Why didn't you go back to Louisville at that point?" asked Edward, rubbing the foot that Hank had put in his lap.

"I meant to. But then Stella died and there was no one there to go back for. And then I found out that Stella had left me a bit of money – nothing anywhere near like you're used to, of course, but a small fortune for me – and Danny – he's the owner of the Redskin – was having some problems and so I bought half the place from him and then I kind of had to stay."

"Wow! You never told me you were a real live entrepreneur! You shouldn't have told me, you know, because now you'll never know for sure if I just want you for your money!"

"Right. Whatever," he said, rolling his eyes, "This goddamned tank you drive probably cost more than I put into that bar. Did you not know that there's a problem with global warming and that we're ruining the planet?"

"Left-wing conspiracy crap," Edward responded again.

"They'll try to make you believe *anything!*"

"My God," Hank said in mock horror, "I accepted that you like the Back Street Boys and that there's the very real possibility that you're an axe murderer, but I never dreamed I've been fucking a *Republican!*"

"I'm not a Republican. I'm an Independent."

"That's what all you Republicans say when you're too goddamned ashamed to admit it."

They rode in silence for a while, Edward rubbing Hank's feet, Hank taking sips of his Coca-Cola, America passing by. Edward was shocked that there had not been a "What the fuck have I done?" moment, a regret at having asked this stranger to share a journey with him. Instead, there was just a kind of ease that made him so relaxed he almost felt sleepy.

"So tell me about Stella," he said, glancing at Hank's tattoo.

"Stella?" Hank smiled that kind of smile that not only suggests happiness but seems to contain it as well. "Well, Stella was basically both momma and daddy to me. My daddy worked on the river with the barges and was never home, and so she – his momma – raised me."

"And your mother?"

"My mother," he said with a snort-like laugh. "Momma had lots of problems, let's just say. Drink. Men. OK, maybe not lots – maybe just two problems – but two bigguns' anyhow. She ran off with – get this – a *preacher* when I was five or six." And then, leaning in conspiratorially, said in nearly a whisper, "a *black* preacher – quite the scandal in Kentucky in those days." He leaned back and continued. "I never saw her after that. Daddy died of pancreatic cancer about fifteen years ago. Stella five years later."

"I'm sorry."

"Yeah, well, everyone's got a sad story, don't they? I bet even Republicans like you."

"*Independents* like me, you mean."

"Right, whatever.

"So yeah, Stella," Hank continued, "She was funny and tough and just one of them people who're filled with life, you know?"

Edward looked at the photograph on the dashboard. "I know exactly what you mean."

"Of course you do," he said, reaching up to touch the photograph. "Of course you do. Stella also knew people really well, it's like she had a built-in bullshit detector. She knew, when I ran off with Chuck, that it would end badly. She could just *see* that Chuck was going to hurt me. And she tried to stop me – God knows she tried – but there wasn't anything she could do. I can be stubborn."

"Good to know," said Edward, smiling.

"Yeah, but she was a great person. We spend all this time in school studying Gandhi and Martin Luther King, and they were great men – don't get me wrong – but sometimes I think they should do classes every now and then on people like Stella, or like your Grams and Gramps. Because, I know Gandhi changed like a billion peoples' lives, but Stella changed mine, you know? And, in the end, I think it'd be good for people to hear more about that kind of thing too." He took another sip. "Can you imagine," he continued, "going to school one day and saying 'I gotta multiple-choice test today on Stella, Grams and Gramps!'" He laughed and let loose a little burp at the same time.

"That'd be great," Edward said, meaning it.

"Anyway, it was Stella who suggested I study to become a nurse. I'd have never thought about it in a million years – I didn't have the best track record in high school –

but when she said it, it just kind of made sense to me. She said that I was always caring for Momma when she would have one of her spells – although I don't remember that myself – and that being a nurse would be a great way to get paid for doing something that I already knew how to do. But then, along came Chuck and that got all blown to hell."

"Well, it's not too late," said Edward feebly.

"Yeah. Right, I'm forty-three years old. I've done nothing but work in a bar for the last twenty-odd years. Do you believe this crap or is it something that people like you say to people like me, like we're in some sort of mother-fucking afterschool special?" He jerked his feet out of Edward's lap and turned away, looking out the window.

"I'm sorry," Edward said, surprised both at Hank's strong reaction and at how hurt he felt by it. "I didn't mean to piss you off. Of course, I don't know the whole situation, but people do things like that all the time. My Aunt Margaret got a PhD in anthropology when she was nearly seventy. It happens."

"Was your Aunt Margaret working in a bar when she got her PhD?"

"No. But that's not the point," Edward said, perhaps more gruffly than he intended.

"Sorry," Hank said, placing his feet back in his lap. "Another few miles and you'll be leaving my ass on the side of the road. I can be a dick sometimes. Don't pay any attention to me."

Edward went back to rubbing his feet. "Hank?"

"Yeah," he said, eyes closed tightly as if concentrating really hard on something.

"Earlier you said that there was still someone back in Kentucky. Who would that be?"

"Well," Hank said, opening his eyes and looking at him. "That would be my daughter."

"I think it's time we got some lunch." Edward responded, looking in his rearview mirror. He knew it wasn't the best response to what he'd just found out, but it was all he had.

They pulled into a Mexican restaurant that had obviously once been a Wendy's. There was a sign which now read "El Bandito" and had a cartoonish Mexican bandit painted on it, running and looking behind him as if being chased by some invisible Gringo. But looking closely Edward could see the outline of a girl with red pigtails, hovering, ghost-like behind the bandit. Everyone runs from their ghosts, he thought, and was about to point this out to Hank but thought the better of it. ("Spark Plug," Gramps used to say to him, "Just because you *got* a thought don't mean you have to *say* it." That particular nugget of advice had gone unheeded far too many times in his life already.)

Hank had become less talkative since the revelation about his daughter, and Edward hadn't pushed him. But now, sitting in front of a frozen margarita the size of a small aquarium, the sound of crunching nacho chips punctuating the silence that had followed them in from the car, he felt a need to speak.

"Hank," he said quietly, "I thought you said you didn't have any children. You know, last night? It's no big deal, really, I'm just wondering why you didn't tell me."

"First of all," he said, "You didn't ask me if I had any children, you asked me if I had ever been married or had a long-term partner and I said no. I wasn't trying to hide anything – I swear – I just didn't really want to get into it last night after all those beers."

"Fair enough," Edward responded, feeling a little foolish. "And you don't have to talk about it now if you don't want to, but just know that you can. You probably feel like

I've been giving you the third degree ever since we left. It *is* possible to talk about the weather or movies or something. We shouldn't let the fact that I'm in this weird, reflective place right now make things too heavy."

"'Weird, reflective place'? Jesus how you talk! Where did I find you?"

"My mother used to ask me that," Edward said, knowing he was on the verge of becoming deep and reflective yet again. "It was a game we played. And I responded: 'In the cabbage patch!'"

"See, that's just it," Hank said, "that's probably why I didn't tell you. Last night when you were talking about your mother you just lit up every single time. That's the way it's supposed to be, I guess, between parents and children. My mother didn't want anything to do with me and I didn't have anything to do with my daughter. What does that say about me?"

"Well, the first part says something about your mother, if it says anything at all. And the second? I don't know that it says much of anything. It depends on the circumstances. There are a million reasons why someone might do that, and most of them are good. I assume your reasons were good."

"Stella used to say 'assume makes an ass out of u and me.' Reasons? I was young, really young – just turned seventeen – and I didn't think I could handle it. I already knew I was gay, of course, and I think I got with the mother – Tracy was her name – more than anything just to see if I could, you know, physically do it and – I thought at the time – live a more normal life. I didn't think much beyond that thought of 'Well, I can get it up for a girl, maybe this will be a solution to my problem of liking dick.' I knew – *Tracy* knew – that it just wouldn't work, and since abortion was out of the question (more for her than for me, but of course it was her who had to make the decision) we decided giving her up for adoption was the only thing we could do."

"That sounds perfectly reasonable," said Edward. "Really."

"Yeah, maybe," Hank said. "But then Tracy dies of cancer at age twenty-nine and I hadn't ever found a guy to love – or who loved me anyway – and I thought if we had just stayed together I'd at least have had someone to care for and maybe that would have given me some stability, a push to make life better. Maybe I would have stayed in college, ended up with a better life."

"Who knows?" Edward said. "Gramps used to say, 'If ifs and buts were candy and nuts, we'd all have a really good Christmas.'"

"I'd have loved your Gramps, I think," said Hank.

"And I think Gramps would have loved you as well." The thought of it, of Grams and Gramps and Stella and Hank all together somehow seemed lovely, one of those manifestations of how-things-should-be that was fleeting but powerful, like the beam of a lighthouse.

"So," Hank continued, obviously determined to tell the tale now, "We're seventeen and pregnant. Stella found the adoption agency, I think, and everything was arranged. Tracy missed a semester of school. I wasn't with her when the baby was born. I think because I didn't get to see the baby it was like she wasn't really a part of me, you know?"

Edward nodded.

"So anyway about seven or eight years ago now, I get this letter from the adoption agency. My daughter – it still sounds funny even saying it – had turned eighteen and was asking to get in touch with me. They had forwarded a letter from her that basically said she didn't really want anything, just wanted to know a little bit about me. She sent me a picture. She's really pretty."

"That's not surprising, knowing her father," said Edward smiling.

"Whatever," Hank said rolling his eyes. "Anyhow, I wrote her back, told her a little bit about myself and that was that. After that we heard from each other a couple of times a year and that was pretty much it until maybe about six months ago when Ellie – that's her name, short for Eleanor – said she would like to meet me."

"Wow," said Edward. "So did you meet?"

"No," said Hank, "we didn't. I didn't really want her to come to Ohio and see me slinging drinks in a bar."

"A bar that you are half-owner of," Edward interrupted. "There's no shame in that."

"I guess not," Hank said. "It's just that she went to college and is an accountant for Humana and I guess at the end of the day I was worried that we wouldn't have that much to talk about."

"And going there? What about you going there?" Edward asked.

"I told her that that's what we would do someday when I got the chance. I went back a few times before and once after Stella's funeral, but besides that I've never been back. I should look in on Stella's grave. Do you know I took some of the money that she left me and paid to have her buried in the same cemetery as Colonel Sanders?"

"Like in KFC?" Edward asked.

"Like in KFC," Hank answered. "Stella just thought Colonel Sanders was the fucking end-all-be-all. He had this huge birthday party at the Brown Hotel years ago and she got to go, through her friend Catherine, I think. There were literally tens of thousands of people there, but Stella swears up and down that she and the Colonel spoke together for fifteen minutes. I always said, 'Stella, you're pullin' my leg!'

but she said it was true, that they talked for fifteen minutes and he was the perfect southern gentleman. So anyway, when I got word that Stella had passed and that she had left me quite a bit of money, I called up Cave Hill – that's the name of the cemetery – and said I don't care how much it costs I wanted Stella to be buried there."

"Pretty impressive," said Edward.

"Yeah, says the guy who owns a whole fucking town!"

"My family does, I don't," said Edward dismissively. "Anyway, back to Ellie. How about we swing by Louisville and see her? And Stella. And Colonel Sanders, of course."

"Of course," laughed Hank. "Just drive to Louisville and look her up and say, 'Hey, I'm in town, how about the two of us get together for a cup of tea? Oh, and by the way: I'll be accompanied by some rich dude who drives a tank who I picked up a couple of days ago.'"

"Why not?" asked Edward.

"I need to prepare," he replied. "And it would be rude to just drop in on her. She's already going to think I'm a skank when she meets me."

"First of all, that's not true. You're not a skank, and she won't think that. Secondly, what do you have to prepare? You call her, you say you're passing through town, and you'd like to meet her. Remember *she's* the one who initiated this whole thing, so she obviously wants to see you." He leaned back with the confident air of a seasoned litigator resting his case.

Hank appeared to study his half-eaten burrito. Edward noticed that his left eye was dancing quickly from side to side, as if nervous. But only the left eye. He thought he had already noted every single detail about Hank, from the way he sometimes bit the inside of his cheek to his strong veiny hands and arms. But just when Edward thought he could sum him up in his mind, describe him to someone if asked, a new detail would surface like an old painting bleeding through a new one, new shapes and colors making themselves known and seen.

"Well," said Hank, "I must be crazy, but ... what the hell! Let's do it. If you don't mind going to Louisville, that is. It wasn't part of your original plan."

"Have you learned nothing about the essence of the road trip?" Edward asked. "It's not about preparation and packing and planning and maps; it's about paying attention to the people you meet on the road. You've met this rich dude driving a tank who obviously stopped at your bar for a reason. Pay attention to him. That's the way it works. And he's saying that we're going to Louisville and we're going to call upon Ellie-short-for-Eleanor and we're going to bring flowers to Stella's grave and say hello to the Colonel when we're there."

"Yes, master," he said.

And they looked at each other, and the words that were not said were nevertheless there. And for an instant Edward asked himself what would happen if he actually spoke the words that were there but weren't. He didn't say them, even though the very air between them seemed to be expressing them in dust and electricity. He could almost see the words now, dancing playfully around them as one dances when they know they are victorious. Or, at least, when they believe they will be.

Chapter Six: 1976

It's my tenth birthday and even though it's supposed to be a happy day it's not happy. It's not exactly sad – it's not like I'm Louis XIV's brother and being forced to wear an iron mask, or young Heathcliff being locked in an attic – but it's not happy because for every birthday I can remember I have been at the Bay (except for the one in Springfield at Mr. Lincoln's cemetery and Bob's Big Boy). This year Daddy has taken me to Boston and Aunt Margaret's house and she – Aunt Margaret – is having a birthday party for me. But what kind of birthday party can it be if it's without Grams and Gramps and Uncle Jerry shooting off fireworks over the bay while giving Grams a big squeeze and kissing her on the cheek before she says, "You smell like a brewery!" and pushes him away? And who's going to make a cake for me like Grams? Certainly not Mildred, Aunt Margaret's cook who told me once "Maybe you run into the kitchen for a glass of milk out in the sticks in Illinois but we don't do that here," and then wouldn't even give me a glass of milk, even though I knew it was right there in the fridge because I had seen the milkman bring it in. (I had also seen the milkman touching Mildred's booby and had half a mind to tell Aunt Margaret.)

And what kind of birthday will it be without my cousins? At Aunt Margaret's there is only my cousin Annabel who is three years older than me and sometimes is nice to me and sometimes is not. She always acts all nice in front of Daddy and Aunt Margaret but when Aunt Margaret says,

"Annabel take your cousin to the playroom" during cock-tails Annabel can turn downright mean. She's a lot bigger than I am and she can hit and pinch and smack pretty darned hard. But Daddy just says that Annabel is rebellious and free-spirited and that I'd know if she didn't like me be-cause Annabel doesn't really hide it when she doesn't like someone and she does like me even if she doesn't always act nice.

I don't tell Daddy but she sometimes calls me names, too. She says I'm queer because I read books all the time and that that's only a thing that little girls or queers do. And she says I'm a hayseed but I know she doesn't know what that means but that she got it from Aunt Margaret because I overheard Aunt Margaret calling me that to her husband Bill once, who is so quiet and weird that I don't even call him "Uncle Bill" but just "Bill" which is rather strange. And now, after all these years, Aunt Margaret has started correcting me when I say "Aunt" like the ants that march around dead trees and not "ahh-nt" which she says is how it's pronounced, even if all of my other aunts are ants and not ahhnts. But whether Margaret's an ahhnt or an ant it still doesn't change the fact that Annabel can be kind of mean to me when we are alone. And when I complain to Daddy about Annabel's meanness Daddy just says "You need to act like a gentleman, EJ" which makes *no* sense at all because Gramps says that you only have to act like a gentleman to ladies and gentlemen and to hell with the rest of them. And Aunt Margaret *may* be a lady, but Annabel is certainly not.

And so it's my tenth birthday and I'm at Aunt Mar-garet's trying to stay away from Annabel like Jane Eyre tried staying away from Aunt Sarah Reed (who was most certainly an ahhnt and not an ant) and from her cousins Eliza, John and Georgiana before Jane Eyre went to

Lowood School where her best friend Helen Burns died right in her arms. I'm in my room and I'm dressing for dinner, which is always a big hairy deal because I have to put on a jacket and tie and shine my shoes and then be expected to go to the playroom with Annabel until cocktails are finished and we get to eat with Daddy and the rest. I hate this dressing for dinner business because it's like the end of the world if I get soup on my tie or something. At the Bay with Grams and Gramps dressing for dinner means coming in from outside and washing my hands and feet if I'm running around barefooted (and I almost always am) and maybe putting on a shirt if it's a Sunday dinner but not even putting on a shirt if it's some other day and it's hot.

There's a knock on the door and it's Daddy who asks me if I'm ready to go to the playroom with Cousin Annabel.

"Why can't I just stay here and read until it's actually time to eat?" I ask because usually Daddy likes it when I use words like "actually" but this time it doesn't work because Daddy just frowns and says, "EJ – now!" and points out into the hallway.

The two of us walk down the hallway with a bunch of paintings of my relatives and go to the playroom. Daddy opens the door and I am really happy to see that Annabel's not there. I hope she hasn't died like poor Helen Burns but if she's gotten a little sick I won't be too sad. Daddy kisses me on the top of my head and says, "Play nice with Annabel" like *I'm* the one with the problems and not psycho Annabel. "Bertrand will come and get you when it's time for dinner. Eddie – this is an important night for me, so please be on your best behavior."

Daddy leaves and I wonder why it's such an important night for Daddy and not *me*, since it's my birthday and all, but Daddy's been acting really weird this trip so

I just let it go like water off a duck's ass, like Gramps tells me to do when I get upset about something that I can't change.

Since Annabel's not there I go over to the piano because it's just an upright and I'm allowed to play it, even though I'm not allowed to play the baby grand that's in the parlor which is silly because they have the same number of keys and everything but that's the rules. I play and sing *Oh, What a Night* by The Four Seasons and get kind of sad because it's the song that Aunt Melinda always asks me to do and I wonder if Aunt Melinda's at the Bay or not. And then I do *(Hey Won't You Play) Another Somebody Done Somebody Wrong Song* by B.J. Thomas because Uncle Teddy always asks for it and sings along really loud and out of key until Aunt Louise says "Jesus, Teddy pipe down! You sound like two goats screwing!" I am just beginning *The Way We Were* because Grams and every last one of my aunts likes that one when Annabel comes in the room, so I stop.

"Only queers play the piano," she says. I know that "queer" means odd or strange – it has come up a lot in the different books I've read – but I'm pretty sure that Annabel is using it in a different way like some kids at school use it and I want to know exactly what it means but I'm too embarrassed to ask her or them. It might have something to do with the post office because Uncle Jerry always calls old Bobo the postman in Bradington a queer but how carrying the mail for someone can be a bad thing I don't know, so I just let it go like water off a duck's ass because – as Gramps also says - "Spark Plug, you can't win 'em all."

I get up from the piano bench and walk over to a red bean bag chair. I wish I had snuck in a book with me because I really don't have anything to say to Annabel and she never wants to play any of my games because they're either baby games or queer.

"Are you queer?" asks Annabel flopping down in the bean bag across from me.

"I know that queer means odd or strange and so I don't think I am queer," I answer in a way that if I said it to Grams she'd say "Don't get snooty!" but in Boston seems to be the way that people talk.

"No, baby, 'queer' doesn't mean odd or strange it means a boy that likes boys instead of girls."

All of a sudden I understands why Uncle Jerry calls Bobo a queer, and I wonder if maybe I *am* a little queer like Bobo, because I'm thinking of Bobo's tan legs in his postman's shorts with the stripes down the side. But I'm not about to say this to Annabel, so I say "I am not queer."

"Do you want to see my pooter?" asks Annabel and I have no idea what a pooter is but I'm a little nervous because I think it has to have something to do with girl parts and sex even if in Chicago we call it a wee-wee or hoo -hah. And I don't necessarily want to see my cousin's wee-wee, hoo-hah or pooter but I'm afraid that if I say I don't want to see it that she'll really think I'm like Bobo the postman so I say yes.

Annabel gets up from her bean bag and stands in front of me and lifts up her dress and pins it to her chest with her chin and then she pulls down her underwear and I see for the first time in my life a real live wee-wee, hoo-hah or pooter. And I'm kind of fascinated by it but afraid of it at the same time, kind of like Space Mountain at Disneyworld. And I am just about ready to reach up and touch it out of interest when she quickly pulls up her shorts again and lets her dress fall back down.

"You're a pervert!" she says to me and I knows what that word means because I heard it so many times in the kitchen at the Bay that I went to look it up in the dictionary. And so I say, "*I'm* not the pervert, *you* are! I didn't show you *my* pooter!"

And Annabel laughs so hard that she falls back into the bean bag and snorts. "You haven't got a pooter, stupid; you've got a prick." And she's still laughing at me and I think that these kinds of things never happen in *Jane Eyre* or *Wuthering Heights* and this is exactly why I like reading books.

"So," she says, all serious now, "now you have to show me your prick."

"No," I say, partly because I think I'd get in trouble and partly because my prick started moving and acting funny when I kept thinking about Bobo's legs and I don't want my cousin Annabel to see it.

"Suit yourself," she says. "I was going to give you a hand job for your birthday but now I won't." She crosses her arms like she's all put out or something, but I'm not going to budge because there really is something going on down there now. I'm not sure what a hand job is but if my prick is involved it sounds like it could be painful. Annabel goes to a school with the Catholics and I think that they sure learn a lot more in that school than I do with the Episcopalians because no one has ever mentioned a hand job or pooter to me before.

"So," she says, "are you ready to get a new mother?"

And I think that as mean as Annabel can be she has never made fun of the fact that I don't have a mother and it almost comes to me to cry but I know if I cry she'll have what Grams refers to as a field day and I don't want to give her the satisfaction so I stay real cool.

"My mother is dead," I say to her trying not to cry. "So I can't have a new mother."

"Lot you know," she says grinning like the cat that ate

the canary (as Grams would say) or with a shit-eating grin (as Gramps and all my uncles would say). "Your father is dating one of my mother's best friends, Leslie. And she'll be your new mother. Mother says they're not talking about marriage yet, but she's sure it'll happen. Then they'll probably move out here to get away from the sticks. Anyway, Leslie is really nice and very pretty and – as Mother says – she comes from a good family, not a bunch of coal-mining hayseeds."

And then I decide to say something to my cousin that I was told to never ever say. The only time I ever heard it was when my ex-Uncle Robbie said it once to my Aunt Melinda right at the end of a big fight they had in front of everybody one summer night at the Bay, and the words were so shocking that Grams starting crying like someone had shot her in the foot or something and Uncle Jerry chased ex-Uncle Robbie out of the house and threatened to break his goddamned scrawny neck if he ever came near his sister again. But somehow, I just know that this is the time to say this phrase because it seems that Annabel is not only being disrespectful to me but to Mommy and Grams and Gramps and everyone. So I look her straight in the eye and say, "Go fuck yourself, you cunt!" and even though she doesn't start crying like Grams did (which I actually hoped she would) her eyes *do* go really big. At first she doesn't say anything, just sits there in shock with her mouth open like a big fat carp lying on the dock. But then she smiles and says, "You're alright, queer boy." And I'm still not too happy to be called queer, but I think if Annabel is smiling then I know I've used the words well and think that sometimes it's not so bad when things happen that never happen in *Jane Eyre* or *Wuthering Heights*.

*

Leslie *is* pretty — I have to admit that — but Mommy was much prettier. Mommy had dark hair and eyes as black as the coal that Gramps chipped from the ground and was thin but not too thin and was even kind of muscular as well. Before she got sick, of course. Leslie has hair so blonde that it almost looks white and she is very very thin and in some places — like her neck — you can see little blue veins near the surface. She smiles but she doesn't laugh much, and even when she smiles it doesn't seem like she's always smiling because her eyes — which are *really* blue — don't seem to match her lips. She wears tons of makeup and always turns her head to the side and touches first one ear then the other, like she's just begging for someone to notice the big honking diamonds that she has there.

Daddy is smiling but not laughing too, and he's acting really nervous, like he's afraid that the chandelier is going to crash down on us all any minute. Daddy keeps looking at me with his eyebrows raised a little bit, like he's wondering what I think about it all, and, especially, about her.

"So, Edward," Leslie says. "Ten years old today. You're practically a man. Your father tells me that you are super intelligent and interested in history and literature. I've arranged for a Dean at Harvard University to take you on a tour tomorrow. Won't that be nice?"

"Yes, ma'am," I say because even if I'm not sure I like this woman with the icy eyes I know I can't be rude or else Daddy will be upset with me.

"I thought you'd like it. Your father thinks you'll particularly enjoy the library. And then, after that, we can have a nice big lunch out and go shopping. What do you think?" She looks at me and smiles but this time the smile doesn't even seem close to a smile.

"It sounds delightful, ma'am," I say and Daddy smiles because I'm doing and saying the right things, which have

95

become a lot more important for Daddy after Mommy died than they were before.

"Can I go?" asks Annabel. Why Annabel would want to go to Harvard University or see a library is beyond me, because I know for a fact that in part she had to go to school with the Catholics because she was having troubles in school because she's clearly not as smart as I am even if she's three years older.

"No, dear," Aunt Margaret says, and Annabel frowns and I want to mouth the word "cunt" to her but I'm afraid of getting caught so I don't.

"Just think, EJ" Daddy says, but like's he's nervous, "in a couple of months our country is going to be two-hundred years old. Isn't it great to be out here where all that history started? This is certainly a great time to spend some time in Boston, that's for sure. I'm sure Boston will put on a fireworks show like you've never seen before – I can't wait for you to see it."

"What about the Bay?" I ask, even though I know I should have said yes sir that will be great sir.

"Don't worry, sport, you'll make it to the Bay for Labor Day. But I thought that for the summer – since it's such a special summer out here in Boston – that we would spend more time here. Between Leslie and your Aunt Margaret, there are so many things planned that you won't even miss the Bay."

I'm trying not to cry because I know I'm ten years old now and probably too old to cry and also that Aunt Margaret has a thing about crying and also I don't want Annabel to see me cry (and she's leaning forward on her seat looking at me like she's expecting the tears at any minute). And I think if I look at Daddy I'll start crying so I look instead at Leslie and decide to talk to her like the others aren't even there.

"I'm very excited about Harvard, ma'am. Even if Daddy and Grandfather Bradington went to Columbia, I know that many of Grandmother Allerton's people went there so I want to see it. And I do like libraries very much, so that will be really neat. Thanks." I can feel Daddy smiling but I still can't look at Daddy or I might start crying.

"Your father was right," says Leslie, "you are quite the little gentleman."

I think she might be smiling with her eyes this time and not just with her mouth, so I figure I can continue and really try and talk to her.

"But I always spend my summers at The Bay, which is this house that my family has just off the Illinois River in a town named Bradington, which you've naturally heard of. My Grams and Gramps are the caretakers of the place and I really like going there because they're the absolute best people in the world. And I get to see my cousins and aunts and uncles and go swimming and out in the paddle boat and Grandfather Bradington had a really big library there – surely not as big as Harvard's, naturally – but big enough that I can always find an interesting book to read. And Snickers – he's my dog – loves it there too because Grams gives him all kinds of things that our cook in the city won't give him and he can jump into the bay and swim to his heart's content and when he does his tail goes around and around like a helicopter."

I know I'm probably talking too much, but I keep going because I'm pretty sure that Leslie smiled once with her eyes as well as her mouth and I think that if I just keep talking then maybe she'll be convinced and she can convince Daddy to let me spend the summer at the Bay. I keep *not* looking at Daddy or Aunt Margaret or Annabel or weird Bill who hasn't said a word the whole meal and is just staring at his plate like it's a Martian or something.

"And my Mommy is buried there, you see, and when I stay there my Gramps and me – excuse me, my Gramps and I – we go every day to the cemetery to take flowers to her and he tells me all kinds of stories about her so that I won't forget her and I'm afraid if I stay away the whole summer that she'll think I've forgotten her."

And now, thinking about walking to and from the cemetery holding Gramps' hand (even if I might be getting too old for that) and putting flowers on Mommy's grave and hearing all about Mommy when she was a little girl and even a grown-up I'm *really* worried I'm going to start crying because I'm suddenly very sad and I don't want to be sad on my birthday which makes me even sadder somehow. But I look up at Leslie and see that she's crying – not big boo-hooing like Grams does but a couple of tears running down from her blue blue eyes. And the fact that Leslie is crying makes it easier for me *not* to cry for some reason.

I look up at Daddy who seems sad too. And then I look at Aunt Margaret who always seems a little angry but looks even angrier this time, maybe on account of the way that she hates crying and all. Annabel is looking like she's confused, and Bill is still looking down at his plate.

Leslie reaches across the table and grabs my hand. "Edward," she says, and I think she's saying it to me but she's actually looking at the other Edward, my father, so I'm not real sure who in the hell she's talking to, "The Bay sounds just wonderful, and I think – if your father agrees – that it's the perfect place to spend a summer. Boston will always be here, right?"

"Right. Is that OK, Daddy?"

Daddy says it's OK by him. Aunt Margaret looks at me like she's mad but I don't care because it was *her* friend who cried, not me. Annabel looks at me and when she's sure no one is looking sticks out her lower lip like she's a baby and mouths the words "boo hoo." I look at her and mouth the words "fuck off cunt" and Annabel smiles and gives me the thumbs up. Then I look over and realize that Bill is for the first time looking at me and I'm worried that Bill will give me the what-for for saying such a thing to his daughter. But Bill just chuckles and then looks back down at his plate, less like it's a Martian now and more like it's an old friend.

Daddy was supposed to fly out to Chicago with me but he said he had some urgent business to take care of, so I'd have to go on my own. Annabel told me that was a lie, that she heard her mother say that Daddy's urgent business was trying to patch things up with Leslie on account of the fact that I'd ruined things by my antics at that supper where Leslie cried. Annabel said there was no way in hell that Leslie would marry Daddy because she'll always be second fiddle, and what woman wants to play second fiddle to a brat? She's telling me this like I should be sad or sorry or scared or something, but I just feel OK because even if Leslie seemed like a nice lady she wasn't the right lady for Daddy.

I've taken the airplane lots of times, but I've never gone by myself so I'm excited but a little afraid as well. In the past, every time that the plane took off and landed I would get a little nervous and so I would reach over and hold Mommy's hand or Daddy's hand after Mommy died. But now I'm just on my own and though there is the pretty stewardess who is as tall as a basketball player and smells like powder I don't really think I can ask her to hold my hand. That just leaves the fat man two seats over who is sweating like a pig and breathing through his mouth with a wheeze so loud I can hear it over the plane engines. Better not to even ask that guy, so I just close my eyes real tight when the plane takes off and make the best of it.

A little later the pretty stewardess comes by and gives me peanuts and a Coke and a little while after that she comes by and pins some wings on my shirt and tells me how brave I am to be flying all alone. I look over at the wheezing fat man after she goes and give him a smile because I'm quite proud of my wings. He acts like it's no big deal but I think that's probably because he's a little jealous because he's been watching the pretty stewardess like a hawk and she never gives him wings or anything but peanuts and a tonic water with a couple of tiny bottles of hooch.

I like being above the clouds and I look down and imagine falling out of the plane and being caught by the clouds like a giant feather bed. But since I've read about clouds and know they're basically just mist, before long I have a hard time imagining floating on them and I instead start thinking about how terrible it would be to fall from thirty thousand feet in the air and so I take out my book to read it.

The book is *The Wind in the Willows* and it was the last book Mommy gave me before she died. I've already read it like twenty times, but I just keep reading it over and over again because I really like it and – along with the big green book – I feel closer to Mommy when I'm reading it. It's almost magic, *The Wind in the Willows*, because no matter what is happening in my life it seems that there is a connection between that thing and something in the book. Today, flying above the cottony clouds (that are really just misty water) I'm reading about Mr. Mole and Mr. Rat going off in search of Mr. Mole's home. And isn't it like magic that I am right now heading back to the Bay which is kind of like my home? It's almost spooky how this book works. And it's always right on track.

The pretty stewardess comes back again and asks me if everything is OK and the wheezing fat man gives a little snort, maybe because she hasn't checked on him and he really is jealous. She asks me what I'm reading and I say *The Wind in the Willows* and she says she doesn't know it. I say she should definitely get it because it *seems* like a book for children but it's really not because there are things that are much deeper in it that children can't necessarily understand. And she messes up my hair a little bit and says "I could just eat you up! Why can't I be twenty years younger?"

And I say, "I think it'd be much better if I was twenty years older, ma'am." And then she blushes a bit and touches my cheek before walking away. And I think the wheezing fat man must certainly be jealous because he tried to get the pretty stewardess' attention, but she just walked away like he wasn't even there.

I fall asleep when Mr. Mole and Mr. Rat have just found Mr. Badger's house and when I wake up I ask the wheezing fat man where we are and he says, "How the hell should I know? I'm not the goddamned pilot." But then the goddamned pilot announces in a crackly voice that is real hard to hear that in thirty minutes we'll be landing in Chicago and so I look at the wheezing fat man and say, "For your information, we'll be landing at O'Hare in about thirty minutes" in case he hadn't heard the captain. But the wheezing fat man just says, "Smartass" and I think of what Grams says about white trash people: there's no helping someone who doesn't want to be helped. I don't know if the wheezing fat man is white trash or not, but it does seem clear that he doesn't want to be helped so he could be.

The pretty stewardess comes back to check on me and tells me that I need to wait until everyone is off the plane and she'll walk me to whoever is meeting me, which would be Gramps, but she obviously doesn't know that. The plane lands and I close my eyes tight and try not to be scared because I know there's no way in hell the wheezing fat man is going to help me now.

The landing goes OK and I sit and watch all the people get off and I'm getting really excited because soon I'll get to see Gramps and I feel like it's been forever since we last saw each other, but it's only been about two months. But that's still a pretty long time. The pretty stewardess comes to me and says, "OK, handsome, let's go" and I say "I'll follow you wherever you may go" changing the words a little from one of Aunt Melinda's favorite songs and the pretty stewardess says, "You're a real pip."

We walk up the hallway thing that comes off from the plane and I think it would make a great bowling alley that could move from house to house and I tell the pretty stewardess this and she says that she's never thought of it that way before. We reach the end of the hallway thing and I see Gramps who is standing there in his bib overalls which look a little funny at O'Hare International Airport but that's Gramps.

I wave at Gramps and Gramps waves back and halfway runs up to me and says, "Spark Plug!" and picks me up and swings me in the air even though I'm ten years old and probably too big for such a thing. But somehow with Gramps it's OK.

And Gramps looks at the pretty stewardess and asks, "Now who's this beautiful lady?" and the stewardess blushes and says, "I can see where he gets it from. Mister, I was about half ready to kidnap this boy and take him home with me." She messes up my hair again and I act all shy in front of Gramps, but I like it just as much as the first time she did it.

And Gramps says to her, "How about I give the car keys to the boy and he can drive himself home and I'll go home with you," and he laughs his big open-mouthed laugh and the pretty stewardess laughs and gives him a fake hit on the arm and then says, "Better not. I'm saving myself for the little man here." And then she kisses her finger and puts it on my nose like Mommy used to do sometimes and I'm happy and sad at the same time.

"Goodbye handsome," she says and then walks away.

Gramps leads me out to the car and I'm surprised to see that Grams is sitting in the back seat, knitting as usual. She gets out of the car and kisses me all over my face and says "My baby!" and cries and Gramps says, "Oh for God's sake Lucille!" And I'm probably too old to be slobbered over like that and I'm certainly too old to be called "baby." But somehow with Grams it's OK.

I sit on my knees facing sideways in the passenger's seat so that I can talk to Grams and Gramps at the same time. I tell them about my time in Boston and my trip to Harvard with Leslie who is this sort of nice friend of Aunt Margaret's who apparently will be coming to the Bay to visit sometime soon with Daddy.

Grams says, "I knew it!" but I don't know exactly what she knows. Gramps just says, "Now Lucille," but Gramps says that about a thousand times a day and it never means the same thing twice so who the hell knows what it means this time.

Grams says, "Her body's not even cold," and I have no idea what she's talking about.

Gramps says, "It's almost been three years, Lucille and he's a young man. You can't expect him to stay alone forever."

And Grams says, "Oh can't I?" and moves a piece of yarn around the needle so hard that she hits the window with her knuckle and says, "Crap!"

And Gramps says, "That's what you get."

And I start thinking about what my cousin Annabel said to me, and a few things that Daddy said to me and the way Leslie was trying to be so nice to me and now the things that Grams and Gramps are saying and it hits me like a ton of bricks what's happening: Daddy and Leslie are going to get married. And I don't really know what to think about it, because Grams seems pretty upset but Gramps seems to think it's no big deal.

"Are you hungry, Spark Plug?" Gramps asks me and Grams says "humph" in the back seat because it's even obvious to me that Gramps is trying to change the subject and I'm just a kid. And I've eaten a bunch of peanuts, but I say yes because I know that Gramps will stop at the Oasis and I can get a burger and sit on a bridge right over the highway and watch the cars and trucks go by right underneath me.

Which is exactly what we do. One thing about Gramps is that he never surprises you. If he asks if you're hungry he's always going to stop at the Oasis, even if Grams would rather go to the Steak and Shake further down the road. Some surprises are good (like Christmas presents or how a book might end in a way that you never saw coming, not even in a thousand years) but lots of surprises are so bad that overall it's better to be around Gramps because you always know where you stand and he's not going to throw anything at you that's too shocking, like Daddy getting married or Annabel's pooter.

Bradington town has some fireworks and even though they certainly aren't as big as the ones in Boston they look pretty neat over the bay and all. I'm sitting on the dock with Daddy and Leslie and Snickers and watching the fireworks and thinking how amazing it is that my country is two-hundred years old. And Leslie says to me that what's *really* cool is that when the country started on July the Fourth, 1776, my family had already been there for more than a hundred and fifty years. And I think that *is* pretty cool.

Daddy has asked some friends of his from Chicago to come to the Bay and so the place is filled with these people and not my aunts and uncles, but it's fun anyway. I do kind of miss my cousins because since they're not here there aren't any other kids, but I don't miss being called "Little Lord Fartleroy" or "Bookworm" so in the end I think I might be better off without them. Gramps is sitting up on the screened-in porch and Grams has taken to her bed with a bad headache. But I heard Daddy say to Leslie that Grams is all bent out of shape because he asked Lorraine, the Chicago cook, to come down and oversee the caterers and Grams is insulted, even if she doesn't know anything about catering.

After the fireworks Daddy's Chicago friends have some food even if Grams says it's damn foolish to eat so late at night. Me and Snickers go to the screened-in porch where Gramps is sitting in the dark, all alone on account of Grams' bad headache. I can barely see Gramps' face but I think it looks sad so I ask him, "Are you sad, Gramps?"

And Gramps says, "I reckon I am a little, Spark Plug. I'm thinking about your mother and how much she loved watching fireworks over the bay. And your grandmother's hissy fits aren't helping my mood none, I can tell you that."

And I say, "I miss Mommy too, Gramps. Maybe tomorrow we can go to the cemetery and light off a few firecrackers?"

"Sounds like a great idea, Spark Plug," says Gramps.

"Gramps?"

"Yeah, Spark Plug?"

"Grams doesn't like Leslie very much, does she?"

Gramps lets out a big sigh and runs his hand through his hair like he does every time when something is complicated. "It's complicated, Spark Plug. It's hard for your Grams to see your father with another woman. But she loves your father and wants him to be happy."

I think about that and wonder if it's what is called a conundrum, a word I have written and memorized but haven't had the chance to use yet because I'm still a little unsure about it. But I don't ask Gramps about it because Gramps isn't always the best with words. Or words like conundrum anyway.

"Maybe Grams is afraid that Daddy's going to forget Mommy," I say.

"Well aren't you just the smartest guy in the world! Spark Plug, I'm pretty sure that that's *exactly* what's eating at your grandma."

"Gramps, can I tell you something?"

"Why Spark Plug, you know you can tell me anything. Anything at all."

"I am afraid of forgetting Mommy too. It's already happening. I can't remember what her voice sounded like." And though I'm ten years old and probably shouldn't cry I can't help it, because the thought of forgetting Mommy is one of the saddest I have had in a long long time.

Gramps says to me, "Come over here Spark Plug and sit on your granddad's lap. And before you start saying you're too old for such a thing I say to hell with that. You come over here."

And so I go and sit on Gramps' lap and at first I think maybe I *am* too old to sit like that, but then I feel Gramps' strong arms and smell his Aqua Velva and feel a hundred percent better already. So I think to hell with it.

"Spark Plug," Gramps says to me, "you might forget

little things about your Mommy as the years go by – that just happens. It's a bunch of horseshit that it has to happen, but it does. To us all – even your Grams and me. But the things that are really important about your Mommy you will never forget. Why every time you read one of those books and every time you say one of those big ten-dollar words and every time that you tease your grandma and get her to roll her eyes, you're remembering your Mommy. Those are things that never die, Spark Plug, and those are the things that will make sure your Mommy lives on in you for as long as you live, which might be two-hundred years like America."

I want to say to Gramps that the average life expectancy is way lower, but I know that Gramps is just trying to make a point, so I let it slide.

Then I see a boat out on the bay with a light, and in the light that's coming in off the water I can see sparkles in Gramps' eyes, not like he's crying, but real close. Gramps is always pretty good about not letting me cry alone, and I wonder if maybe this is one of those times.

"And Spark Plug?"

"Yeah Gramps?"

"I'm glad I got my little buddy here with me," Gramps says and gives me a squeeze. "Because when you're here, when we can sit and shoot the shit like we do, your Mommy seems mighty close. Mighty close indeed."

And then Gramps starts to cry for real, and so I know this is one of those important times when Gramps won't let me cry alone. And it's sad but it's not at the same time. Because I really get what Gramps is saying about the reading and the ten-dollar words and teasing Grams and just being together and shooting the shit. Mommy seems almost there, which I guess is probably the most I can hope for.

Chapter Seven: 2012

Edward stepped out on the balcony and looked over the streets of Louisville, at the Ohio River below him. When viewed from up close, from its banks, the river seemed frenetic, rushing with a roar to its unseen end. The scene from above suggested a different story, however, one of an old southern gentleman on an evening stroll, in no particular hurry to get anywhere. It struck him that the river, bathed in the setting sun's orange glow, was meandering in a way not unlike Hank and him.

It was connected, this river to his river, the Illinois. He had begun life thinking that the Illinois was Grandfather Bradington's river, that the power of that frightening and mysterious old man somehow extended over nature itself. And even if his father had shown him on a map how the Illinois connected to the Mississippi, and how it was all a series of interlocking fingers that had been clutching at the land for millions of years, he had never been able to shake the idea that the Illinois River was actually his grandfather's. (Promoted, in no small part by the old man himself, who would frequently order the cook to get some catfish from *his* river for supper.)

But memories of Grandfather Bradington were murky like the river itself, and as he grew up Edward began to so associate the river with his *other* grandfather that it seemed the Illinois was clearly Gramps' river and *not* Grandfather Bradington's. Whereas Grandfather Bradington was the river's detached overlord, Gramps was its brother, its son, who had bathed in its muddy waters, toiled to chastise its encroachment on peaceful shores, battled against its arrogance during floods.

"Penny for your thoughts." Edward looked up to see Hank, toweling his hair dry from a shower.

"I swear to God the older I get the more I seem to indulge in weepy nostalgia. I need to get some help." He turned back around to face the river, a sad smile that he could feel on his face like an embarrassing soup stain.

Hank wrapped his arms around Edward from behind, head peering around his shoulder to enjoy the same sight. "Maybe," Hank said, "weepy nostalgia is the norm – you know – the way people ought to be. Maybe the way you were before wasn't normal."

Edward laughed. "If only you could have told me that twenty years ago."

"Ifs and buts, ifs and buts. Let's just say that you're where you need to be right now and everything you did in the past got you here. It's all good."

Edward looked again at the river below that was connected to Gramps' river and felt that maybe it was, indeed, all good. It was cautious and still partially buried, this feeling; it wasn't yet ready to surge up to the surface and change him completely (nor was he, he admitted, ready to be changed). But it was there, and he could recognize it, nod to it like a stranger on the subway with an open, accepting face. And this – this awareness, this knowledge, this partial acceptance, this hope – was not merely just enough, it was more than he had felt in a long, long time.

"Dial the number, Hank. It's why we're here. You're stalling." Hank was sitting on the bed, flipping through the television channel, and Edward couldn't fully contain his impatience.

"Isn't it kind of late notice?" Hank asked, eyes on the screen. "What if she has plans? I'd be pissed off if somebody just showed up out of the blue and expected me to drop everything and meet up."

"If she has plans tomorrow or the next day we'll just wait until she's free," said Edward. "Remember, *she* contacted *you*. Just call her."

Hank shouted, "Jesus Christ, Edward, just let it go! For fuck's sake!" He threw the remote control against the wall.

Edward sat down, startled. Having spent so much time with Ben – who registered anger in more subtle ways – he was unprepared for a tone which could only be described as visceral. It was raw, Hank's anger, unexpected and intimate, and Edward began to see how very little he really knew about his traveling companion.

Hank looked at him. "I'm sorry." His voice was softer, but something within Edward felt it wasn't quite soft enough, that after such a volatile outburst something more conciliatory was called for. "I'm still worried that we're imposing." He smiled, a pained smile that reminded Edward of something Gramps always said: "Yeah, he's smilin', but he ain't lettin' that grit in his teeth go."

"I don't think we're not imposing," Edward said quietly, cautiously. "To me it seems no different than if you would have called her from Ohio and said, 'Can I come next weekend?' If she's got something going on, we just wait it out until she's ready and we can see the sights of Louisville in the meantime. It's all good, remember?"

Hank sighed theatrically and reached for the phone. Edward turned to go back into the bathroom, but Hank said, "No, stay." The moment of anger had passed, but left something in its wake – a hesitancy, a caution – that Edward hoped would be a small snag which could easily be patched over, and not something that would rip the whole fabric. He sat next to Hank on the bed and began rubbing his shoulders.

"Hello, Ellie? Yeah, hello. This is … Hank Drummond. How are you? Good, nice to hear that. Me? Yeah, I'm good too. Listen. I'm calling from Louisville. It's a long story –" he looked at Edward, "– but one thing led to another and I've made un unexpected trip here. I know it's kind of last minute and everything, but I was wondering if maybe you would have some free time in the next few days to get together. I understand if you're busy, but I thought it was worth a shot anyway."

Edward leaned closer.

"Tomorrow? Yeah – that'd be great. Dinner? Sure. I'm afraid I don't know many restaurants – I spent most of my time at Burger King when I lived here. Maybe you could choose a nice place? OK – Edward remember this: Lilly's on Bardstown Road. Do you mind if I bring my friend? Great. We'll see you there at eight. OK. Bye bye."

He hung up and set the phone on the bed. "Tomorrow for dinner," he said.

"Yeah, I got that," said Edward with a smile. "Now that wasn't so difficult, was it?"

"Wipe that fucking smug look off your face," came the response, which Edward knew meant, *no, it hadn't been difficult at all.*

The next day the warmth of the Indian Summer had disappeared, leaving in its wake the first proper fall weather of their journey. The cooler weather had a sobering effect on Edward, and he felt that the colorful leaves shone less brightly than they had the day before, seemingly more aware of their oncoming descent to the ground than they had been in the previous days' warmth.

Death was, Edward thought, in the air, and not just

because the day's program was to lead them to the cemetery where Stella was buried. The night before he had dreamt long, senseless dreams filled with images more than linear stories, and all the images were connected to people who had died. Strangely, though, he didn't find the images sad, but instead comforting, like the scent on the pillow of someone whose head rested elsewhere. And this lingering presence, this sober collection of ghosts, was beautiful somehow, seemed to make him feel calmer than he had felt in years.

Edward's point of reference for all cemeteries was his family's private cemetery at the edge of the Bay. There three enormous mausoleums jockeyed for position in the shade of giant oak trees. The overall effect was one of clutter, as the hulking edifices were too large for the space, enclosed on all sides by a sandstone wall and covered above by the overly solicitous trees. So many times he had walked, hand in hand with Gramps, to lay flowers at the iron door of his mother's mausoleum, guarded by two enormous angels, and instead of pondering the vastness of eternity the sense was more of entering into confinement.

Grams and Gramps, not being Bradingtons, didn't have "the right" (his father's words) to be buried in the private cemetery. Thus, when their times came they were buried in the Bradington Municipal Cemetery on the outskirts of the town itself. Although much larger, it boasted no mausoleums and very little vegetation. It was, instead, cramped with row after row of similar-looking gray grave markers, nearly anonymous, and the only time he had visited the cemetery it also gave him a sensation of captivity, the stones themselves lined up like prisoners at roll call.

Cave Hill Cemetery couldn't have been more different. It was expansive and lush, trees and flowering bushes dotting sloping hills on which the graves seemed to have been lightly sprinkled from above. It was calm and curvy, a great swath of green velvet adorned with colorful stones.

"Now *this* is a place I wouldn't mind being buried in," he said to Hank, looking a little lost and unsure where to go.

"I suspect you won't really care where you're buried because you'll be dead," Hank said, changing directions and charging ahead like a tour leader on a schedule.

"I think you're full of shit," challenged Edward, "Why was it that you had Stella buried here? What's it matter? You could have just had her cremated and scattered in the river. No, you *wanted* Stella to be buried here because you know – deep down – that there is somehow a connection between those of us here and those who have moved on."

Hank stopped walking and turned back to look at him. "Jesus, how you go on! Do you plot out that bullshit or does it just come to you naturally? OK. First of all, Stella would never have been cremated – she didn't believe in it and even though she's dead I still think I have an obligation to honor her beliefs. Secondly, even if she did, I don't think Catholics can just scatter their ashes anywhere they fucking please, so you're clearly talking out of your ass on that one. And thirdly, the money to plant Stella here and the money to keep her here comes from Stella herself. And being buried here is a thing that she would have spent her money on if she could have. But she couldn't because she's dead. So I took her money and spent it where I thought she would have wanted it to be spent. End of story."

"Calm down, Snarla!" said Edward. "Are you nervous about meeting your daughter tonight or are you just feeling particularly cunty?

"How about neither?" responded Hank, not even looking back. "How about you're just talking complete shit and need to be called on it? So just back the fuck off with your dime store psychology. I just want to visit my grandmother's grave. Let me have some motherfucking peace!"

Edward spoke quietly. "I believe Mother Teresa said the same thing when she accepted the Nobel!"

Hank began laughing, a small rattling that began in his belly and had grown enormous by the time it was finally liberated from his wide-open mouth. He laughed so hard he doubled over and sat down on the grass, tears of laughter combining with other, less joyful tears.

Edward sat beside him, feeling the shaking of his tears, aware of being privileged to be doing so. The mourners nearby turned away, perhaps ashamed of being rash to judge; "everyone mourns in his own way" Edward could almost hear them think.

"I'm so full of shit," said Hank, wiping his nose. "I know there's a connection and of course that's why I buried Stella here. I just feel like crap that I haven't been back to visit her, that I abandoned her. And here we are on the same-ass day that I am going to meet my daughter who I basically abandoned as well. It's just a little too much."

"Listen," said Edward, taking his hand, "you haven't abandoned Stella. She's been on this crazy trip with us every step of the way. Along with my mother, Grams, Gramps, and all those Bradington and Allerton ancestors. Thank God I've got such a big-ass car. And you didn't abandon your daughter; you gave her what you thought was a better life. So enough with this pity party! Are you going to show me Stella's grave or do I have to find it myself?"

Hank stood up and kissed him lightly on the cheek. He pointed to a larger-than-life size bronze statue of a man in a tuxedo and cape. "There it is," he said.

"Stella was a man who wore a cape?" asked Edward.

"No, of course not. I just always know where to turn when I see that grave. Pretty sweet, huh? He was a magician, I think. If you keep going that way, you'll run into the Colonel himself."

"That will be stop number two on our tour here today. Is his grave a giant bucket?" Edward grabbed Hank's hand and they turned to walk away from the bronze man in the cape. It struck Edward that he had never held another man's hand in public before; doing so made him feel young and strong.

They arrived at a simple gravestone which was deep red and had roses etched into it. In a curly script not unlike that of Hank's tattoo was written *Estelle "Stella" Marie Drummond: 1911 - 1993.*

They stood in silence for a few moments until Edward asked, "And your grandfather? Why is she buried alone?"

"My grandfather left her when my daddy was just a tyke, back in the thirties sometime."

"And she was alone all those years? She never remarried?" The loneliness of the scene felt like a weight on Edward.

"Stella was Catholic; marriage was forever. I remember when I was in high school, she went on a few of those elder hostel trips – nothing too far, I think St. Louis was the farthest they went. There was this nice old guy named Maurice who went on all the trips and was obviously sweet on her. She was sweet on him, too, but it never went anywhere because she always said, 'I'm a married woman!' And I'd say 'Stella you ain't seen your husband since before World War II broke out. How can you say you're married? Hell, he's probably dead by now.' But she just said that he could still be out there somewhere, and he was still her husband in the eyes of God. So that was that."

"Your family have had some bad luck in the relation-ship department, haven't they?" Edward asked and immediately regretted his choice of words.

"You think?" asked Hank with a chuckle. "First Stella's man leaves her, then Daddy's wife leaves him and then Chuck leaves me. I think our family is just cursed."

Edward put his arms around him and said, "Well, you know how that works: to break a curse you need a kiss from Prince Charming. So pucker up, handsome."

Hank didn't kiss him but instead turned his head towards the grave once again. "What's that, Stella?" he said, cupping his hand to his ear. "Yeah, I know. You're right: he's full of shit." And then, to Edward: "OK Romeo, let's go pay our respects to Colonel Sanders." Hank turned and walked away, leaving Edward standing at the grave alone. Hank never looked back, something that Edward felt was significant but was not exactly sure why.

It was still early, so they decided to walk around a shopping mall. The presence of angled glass all around them made Edward think of an aquarium, and the colorfully dressed people walking past them seemed like fish moving in vari-ous jet streams. He marveled at all the stories that must be swirling about him.

"Let's play a game," Edward said.

"Like Monopoly?"

"No, not Monopoly," replied Edward, rolling his eyes. "When I was a little boy and my mother was in the hospi-tal, there were a lot of times when I couldn't go up to her room – at the time the entrance age was ten years old and I was like five, six, seven at the time."

"That seems a little harsh."

"Yeah I suppose it does. I think they've changed the rules now, but anyway that's the way it was way back in the

Dark Ages. So I'd go to the hospital and if my mother was feeling up to it Dad would go up to her room and bring her down to the lobby to see me."

"And if she wasn't feeling up to it?"

"Then I would have to sit in the lobby until he was finished."

"I'm not real sure what this has to do with playing a game," said Hank. "But it sounds like it could be the saddest fucking game ever invented."

"Just wait," laughed Edward, "we haven't got to the game part yet. So, there was this nun there, Sister … Sister … I can't believe I don't remember her name! She seemed old – everyone seems old to a little child, I guess – but, in the end, she was probably a little younger than I am now. It was hard to tell because this was back when her cadre of nuns still wore the whole getup."

Hank smiled. "I believe they're called 'orders' and the 'getup' is called a 'habit.'"

"Are you Catholic?" asked Edward, slightly shocked.

"Recovering," responded Hank. "Twelve years of Catholic school are enough to turn anybody off. But continue. We've got a young boy who isn't allowed to see his dying mother and a nun so far. This is going to be one kick-ass game."

Edward laughed. "Anyway," he continued, "Sister would come and sit with me in the lobby and the game was we would make up stories about the people we saw walking by. Sister's stories were usually boring, as I remember them – you know, nice nun stuff like 'His wife has just had her first child and he's taking flowers to her' or 'Her husband broke his leg skiing and she's going up to show him the pictures of the vacation she got developed so that he can remember how much fun they had before the fall.' Things like that. Now that I think about it, maybe since she

117

worked there, Sister wasn't really making up stories at all, but just telling what she already knew about the people."

"That cheating bitch!" responded Hank in mock indignation. "So if Sister's stories were boring, what did you come up with?"

"I don't know," Edward responded, looking up into the air. "More exciting things. More creative things, I guess I'd say."

"So basically, you're saying that even though Sister was a big fat cheater, you still completely managed to kick her ass. Do you remember any of your stories?"

"Just one of them. I have no idea why I remember this one and not the others. Anyway, there was this really fat woman who was walking through the lobby with a full-length fur coat on – this was, of course, also back when women wore furs. Sister asked 'What's her story?' and I said that she was going up to see her husband who was a Russian defector who had escaped from a gulag in Siberia and would have frozen to death had he not been able to kill a bear with his bare hands, skin it with his teeth, and cover himself with its fur. He managed to make it to Kamchatka where he found a pirate ship that took him to the shores of Alaska, where he worked as a lumberjack until he saved up enough money to go to Springfield, Illinois, where he had always wanted to go because he had got his hands on some illegal history books in Russia and had read about Abraham Lincoln and naturally wanted to visit his tomb. So he makes it to Springfield and falls in love with the cemetery caretaker's daughter and they get married and he eventually takes over running the cemetery. In the meantime, he has always carried around this bear pelt with him and he gets it made into a coat and gives it to his wife, who was coming to visit him in the hospital because a tombstone had fallen on his foot and broken it."

"*That's* your story?" asked Hank incredulously. "How old were you?"

"I don't know. Six. Seven maybe. No, I would have had to have been six because it was obviously cold outside and my mother died the summer I had just turned seven. Yeah, definitely six. Or maybe five."

Hank stopped walking and turned to look at him. "How the hell did you come up with that?"

"I don't know. Sister always asked me the same thing. Well, without saying 'hell' of course. I read a lot when I was young – probably, sadly, much more than I do now. Kamchatka I must have gotten from that board game Risk that my cousins and I used to play at the Bay when it rained and we couldn't be outside. And it was during the Cold War when everyone was talking about Russia and defectors. I guess I just sort of put it all together."

"I feel so sorry for that nun," said Hank. "She had already drawn the short straw and couldn't ever have sex and in addition she gets her ass whupped by a small child. Poor thing."

"Oh, I don't think Sister took it too badly. She would always say 'Wowzy wow!' and call me 'Einstein.'"

"I'm not surprised."

Edward, stopped to look in the window of a book shop. "I haven't thought about her in years. If she was – let's say, forty – back then that would make her something like seventy-eight or so now. I wonder if she's still around."

"In my experience," said Hank, "nuns tend to live to be about a hundred and fifty, so I'd say odds are good that she's still kicking." And then he added excitedly, "We *so* have to go look for her!"

"That's ridiculous."

"I'm serious!" he said, tugging at Edward's sleeve like a child. "You're all busy talking about 'road trip this' and 'quest that' and you're certainly not shy about telling me where *I* should be going and what *I* should be doing. So now, as the official buttboy of your journey, I am commanding you to try and find this nun."

"Can buttboys command anything?" asked Edward, smiling. "Don't they just have to do as they're told?"

"Fuck you. Lot you know about the world. We buttboys fucking rule the world, I can tell you."

"Well I hope to hell that you're also omniscient; we don't even know this nun's name!"

"How hard can it be to find out?" asked Hank. "We go to the hospital. You tell some nun there your story. Come on – a kind nun, a dead mother, a little boy who has turned into this hot man – those old girls will be creaming in their panties to help you."

"I'm pretty sure that nuns don't cream their panties."

Hank rolled his eyes. "Lot *you* know about nuns. Trust me: they'll eat this shit up. It's a done deal. We are adding this to our road trip. End of story."

"OK," Edward replied smiling, "We'll make a trip to Springfield in search of this unnamed nun who probably won't even remember me – if she's even there or alive. But – you're right – it is well within the parameters of a classic road trip, so I acquiesce. Now: are you ready to play the game?"

"Not on your fucking life," answered Hank, walking away and leaving him looking at a life-size cutout of Rachel Ray in the book shop window. Edward shook his head, looking at the cutout and pleading with his eyes for some support; but Rachel clearly seemed to be saying "I'm with Hank on this one."

"This isn't *Pretty Woman* you know; I *can* buy my own goddamned clothes." The anger had returned to Hank's voice. He assessed the trousers and jacket he was trying on while Edward looked on, trying to adapt an air that said he was interested in his choice but ultimately without a real opinion.

"Again with the romantic comedy references from a crusty person who claims not to watch TV," Edward replied teasingly.

"Crusty? What the hell does that mean?"

"I think one definition would be someone who is offered something and says 'I can buy my own goddamned clothes.'" Edward would *not* be timid as he had been earlier in the hotel; if Hank wanted to come unglued in a public place he could have at it.

"I can, you know," he said curtly, voice registering something which sounded to Edward like disapproval, like that first small fissure in a bigger tear.

"I know that. Jesus – what's the big deal? This place we're going seems a little nicer than the clothes either of us brought, so I thought, 'Gee, since I need to pick something up for myself maybe I could buy something for him as a small token of my affection and in gratitude for joining me on my weird road trip' but if it's a huge fucking issue forget about it." He was surprised at how disappointed he felt, an odd sensation creeping from somewhere deep inside that hadn't surfaced in years.

Hank walked over to him and stroked his cheek. "You're absolutely right, I'm being an asshole. It is very nice of you to offer, and I should accept it nicely. Stella used to say that anybody can be gentlemanly in giving things out, but only a true gentleman can accept with grace something given to him. Of course, Stella wouldn't have known a true gentleman if he came up and pinched her tit. But the saying's good anyway, isn't it?"

"Sure as hell is. Well then, good sir, is this the

ensemble or shall we look elsewhere?"

Hank turned back to the mirror. "Well," he said, "it kind of makes me look like a fucking Republican on the way to the club, but besides that I think it's OK." He took the jacket off and walked back towards the dressing room.

"Your ass looks fucking fine in those pants," Edward shouted after him just as a stern-faced woman exited a dressing room. She seemed to look at him with disapproval if not downright judgment, but Edward thought she was probably just upset because no one had told her such a thing in a long time, if ever.

"She wrote a smiley face," Hank said with crinkled brow, looking at the message on his phone as if it were a strange specimen of insect. "Who writes to say that they will be forty-five minutes late and then puts a smiley face afterwards? That's just weird. And wrong."

Edward smiled. "It's not weird and it's not wrong. She's probably mortified that the first time she meets her father she's late. The smiley face is a way to say, 'I hope we can laugh about this together one day.' I think it's cute."

"Cute? Jesus! I'm pretty sure that I have not heard a grown man use the word 'cute' in … I'm not sure I've *ever* heard a grown man say cute. Maybe when talking about a baby or a small child. But in ordinary situations? No. Never." He took a sip of his wine with one hand and picked an imaginary piece of lint of his lapel with the other. "Never," he repeated nervously.

Edward looked around the restaurant, not entirely sure how to respond, or, indeed, if a response was even called for. Small white lights were arranged all over the place – on the piano in the corner, on the bar, on the walls – and their presence infused the room with a holiday feeling, bathing everyone's face in happiness. He admitted to himself that it could all be an illusion – maybe the happy-looking couple next to them were actually breaking up and chose a public place so as not to raise their voices – but he knew that sometimes illusions weren't so bad, could be used as seasonings to cover the all-too-bitter taste of reality.

But even the sparkling lights could not soften Hank, who sat before him with a face as stern as one of those old Russian propaganda posters. He frowned; he twitched; he looked around nervously.

"It's just a smiley face," said Edward.

"Tell me," said Hank, waving a breadstick in his face. "What's the secret? I mean, you know, the smiley face secret. There seems to be folk – like you, and obviously like Ellie, too – who see that motherfucking smiley face everywhere and then there are others – like me – who don't get it. And when we see it – people like me, I mean – we want to poke its black little eyes out and carve up its face with a cheese knife."

"Does it have to be a cheese knife?" asked Edward mockingly. "Or would a bread or steak knife do as well?"

"Fuck you," said Hank. "I'm being serious. Take Ellie, for instance. She's coming here to meet a father who for all practical purposes abandoned her, who just up and gave her to someone else. Who could be a dick, for all she knows. And yet she writes the longest fucking text-message apology for being late that I have ever seen in my life as if *she's* the one who has done something horrible. And then she ends with a smiley face. I genuinely want to know how you people see this smiley face everywhere. Is it something you're born with? If that's the case, Ellie obviously got it from her mother. Or can you develop it somehow? I really want to know."

Edward reached out to touch his cheek, a gesture that was not blocked but didn't seem fully received either.

"Maybe both. I mean, I think there are some people who are just naturally born cheery and live the rest of their lives seeing the smiley face, as you put it. Others learn it. You can learn it, I think."

"And which are you? A naturally born smiley face guy or one who learned to be a smiley face guy?"

"I'm not really sure," Edward said. "I think I was a pretty cheerful child – even in the midst of all the shit I had to put up with – so maybe I was born that way. But now that I'm thinking about it – and I can assure you I have never given this any thought before tonight – I think it's a little like a muscle. You have to exercise it. Probably in early adolescence I didn't do much exercising of it, although probably no one does in early adolescence. And then I fell in love and, well, smiley faces seem to come with that. Until they don't of course. I was too stoned and angry in college to be a smiley face guy, and afterwards I guess I just stopped trying – I mean, how many smiley faced lawyers do *you* know? But now, well, it seems I've started looking for it again. Just recently really. Like, I don't know, four or five days ago."

Hank sipped his drink and considered his words. "I just don't know how to do it. I'm not sure I ever will."

"When I was seventeen," Edward continued, "I got into a little trouble – at the Bay, actually. A delicate situation with the wrong kind of person, as my father would say. I have wondered since then if he wasn't maybe the right kind of person, if maybe I should have fought harder. Ifs and buts, I guess. Anyway, things were taken care of and I was forbidden from ever seeing him again. My father's wife found out about it and kicked me out of the house, since I was not only a fornicator but a faggot as well."

"My God! That seems kind of harsh."

"Well," continued Edward, "in practical terms it wasn't

as harsh as it sounds. I was already in boarding school, and it just meant spending more time at my Aunt Margaret's house and the Bay – but strictly supervised, of course. She's a gold-digging whore and I think she was just looking for an excuse to get rid of me."

"Jesus – no smiley face there!" said Hank, smiling.

"Not at all," laughed Edward. "So anyway, the next summer I'm still not over Jeff – that was his name – and my father knows this but doesn't really know how to handle it because Jeff's a guy and all, so Dad says I can go with a couple of buddies to do the whole backpacking-in-Europe thing. Now these guys came from rich families, too, and we could have stayed in beautiful hotels, but we all decided to do it like regular people do."

"I don't think *real* regular people go backpacking in Europe."

"Whatever. And I was Mr. Mope. Here we were, seeing some of the most beautiful sights in the world and I was always in a bad mood, feeling sorry for myself, and this was all multiplied because my buddies didn't know I was gay and so I felt I couldn't really talk about what was going on, what I was feeling. *Now* I know what an opportunity such a trip was, but at the time I was just too caught up in my own shit and how the world sucks and there's nothing good in it."

"Poor little rich boy," said Hank.

"We were in Budapest, staying at this horrible hostel that smelled and I'm pretty sure had rats. Budapest is gorgeous now, but this was back under communism and it was a little rough around the edges to say the least. Anyway, it was hotter than hell and I couldn't sleep, so I got up and sat in the window to try and get a little air. Below the window we had the view of an alley with dumpsters that hadn't been emptied in a while."

"Lovely scene," said Hank. "You should write travel books."

"Exactly. So, there I am, the sun is just coming up outside, but the alley is still kind of dark because of the buildings surrounding it and I'm looking out over mounds of trash and thinking about how my life is over, ruined, and that I maybe have ruined another person's life as well and how I am a fraud and dishonest because I am hiding who I really am from my friends (one of whom, by the way, I discovered was also gay – but much later). Anyway, then, as if the whole scene wasn't depressing enough, a young boy – seven, maybe eight – comes into the alley and starts going through the trash. He was a Gypsy, I think. And I'm sitting there thinking that *this* is what the world is really about – not my cushy existence and hiding – but *this*: heat and smell and trash and hungry children and lost love and regret."

"Wait," said Hank, "don't tell me you're somehow going to find a smiley face here?"

"Why yes I am," answered Edward with a chuckle. "Because just as I was wallowing in the deepest of self-pity and ain't-the-world-shit thoughts, the boy began to sing. That's right – sing. As I tell this story now, I think I have romanticized the scene somewhat and I hear him in my head with the voice of an angel. Who knows? Maybe he sang beautifully and maybe he didn't. But the point is that there, on top of his mountain of garbage, he sang. And I just sat up there in that horrible room, my buddies snoring and sweating nearby, and watched and listened to this little boy and thought that I hadn't heard anything so beautiful in a long, long time – probably not since my mother died. And that's it. That's how I got the smiley face back, I guess."

Hank looked at him, face a mixture of affection, suspicion and something else Edward couldn't entirely read. A small taste of regret began to form on his tongue; had he shared too much?

"You're a strange one, Edward James Allerton Bradington the Fourth," Hank said. "I keep thinking that you really are too good to be true, that something must be wrong with you, something I'll find out later. But I want to stick around, even if I know this could end badly. I can't *not* stick around."

"Well we're supposed to stick around for it all. But – let me just put your mind at ease – I don't think it'll end badly. I think the worst that can happen is that you'll begin seeing the smiley face a little bit more, that's all. Now that wouldn't be too bad, would it?"

Hank didn't answer him, simply stared silently towards the door. Edward turned around, following Hank's gaze to a young woman with familiar eyes standing in the doorway, mirroring the sparkly lights all around. As Edward turned back around to look at Hank, he swore he could almost hear that little Gypsy boy singing over the notes of the piano.

Edward watched Hank as Hank watched his daughter come towards their table. Ever the lawyer wanting to facilitate communication, he sat up ready to do his magic so that Hank and Ellie could get beyond their awkwardness and really talk to each other, could find in each other what was missing, what they were looking for (even if they didn't know exactly what that was). But Edward knew this wasn't his story to tell. And as father and daughter met, he let go of words he may have said for a silent hope that Hank could somehow hear the singing too, or, if not, could begin to consider that maybe such music existed somewhere.

Chapter Eight: 1982

There are basically two reasons I like wading in the shallow, reedy part of the bay that borders the woods, and they just might both have to do with sex. First of all, I like the feeling of the mud oozing through my toes. Hours after wading into the mud, feet washed and put into shoes, I think about that feeling, the squishiness, and I smile.

I think it might be sexual because on my way to the Bay this summer I boldly walked into a book shop in Boston and bought a value-pack of three old copies of *Honcho* magazine stuck together in yellowing cellophane, although the old woman at the counter gave me quite the hairy eyeball, and probably would have told me to get out of there had she not choked on something and started hacking up a lung. But she took my money and waved me away, hand jerking as she coughed, and I was so happy and nervous that I didn't even wait for change, just ran out into the sunshine that bounced off the cellophane like laughter.

And it was in one of those magazines that there was a photo spread of some guy with a huge dick arching his back like he's having a spasm while some other dude with low-hanging balls is bent over him and licking in between his toes. And even if the dude with the big dick's body looks like he's in a lot of pain, all arched and tense, his face looks like one of those ecstatic saints that was painted in the fifteenth-century frescoes I studied in my Art History class. And so I think there's got to be something to this in-between-the-toe thing and even though I don't have some guy with low-hanging balls licking in between my toes, any-thing I put there feels pretty damned good.

And so the mud oozing through my toes feels really nice and when I'm wading there, barely in sight of the big house, I remember the look on that guy's face and completely get it and wonder if I will ever find a man with low-hanging balls to lick in between my toes. I think about it a lot, wonder how well I would have to know someone to ask him to lick in between my toes, wonder exactly how you go about asking such a thing, whether you just come right out and say, "Yeah baby, lick between my toes!" real smooth like Richard Gere might do if he was ready for a little in-between-the-toe action or whether you try and make it a joke like "Hey, I know this guy who likes to have someone lick in between his toes; isn't that the weirdest thing ever?" And then, maybe the guy would say, "Well, no, I don't think that's strange at all" and start moving down the bed while I wiggle my toes.

So that's the first reason I like wading in the mud, and it's definitely sexual – there's no denying it.

The second reason is not overtly sexual if you just look at it on the surface, but if you dig a little deeper it just might be. Because I also like walking in the mud because it's a thing I can do without any fear of having to get too close to my cousin Annabel who is staying at the Bay that summer with a pack of her awful friends. Annabel loves tormenting me – it's basically been her only hobby since like forever – and I hate it and like it at the same time because she's solid, my Annabel, and I know she gives me shit because she loves me. I try to do the same to her but I'm not as clever as she is – that chick is wicked funny. She's always teased me about sex but now that she's in col-lege and has obviously had loads of sex she's upped the level of her sexual teasing, specifically in my case about my lack of sex. Even though I deny it she keeps teasing me because I'm a virgin, which, of course, I actually am but would never admit because I think it's strange being a virgin at age sixteen. But there's no way in hell I would ever let Annabel know that I'm a virgin, so I talk like I'm an old pro, a veritable gigolo. But no matter how many stories I bring up about the loose girls I know she just smiles and shakes her head and says things like, "Whatever, Romeo" or "Beating your meat with your roommate Biff doesn't count, virgin boy."

And the problem is that one of Annabel's friends – a guy everyone calls Red – is quite a looker and seems to be teasing me too, but in a different way than Annabel does. And even though it's all just teasing, being teased by Red about sex makes me think about sex with Red. A lot.

So even though Annabel and her friends won't follow me to wade out in the mud they're still somehow connected to it – at least Red is – and that connection with the feeling of mud between my toes is definitely sexual if you think about it.

I know I probably *could* have sex, because there have been many, many girls who have let me get to second base and maybe third base if you count over-the-underwear touching. But I don't really want to have sex with the girls who throw themselves at me. I'm just not interested in girls, although I feel like I have to play the game so that people won't think I'm a fag. At boarding school loads of guys brag about diddling this girl or that girl but I really don't know how they manage it. I think in reality they're just jerking off in the bathroom stalls like I am – maybe thinking about me as I am thinking about some of them. But besides that, there's just too much going on. Between classes, tennis, and swimming, and basically being locked down, I don't really feel like I could find the time to get down to some serious diddling of my own.

Which leaves summers. But most summers I'm either at the Bay, where there are only my cousins there – and very occasionally at that – and there's not a one of them who is foxy enough to tempt me into the dark territory of actually diddling a cousin. I do love my time at the Bay, love shooting the shit with Gramps while fishing; and I love sitting in the kitchen and watching Grams cook and hearing *her* take on Gramps' stories (which are sometimes the same as Gramps' and sometimes not). And I love that I have time to lounge around and be lazy and write – I'm trying my hand at writing some short stories and I think I'm not half bad.

But there are no boys. And having no boys around is probably worse than having too many boys around, at least in terms of how much I think about sex. Just wading in the bay with the mud through my toes thinking about Red who is sunbathing on the dock listening to Duran Duran, lying on his back so that the lump of his dick is clearly visible – this combination of things has given me an uncomfortable stiffie that will not go away, no matter how hard I try thinking about starving children in Ethiopia. So I think that maybe diving into the bay full-on and swimming around a bit in the muddy water will help ease the tension down there.

And so I completely immerse myself in the water and go really deep down to where the water meets the mud, where the water is the coldest, and I grab a handful of the mud. It naturally doesn't quite give the same thrill as in between the toes, but it's nice anyway. I emerge from the deep and pretend I'm Aquaman on some kind of mission, even though I know I am likely way too old to be pretending like that. But I can't help myself, it's too fun, this imagining that I'm a superhero and can breathe underwater, and I even do the butt-up-in-the-air swim move, even if while I'm doing it I realize that it's the move of the Man from Atlantis and *not* Aquaman.

And I swim and swim – further than I ever have before and dive down down down until I get under the divider that makes our part of the bay private. Coming out and up on the other side, I continue around a bend, and aren't I shocked as shit as Gramps would say when I get around the bend and there on the shore is a beautiful boy with two girls, lying out in the sun. And though I've gone further than I'm allowed – you can't even see the house from where I am – I say to myself that neither Aquaman nor the Man from Atlantis have to be slaves to such boundaries, so I decide to swim up to the shore to say hi, reaching down first to make sure that my stiffie is gone, which it is, thank God.

I swim up (but not using the butt-up-in-the-air swim move, rather a breast stroke) and walk out of the bay to where the three are lying, trying not to think too much about the mud oozing through my toes because I don't want to get a stiffie in wet trunks in front of total strangers.

"Hi," I say real smooth-like and the two girls just look at one another and giggle but the boy shields his eyes from the sun and says hello.

"Nice day, huh?" I say, because I don't really know what else to say.

One of the girls giggles and I think that maybe I haven't been as smooth as I wanted but the boy looks at me with curiosity. "It's great," he says. "Where did you come from?"

"I swam from the house over there," I say, indicating the direction of the house and slightly flexing my arm at the same time because I know I've got some pretty wicked muscles and I think they should notice and then maybe the chick who giggled at me would think twice about doing it again.

"You mean the Bradington place?" says the giggler, suddenly all interested now. I'm not sure whether it's that I'm from the Bradington place or my muscles that has brought this change about in her, but – just in case it's the muscles – I point in the direction of the house flexing again and say, "Yep. That's the place."

The giggler immediately jumps up, tugs her bikini bottom out of her crack and says, "Hey. I'm Linda Shamansky. These are my friends Kim Dawson and Jeff Marks. What's your name?"

"Edward," I respond real cool-like. Aquaman and the Man from Atlantis aren't big talkers, and I think that I should follow their lead.

"Edward what?" asks Kim.

"Uh ... Edward Bradington," I say.

"Get the fuck out of here!" says Linda, like I've just told her I'm David Bowie or something.

"No, it's really my name."

"Like of *the* Bradingtons? Do you live in the mansion?" asked Kim.

"Well, I don't live there – I go to school out East and my main house is in Chicago. But, yeah, I stay there a lot in the summer."

"Well I'll be damned," says Linda. "I only ever met a real Bradington one time, when I was a little girl, when my family was asked to be one of the families for the Collection at Founder's Day. Was that your Dad who took the cash?"

I'm thinking I maybe don't like Linda too much, because I'm embarrassed by the whole deal of the Collection and think people shouldn't ask about it, and yet she brings it up like she's talking about the weather. And

Kim is smiling like the cat that ate the canary, like she knows Linda's yanking my chain and she's enjoying it. Only Jeff doesn't seem to be playing along, and I decide that I really like him for that (and for his smoking hot suntanned body).

"Dunno," I answer real cool-like, "it'd either be my father or my grandfather. Depends on what year you're talking about. Grandfather died when I was five, but you look a lot older than I do so maybe you would have been around for him, too."

Linda smiles like she appreciates my slam, even if I can tell she doesn't like being called old, even though she is clearly five or six years older than I am. Jeff starts smiling now too – I can just see it on his tanned face forming like a sunburst behind clouds. (Like a sunburst behind clouds – I need to remember that one.)

"How old are you?" asks Linda.

"I'm sixteen," I answer, flexing my stomach muscles a little bit so that she knows that even if I'm only sixteen I'm clearly a man.

"Fuck, I could be your auntie!" shouts Linda. "Wanna come sit on auntie's lap, little boy?"

And I laugh because I know she's teasing me kind of like Annabel teases me, which I guess is just what some girls do.

"God, Linda – leave him alone," says Jeff, shaking his head. Then I turn to look at him and I see he's got huge blue eyes that are as clear as the bay should be but isn't. He gets up as quick as a whistle and doesn't need to pull his trunks out of his crack. He holds out his hand and says, "Forgive my friend. It's nice to meet you, Edward."

I take his hand and as soon as we touch it's like I can feel that mud in between my toes and I see the picture of the big-dicked man and the man with low-hanging balls in my mind's eye and I'm praying to God that I don't get a stiffie right then and there. God seems to answer me, because although I can sense a few stirrings down there it remains kind of in between flaccid and hard – flard, we call it at school because Stevie Barnard is always walking around that way in the locker room and we've pretty much had to invent a word for it because he's that way every day.

"Are you from Bradington?" I ask Jeff, feeling a little silly because it's my name and all.

"Born and bred," answers Jeff. "These two also."

"Yeah, but at least we got out of this fucking town," says Linda while Kim nods like the Chihuahua in the back of Uncle Jerry's Buick. "We go to cosmetology school over in Decatur," she says, looking at Jeff kind of snarlishly. (Which I know isn't a word but I'm determined to invent because Shakespeare invented thousands of words and I think I want to be a writer too, so why the hell can't I invent words too?)

"I'm still in high school," I say to Jeff as if the other two aren't there. "No college for a couple of years yet."

"Me neither," says Jeff and I like that he pronounces it *neether* like my mother's family and not *nyther* like my father's family. "But I want to go part time over in Springfield and work in politics at the same time. I want to major in political science."

"Cool," I say feeling kind of lame.

"Where are you going to college, Eddie: Harvard? Yale?" asks Kim, who is beginning to seem loads more unlikeable than Linda and certainly less likeable than Jeff, who I think would be really likeable even if he wasn't such a fox. But he *is* a fox.

I kind of want to shout at Kim "Why do you have to be so bitchy?" but would never do such a thing. But I still think about it. Instead, I just say, "Maybe Harvard. Most everyone in my family went there. But some went to Columbia and I'm thinking about going there because I think it would be cool to live in New York. I'm a little tired of Boston." I say that last sentence all snooty-like, looking at Kim, because Gramps always says you got to treat ladies like princesses unless they act like frogs, and Kim is practically fucking *croaking*.

We all just sort of sit and stand around saying nothing for a few minutes. Linda seems happy enough to just look out at the bay. Kim seems maybe offended. And Jeff and me seem to be happy just standing there smiling at each other.

"So," says Jeff, breaking the silence, "got plans for tonight? A few of us are meeting up and we're just gonna drink some beer and shoot the shit. You wanna join us?"

Before he can even answer Kim says, "Now Jeff – you know the Bradingtons aren't allowed to mingle with us hillbillies."

I ignore her. "Sounds great. Like after supper?"

"Yeah. Whenever. We're here. Any time."

"Cool," I say. "I'll come back after supper then."

"Oh, poor thing," says Kim, *really* getting on my nerves now, "servants expecting you for supper?"

"Yeah, something like that," I reply with a smile and then wink at Jeff, who blushes. I'm really beginning to like this boy, more than any other I've ever met, I think. Then, flexing my muscles once again, I say, "Well, I better be getting back home. Like you said, the servants are expecting me. Later." Jeff and Linda laugh and Kim frowns.

And I jump in the water and swim away – the side stroke so it looks like I'm in no hurry to get anywhere. And as I look up at the tree line as I glide off, I think that – at that moment, anyway – *neether* Aquaman nor the Man from Atlantis got anything on me.

*

Lorraine (Quiche Lorraine Annabel calls her which fucking slays me every time) has the evening off and so Grams is doing the cooking, which is a good thing, because Grams and Lorraine get along like oil and water and meals where they are both present tend to be tense, to say the least. Grams thinks she can cook better than Lorraine (which she probably can) and Lorraine thinks she's queen of the world because every summer she is flown – first class – to the Bay even if there isn't a single Bradington there to cook for, and she refuses to serve Grams and Gramps because they're not Bradingtons. So when there aren't any other Bradingtons around I hate dinner, because it means that I have to sit in the huge dining room by myself while Lorraine eats in the kitchen and Grams and Gramps eat in their sitting room.

But Lorraine's got her day off and Annabel and her friends have gone to Champaign for the night, so I get to eat in the kitchen with Grams and Gramps and it's much more pleasant than sitting by myself. And this evening Grams has cooked fried chicken with mashed potatoes and gravy and green beans and corn on the cob and biscuits. And Grams is quizzing me on what I am going to do in the evening, hinting that she would like to do something with Gramps and me.

"I've been invited to a little party," I say nervously, because Grams is nothing if not protective of me.

"Where?" she says kind of suspicious-like, looking at Gramps as if he's in on it, which – just this time – he isn't.

"Just around the bend on the bay. I swam there today and met some kids from the town." I begin making a perfect lake out of my mashed potatoes, getting ready to fill it with gravy.

"Your father doesn't like you mingling with the kids from the town," Grams says, and I can't tell whether she's on my side or my father's, which – just recently – have emerged as two very distinct sides. "Maybe it would be best if you just stayed in tonight. We were thinking about playing Yahtzee." She's definitely on my father's side here.

"You got a mouse in your pocket, woman?" asks Gramps. "Who's this 'we' you're talking about? I was going to watch TV and then go to bed. If you want to go, Spark Plug, go ahead. Just be careful."

"Thanks Gramps," I say and then, to Grams, "Why don't we play Yahtzee tomorrow?"

"Well, I don't know," says Grams with that whiny voice she always uses when she's offended or hurt or just pissed off, "I've got a lot to do tomorrow."

"What in the hell have you got to do tomorrow?" asks Gramps, looking at her like he can't believe she's just said that.

"You don't know all I do," says Grams to Gramps, this time with a voice between a whine and something a little harder. And then, to me, again with the whine "We'll see about Yahtzee tomorrow. You go to your party. Don't you worry about us." Of course, the way she says "Don't worry about us" makes it pretty clear that she *wants* me to worry about them.

The rest of the meal is pretty much in silence, except for Gramps, who every now and then just starts whistling a little tune for no reason. I can't quite make out Gramps' tune, but it seems happy. The same cannot be said about Grams, who's raising her eyes so high that it looks like they're going to go all the way to the back of her head. Grams does that when she's pissed off. But Gramps always just whistles, which I figure is how I would like to be some day.

*

Getting back to the party spot is proving to be a little tricky. I don't want to swim there because I'm afraid that the others won't be in swimming trunks, and I already feel like I won't quite belong there and being the only one in swimming trunks will make it even worse. But I'm wearing my Speedos from school under my shorts, so if people *are* in swimming trunks I at least have those, which might not be what people swimming in muddy Bradington Bay wear but I don't care so much about that because I've been told I look pretty wicked in my Speedos so what the hell.

But I've never been in the woods before – never been allowed to – so finding my way through them is not easy. I think I'm heading in the direction of the bay but when I keep walking and never find it, I have to admit that I'm wrong. I'm just about to say *the hell with it I'll swim* when I hear voices and I walk in their direction.

There's a bright full moon – I bet it'll look pretty damn cool when I finally reach the water – but with all the trees there's not much light where I'm walking, so I'm going pretty slowly. Eventually the voices I am trying to follow get louder and so I start speeding up again, and before I know it, I reach a clearing which the moon is hitting, and I see the back of some guy and the face of Kim, head tilted up to the moonlight. I get a little closer and I can see that this guy almost certainly is getting to third base, and Kim is too (if girls get to bases as well – which I'm not really sure about but know that Annabel would know).

Now I'm in a bit of a dilemma because I don't want to interrupt the third-basing, but at the same time I really need to ask them the direction of the water. So I cough really loudly and when they don't hear me I do it again and try to hack up a lugie, although I don't get any lugie-stuff in my mouth, so just make this strange noise that sounds like a donkey.

The guy in front of Kim turns away and his pants are undone (Kim was definitely third-basing) and Kim buttons up her jeans (he was certainly third-basing too) but the guy doesn't, like he doesn't care that his pants are undone and his white underwear are almost reflecting like bicycle brake lights in the moon.

I step out into the clearing and nod at Kim. "Sorry to disturb you," I say politely, "but I think I'm lost. I've never been here before." I'm a little embarrassed but not too much, because even if I am lost in the woods *my* pants are not unbuttoned so things are pretty much equal, in my way of thinking.

Kim looks at me annoyed-like and points to his left. "There's a path that goes to the water."

"Cool, thanks."

The guy with Kim looks at me with this "who the hell are you?" expression.

"I'm Edward," I say and though ordinarily I would shake hands like a gentleman should, I don't this time because this guy's just had his hand down Kim's pants.

"Edward?" says the guy with a smirk. "I'm Bill. No, wait: *William*!" Bill and Kim laugh like it was really clever.

I just shrug and say, walking away, "Ever so pleased to make your acquaintance, William," with an English accent because, as Gramps says, sometimes you just got to give assholes a little show to let them know that *you* know they're being assholes.

I find the path and start walking. I wonder if I should maybe introduce myself as "Ed", but I don't really *feel* like an Ed, so then I think about "Eddie", but I don't really feel like an Eddie either (even if sometimes people in my family call me that). No, unfortunately, I feel like an Edward and have never thought of it as a funny name, especially since there are boys named Attila and Hillary at my school.

After a few minutes I can hear Joan Jett singing *I Love Rock and Roll* and I figure I'm heading to the right place. But when I get there, I am a bit surprised to see only the two others from before – Linda and Jeff – with just one other guy. They're sitting around a small fire and no one is talking – they're all just staring into the fire like Joan Jett-listening zombies. I cough again and this time they look up.

"You made it!" says Linda, a lot friendlier than before. I think I could learn to like Linda.

"Yep. Here I am," I say, not really knowing what else to say. Linda comes and gives me a hug like we're old friends.

I walk over to where Jeff is sitting on the ground and smile and say, "Hey Jeff" and offer my hand. He shakes my hand and looks up at me and smiles a smile that I can also see in his clear blue eyes. I hang on to Jeff's hand a little longer than is necessary, but he doesn't seem to mind.

"This is Bart," Jeff says. "Bart, this is Edward."

"Some people call me Eddie," I say, trying it out.

"Nah," says Jeff, "You seem more like an Edward than an Eddie."

I smile, thinking that maybe Jeff gets that I *feel* more like an Edward and that's pretty damned cool. Bart nods and grunts and what with a forehead that juts out like some Mexican cliff and the grunting Bart really *does* seem a bit like a zombie and I can't help but smile.

Linda comes up to me and offers me a can of beer. "We decided in the end to make the party a little smaller. I hope that's OK." She shoots Jeff a look like maybe they're in on something, but something nice.

I go over and sit on the ground next to Jeff, and though I don't look at his face, I'm pretty sure he's smiling.

I just know it somehow.

"What did the cook fix you for dinner?" Jeff asks in this fake British accent, but the way he says it I know that he's making more fun of Kim's behavior that afternoon than my having a cook.

"In the end the cook had the evening off," I say with a smile, "so my grandmother made fried chicken." A grandmother frying chicken seems to be about as normal as you can get, and I really want Jeff to think that I'm normal.

Bart says "Fried chicken" in a voice not unlike a zombie saying "Brains" and Jeff smiles and does the tipping-the-bottle action and we both laugh. Linda laughs too and she goes and sits next to Bart, who doesn't appear to even notice her there.

"So you go to a boarding school," says Jeff, drawing out the first syllable on boarding so it sounds more like boring. "What's that like?"

"It's OK," I say, realizing that I've never really thought too much about it, in that way that I often don't think about things that just are and always have been. "I like it well enough."

"Is it just boys?" asks Jeff.

"No, we've got girls in our classes. But obviously I only live with boys."

"Don't you ever miss girls?" I notice that Jeff's eyes are now darker, and wonder if they are connected to the bay somehow, like they know when the water itself turns dark.

"Not really. Like I said we've got girls at my school, we just don't live with them. So there's not really anything to miss in that sense. And we have dances and stuff like any other school. And we're free on certain weekends and I usually go to Boston and there are tons of girls in Boston. So, you know, it's not like I never see girls; I just don't live in the same house with them. What grade are you in?" I kind of want to change the subject because I don't really want to talk about girls.

"I'm going to be a junior," Jeff says.

"Just like me," I say maybe too excitedly and immediately worry that I sound a bit nerdy.

"Cool," says Jeff. "Linda's in cosmetology school – as you know, I think – and Bart just graduated in May."

"Cool," I say, and then, addressing Bart, ask, "Where are you going to college?"

"I'm not going to college," he slurs, "my Uncle Wally got me on at the county."

Linda looks at me like I'm a dick for having asked about college and I get it as I feel a little like a dick for having automatically assumed he would go to college. But Bart doesn't seem to mind, just keeps drinking his beer and looking into the fire like he's expecting a genie to hop out of it any minute.

Just then Kim and Bill come back. I'm a little disappointed because it was nice just shooting the shit with Jeff and Linda and even drunk Bart.

"So Edward," Kim says, sitting next to me, "do rich people smoke pot or do they just pay other people to do it for them?" No one laughs since it's not really funny or clever to bring up the fact that I'm rich. It's not like I haven't heard crap like that my whole life from my cousins.

"That doesn't really make much sense," I say, trying to take the wind out of her sails as Gramps says, or take her down a notch as Grams says. "Why would we pay someone to do something that feels good?" I'm thinking I *really* want to say "What the fuck did I ever do to you, bitch?" because she's being awfully nasty but, of course, I don't.

"Yeah, well," says Kim like she's saying something really clever. "Bill can get some pot, but you'll need to chip in. How's twenty bucks sound?"

"Twenty bucks?" says Linda before I even have a chance to say that it's OK. "There are five of us. Don't tell me that he's going to get a hundred bucks worth of pot."

"I was thinking that since he owns the fucking town we live in he could pop for the pot tonight," says Kim.

And even if I don't like Kim and Kim clearly doesn't like me, I can't really think that she's off track on this one. Twenty bucks is nothing to me and it just might be to the others – I don't really know – so I wouldn't mind paying twenty.

Jeff stands up and although he is the youngest, he is clearly taking charge of the situation. "A fiver from everyone will give us twenty-five," he says and walks around with his hand out like he's one of those Salvation Army dudes that is always ringing a bell outside of Marshall Fields at Christmas time. Except Jeff isn't ringing a bell, naturally, but I think about him ringing a bell and let out a little chuckle. And Kim looks at me like I'm laughing at her, but in a bad way, because her eyes go all small and piggy. "Spark Plug, you can't win for losin'!" I can almost hear Gramps saying in my head.

Jeff gives the money to Bill, who grabs Kim's hand that just minutes before was down his pants and probably around his crank and they start off through the woods. Linda yells, "Wait a sec!" She winks at Jeff and grabs Bart's hand (who seems startled like he's heard a shriek in a graveyard) and they scurry off like cocaine-snorting mice, leaving Jeff and me alone.

"Sorry about them," Jeff says as soon as they have disappeared into the woods. "I sometimes wonder why I hang out with them."

"Why do you?" I ask in a way that I hope doesn't sound mean or snobby.

"Well my two best friends – Abbey and Jennifer – are both working at a Christian family camp this summer, so there aren't that many people around to hang out with. Linda's my neighbor and she's not so bad. But Kim? Well, you see how she can be. Sorry."

"No biggie," I say. "I get a lot of shit from my cousins so I can say I'm pretty much used to it. I just let it go off me like water off a duck's ass." I hope that using one of Gramps' lines will make me seem cool like Gramps.

"I guess that's all you can do," says Jeff like he didn't think the line was cool but more like he thought it was deep. (I think if I can't be cool, deep will work just fine.)

We sit in silence for quite a while, even though I have a million questions I would like to ask Jeff. Mosquitoes are buzzing around us but they don't seem to be biting, so I kind of like the sound, like little violins serenading us.

"You feel like getting in the water?" asks Jeff.

"Sure. If you do," I respond, already beginning to worry about the combination of the violin-playing mosquitoes, the mud between my toes and a hot boy under the moonlight. If there was ever a recipe for a stiffie, that was it.

Jeff gets up and takes off his t-shirt and jeans, and he's wearing white underwear. They seem to glow in the moonlight.

"I've got swimming trunks on," I say apologetically, because I'm nervous and don't want to give Jeff any ammo at all for not liking me. I take off my shirt and shorts and kick off my boat shoes and am standing there in my Speedos, and I worry that I was a little too fast in doing it all, like I was desperate or something.

"Wow!" Jeff looks at me like he thinks I'm a fox.

"Wow!" I say looking at Jeff because I think he's a fox.

We walk into the water, which is warm and still. The moonlight is making a giant streak on the bay, and it seems like a spotlight shining on us. I am trying not to think about the mud between my toes.

We walk out far enough that the water comes up to our chins, not speaking, just looking at each other and enjoying the water. I can no longer ignore the combination of the violin-playing mosquitoes, the mud between my toes and a pretty boy under the moonlight, so I've got a stiffie but I'm not too upset about it because the water is so muddy that there's no way Jeff could see it, even if he dove under and opened his eyes, which he probably wouldn't do in that water.

"Do you want to kiss me?" Jeff says, finally breaking the silence. No boy has ever asked me that, and I'm impressed by just how easily Jeff has asked me.

"Yes," I say. "Of course. But what about the others?"

"No worries," says Jeff. "The girls know I'm gay and the boys suspect it, so it's all good."

And Jeff kisses me, and I kiss Jeff back. He tastes like beer and bay water and even if that doesn't sound all that great, I think it's fantastic. We kiss and kiss, and I'm trying to hold back because I've never done this before – not with a boy – and I've just met Jeff, really, and I don't want him to think I'm some kind of a sexual pervert. So I kiss Jeff really light and cool like they do in the movies and not like I imagine kissing really happens, all wide open mouth and slurping tongues.

And then Jeff grabs one of my hands and puts it on his dick, which is a lot bigger to the touch than I imagined. And I try and make sure that my touch there is as light as my kissing is, but it's not easy because I want to maul him like a bear, want to rip off those white underwear and kiss him and taste the bay water there.

And then Jeff does something that I am so not ready for – he goes to third base on me. And I'm slightly embarrassed that I'm so hard, but Jeff doesn't seem to care, just says "Wow!", which I take as a good sign. And then he starts slowly stroking up and down and it's the first time anyone has ever touched me there before and it's a bit like I'm jerking off with my left hand only much, much better. And I'm really liking it, but I feel like I should tell him to stop because if he doesn't stop I'm going to spoo right there in the bay in like twenty seconds which I know from having watched a few porn movies is *so* not long enough a time to go before spooing. But before I can tell Jeff to stop for a bit I know it's too late and I feel that familiar feeling coming upon me, but this time it's like a million times more intense because it's not my hand and I'm in the water with this beautiful boy and there's mud oozing through my toes.

And it happens. And my legs go all weak and I kind of slump down a bit, so much that my nose goes under water and what with the heavy breathing I'm doing I snort in like ten gallons of bay water and start choking. So now I'm not only embarrassed because I spooed so quickly but also because I'm coughing and gasping like I'm having a heart attack or something.

Jeff just smiles at me and pounds me on the back like I'm a toddler who's got a piece of chicken wedged in his throat and this makes me even more embarrassed, if that's even possible. And after a long, embarrassing wheeze I'm finally able to speak and I say, "Sorry." I don't specify if I'm sorry because I spooed so quickly or because Jeff had to hit me on the back like a toddler, but in my mind it's all included.

"What for?" asks Jeff smiling.

I wish I hadn't said that because now I have to actually say that I spooed too quickly. "I think I finished a little too early," I say, deciding not to go into the choking as well. "I guess I was just a little surprised. Sorry."

Jeff kisses me softly and says, "I'm no expert, but I don't think it matters how fast it happens if it's a hand job. If we were fucking it would be a different matter. But hand jobs can go really fast. It's OK."

I just nod because I now have to add the fact that Jeff seems to know *way* more about sex than I do to my tally of embarrassment. And I wonder if he's brought up the subject of fucking because that's what he wants to do, so I say, "If you want to – you know – fuck, I'll be ready to go again in about three minutes. Or do you want to fuck me? I'm clueless about how all of this is supposed to go – I'm sorry. I feel like an idiot."

"Don't worry about it," he says with that killer smile of his, "Maybe you could just return the favor? I probably already went a little too far for just having met you and all, but it just happened before I knew what I was doing. You probably think I'm a slut. I'm not a slut – I swear."

"I don't think you're a slut," I say. And I don't. In fact, I'm amazed at how little I'm thinking about sex at all. I'm looking into Jeff's eyes (which have changed again) and see in them something that has been constant: I see someone who, amazingly, seems to understand me in a way that I have never experienced before. And, sure, the hand job was nice, and I would most certainly like to take it further, but I think that it's all pretty nice – no, it's fanfuckingtastic, to be more accurate – to be able to look into someone's eyes and know that they get you. And I think, looking into Jeff's eyes, not saying anything, that maybe I get Jeff as well.

I reach down and do a little third-basing. And instead of looking away, or being embarrassed, we both look at each other without flinching, eye contact not being broken until Jeff closes his eyes and shudders with a moan. And then we just stand there in the water, hugging each other, listening to the violin-playing mosquitoes that seemed to follow us from the shore, feeling the mud between our toes, and thinking that where we are is not a bad place to be at all.

Chapter Nine: 2012

Edward hadn't noticed when it had happened, but at one point the hills had disappeared, the monotonous road seemingly bleeding into the scenery. Had the change been gradual? Had the hills quietly crept away, tiptoeing so as not to make their absence known? Or had there been a moment – a moment Edward had obviously missed – when they ended abruptly, when they no longer had the strength to continue their swirling play, when they could no longer keep up with the road's unyielding sense of purpose?

Edward wished he had been more observant, wished he had seen what had happened to the hills. And now awareness of their absence weighed heavily upon him. The lack of the soft, seductive folds that allowed him to think so symbolically and poetically about his journey meant that he could no longer ignore what the road was telling him: he was really going back to the Bay. And he was suddenly unsure whether the whole trip was a monumentally bad idea, an uncharacteristic lapse in what had always before been fairly sound judgement.

The evening before, watching a father and daughter come together after so many years, he felt he was on the right track, thought that this strange journey which had begun with the ill winds of a hurricane was just as mythic and significant and changing as such journeys should be. Even if Hank – in the end – could be seen as no more than demonstrating a reserved politeness which perhaps bordered on affection towards his daughter, he knew that these things took time. The seed had been planted; the journey had done its magic.

Sure, Hank was quiet and didn't seem to be acting like someone who had just had an epiphany of sorts, but that didn't mean anything, did it? Maybe the epiphany was so grand, the light so startling, that he needed time to take it all in, to allow the wonder of what had happened to cascade over him. Maybe Hank was just tired. Maybe silence was how he registered emotional insight and Edward just didn't know him well enough to know this for sure. And driving through the hills allowed Edward to continue in this strain of thought, their jumping and skipping presence affirming him, comforting him.

But now the hills were gone. And Hank was still silent. And Edward's sparkling memory of the evening before was fading as well, replaced by a doubt as constant and unswerving as the road.

"I think we should get off the interstate," Edward said as they drove by what looked like a refinery of some sort, smoke belching into a cloudless sky. "I mean, we're not in any hurry, are we? Why the rush to get there?"

"Why the sudden change?" responded Hank. His voice sounded suspicious, as if he already knew the answer. "I thought you said we'd take the interstate to St. Louis and then from near there get on the Great River Road and go north."

"Well just look at this," Edward said, holding his hand out to indicate the road in front of them. "There is absolutely nothing to see here. It's ugly and depressing. The whole point of the journey is to see things along the way. This way we're only seeing semis and cars."

"*I* thought the point of a journey was to get where you want to go. And this road leads us to the road that will lead us along the river which will then lead us to another road going through a bunch of podunk towns – 'jewels of America' I believe you called them – which will lead us to Springfield which may lead us to the nun. And then, from Springfield we'll go through the country – 'I know I still remember the way because it's in my blood!' you said – and we'll end up at the Bay. That was the plan. Now I personally don't give a rat's ass how we get there, but you mapped this out, and I guess I'm a little curious as to why you want to change it now. And why you seem to have something shoved up your ass."

"Are you even going to call her?" asked Edward, looking straight ahead.

"Is that what this is about?"

"*This* isn't about anything. I'm just asking: are you going to call her?"

"I don't know. I'm sure I will when the time's right, when I think I'm ready. But if you mean am I going to call her this minute, or even tomorrow or the next day then the answer is probably no, I'm not." Hank opened his window slightly, turning his face away.

"I don't buy it, you know," Edward said. "This whole 'I'm fucking strong like Hercules and nothing gets me down and I just shrug things off and move forward' thing you're trying to do. I don't buy it. You *have* thought about it and it *has* affected you and brushing it aside is not a sign of strength, it's a sign of weakness. You're being weak. Scared."

"I had no idea I was going to be road-tripping with Sigmund Fucking Freud!" Hank said coldly. "Thank you so much for unpacking my essence for me, doctor; I would have never been able to figure anything out without you. It's amazing how you can tell me my business when you haven't even known me a week. You really are a genius."

"It doesn't take a genius," said Edward, "just eyes and

ears. You've shut yourself up in some little town in Ohio where you are basically married to your business. You – by your own admission – don't see anyone, don't really have anyone you spend time with outside of the bar. Then, a person who actually has a connection to you – and there is no stronger connection than blood, I can tell you that – wants to become a part of your life and you have to *think* about it? And it's not like she was some horrid person, and it's not like she's even particularly needy or anything. She's an adorable young woman who just wants to know a little more about where she's come from. What's the harm in that? But you're too scared to even *consider* it."

"Again," said Hank, tinny voice rising in pitch and volume, "I thank you for your wisdom. It's amazing that you have all the insight into *my* life but don't seem to be able to figure *yours* out."

"What the hell is that supposed to mean?"

"Never mind." He reached to turn the radio on.

"No," Edward said, blocking his hand, "I really want to know. Tell me: what is my life about?"

"Well," he said, turning to face Edward, "you have been in an unhappy relationship for three years. You're bored with your job. You resent your family. And you're so fucking scared of dealing with any of that that you just up and leave everything and drive across the country. But here's the thing about you, Edward: you're even scareder – more scared – of being alone. So you turn on your charm and pick up some guy along the way and talk about your dreams and this whole fucking stupid idea of a journey and you convince him to come with you, because you can't bear the thought of being alone. 'Cause you see, if you'd made this trip alone you might just have to discover that you *can't* go back again, that your life *doesn't* have all this great meaning, that you *are* alone and that sometimes – just sometimes

– the road takes you from point-fucking-A to point-fucking -B and nothing more."

Edward said nothing. The road and the prairies seemed to be watching him, expecting him to respond. He missed the hills.

"Listen," Hank continued, "I'm sorry – there's no need to be a dick, I know. Here's the deal, Edward: things with Ellie aren't as simple as they seem. She *is* lovely and I know that she's not some emotional cripple who's going to suck me dry. But Ellie represents for me a place I'm just not ready to go to right now. It has taken me a long time to get to the point where I didn't wonder every single day whether I should have just tried to raise her with Stella's help. Maybe she would have been happier. Maybe *I* would have been happier. But I didn't do that, and so it don't do no good at all even *thinking* about it. And last night, at the restaurant, the old thoughts started coming up again, that I'd made a huge mistake. And it hurts like a motherfucker – this regret – and I just don't know if I got the strength right now to get into it again."

Edward reached out and stroked his hair. "I'm sorry," he said, and marveled at how limp words could be. He wanted to convey that he was more than just sorry, that he understood living with regret, that everything Hank had said about him was true. But he also knew that if he said those things he would have to say more, explain. And just as Hank was not ready to invite regret back into his life, Edward knew that he wasn't either, didn't want that particularly ugly companion on this trip. And so he just said "I'm sorry" again and stroked Hank's hair.

A sign for an exit came up that promised a scenic route, but Edward ignored it and continued driving on the interstate. The absence of the hills no longer bothered him, and the flat prairies suddenly seemed less antagonistic.

They were not as happy and dancing as the hills had been, but they were constant, and seemed to be saying to him "We'll support you."

Which is just what he needed.

St. Louis was a disappointment. In part because the words spoken on the way lingered, casting everything in a somber light that made the city look gray, tired. Even the sparkling downtown with its buildings casting geometric shadows on the Mississippi below seemed dull and lifeless. If the Ohio River seemed to animate an already lively Louisville, the Mississippi seemed more an IV hooked up to a barely breathing body.

In part, though, Edward knew that St. Louis failed to impress because a city wasn't what they needed right now. He had nothing against cities – he lived in the heart of the world's most exciting metropolis – but cities were like colorful rattles in the hand of a baby: distracting, noisy, entertaining. Neither he nor Hank needed such things right then.

And so, stopping only long enough for Hank to take a picture of the Gateway Arch, they continued on, retreating from Missouri back into the comfort of Illinois. "A river forces an 'us and them' notion" Gramps used to say looking across his river to the other side; Edward longed to be among the *us.*

He knew he had to find Alton to get on the Great River Road, but Alton ended up being much larger than he remembered as a boy, and the river not as easy to find as he had imagined. "It's hard to lose the Mississippi River" said Hank, noting that they had perhaps driven by the same convenience store three times. Edward considered turning on the navigating system, but Gramps seemed to be saying to him, "Damn it, Spark Plug – you shouldn't need a highfalutin gadget to find the biggest river in America!" so he drove on, even rolling down his window so that the air's scent might give him some clues.

They turned onto a tree-lined street that boasted a few buildings that seemed older, so he figured he must be getting closer since the city had most certainly sprung up from the river.

"What the hell is that?" asked Hank, pointing off to the right, where a giant bronze statue was set off from the road in a small park.

"It's Robert Wadlow!" said Edward excitedly.

"Who?" asked Hank.

"Robert Wadlow. He was the tallest man who ever lived. He came from Alton. Let's stop!"

He parked the Range Rover at the side of the street. As they walked up the path it became evident just how tall this man had been; the life-size statue was massive.

There was a young couple taking pictures of each other at the statue. The girl had a pretty face framed by a mass of shiny black curls, and as they got closer Edward could see that her body was twisted as by some disease. Standing there in front of the "Gentle Giant" – he was so tall that she only came up to his crotch – Edward could see that her face was luminous, radiating a happiness that seemed perfectly natural. She was holding on to one of the statue's legs – her crutches were on the ground beside her – while her friend took one photo after another.

Edward watched them, transfixed by the simplicity and beauty of the scene. Here was a girl, he thought, who did not live with regret. And though not religious, he shocked himself by saying a prayer to God right there on the spot that she would be allowed to always live that way – without regret – clutching to the people around her to support her and help her in her happiness.

Photographs finished, the couple moved off to another bronze sculpture – a life-size replica of a chair which had been built for the giant. The young man helped the girl up into the chair for more photos.

"OK," said Hank, grabbing his phone, "your turn."

"Are you kidding me? You actually want to take a picture of me standing next to him? It seems kind of cheesy, doesn't it?" He was slightly embarrassed.

The girl, legs sticking out in front of her in the giant chair said, "Of course it's cheesy! Duh! That's the point!"

Her boyfriend said, "Jennifer!" in reprimand, but Edward just said to her, "You are absolutely right. Thanks for the reminder" and walked up to take his place next to the statue. His head arrived at the giant's stomach.

"Take his hand!" yelled Hank.

Edward reached up and took the enormous hand while Hank took photos. He felt like a child, the large cold hand dwarfing his own, and it was a very nice sensation indeed. Childlike wonder cropped up and left you feeling weak but safe, insignificant but important somehow. He liked standing there, feeling like a little boy, but Hank had finished with his pictures and had moved on to read a nearby plaque, and Edward had to let go of the hand and join him.

"If I continue on in that direction, will I find the river?" Hank asked the statue, neck craned upward in anticipation.

"Yep, it's about five minutes away," answered the girl Jennifer, walking past him with great difficulty, metal crutches scraping against the concrete.

He grabbed Edward's hand and they returned to the car. "A giant and a beautiful princess," Hank said, looking back at the scene. "I'd say we're back on track in terms of the whole journey thing."

Edward nodded, getting in the car and starting the

engine. But, looking at the faces of Grams and Gramps looking at him, he was pretty sure they had never really been *off* track.

The afternoon sun was setting when they decided to stop for the night in a small riverside town called Elsah. If their goal was to escape urban settings, they couldn't have chosen better. Sitting underneath a bluff, the village had the feeling of a different time and place, when the river passing in front of them would have been dotted with riverboats carrying gamblers – scoundrels! – on their way to the brothels and gambling establishments of New Orleans. There were only two streets in the village, and he drove up one and down the other until he found a large, old, barn-red two-storey house, surrounded by a pristine white fence. Over the main porch hung a sign that read "Green Tea Inn." Edward pulled in.

They entered the front door and were met by a kind-faced old woman, who before Edward had even spoken said, "You're *very* lucky. We had a cancellation in the Hummingbird Garden Room if you want it for just one night. Otherwise – you're out of luck. The whole town's booked." She smiled at them expectantly, looking from Edward to Hank as if anxious for one of them to answer her.

"We'll only be staying the one night, so it sounds like we've hit the jackpot," answered Hank. "Honey, why don't you take care of the details and I'll go out and get our things," he said to Edward, who was confused because Hank had never called him "honey" before and wondered why he was playacting.

They were led to a large room with pale green walls, white furniture, and bright yellow quilts and fabrics. If outside the setting sun was slowly ushering in night, here it seemed as if the morning was just beginning.

"Wow, it sure is bright!" said Edward with a grin.

"Thank you," said their hostess, who had obviously chosen to take his comment as a compliment. "Breakfast is from seven to nine, checkout at eleven. Just holler if you need anything." She closed the door, and they were alone.

"Listen," Hank said, "I don't really feel like going out tonight – I'm beat. Why don't I hop in the shower while you find a supermarket somewhere and buy some sandwich -things so we can just have supper here in the room. Sound like a plan?"

"Yes, honey," said Edward.

"Yeah … that. I don't know what got into me. It's just we're in this beautiful old-fashioned house and there was this sweet old lady in front of us and I guess I just didn't want her to think we were, you know, like sordid gays stay-ing for a one-night orgy."

"First of all, I don't think we seem too sordid," said Edward, shaking his head. "But – more importantly – I doubt whether the sordid gays of the orgy scene have really embraced the Green Tea Inn. Colorful quilts and fisting rarely go together."

"Fuck you," Hank said, throwing a quilted pillow at him. "Just go get something to eat. I just *might* be a prude tonight if you give me any more lip."

Edward got back on the river road and headed north. To his left, the sun was setting, and its reflection seemed to cast the river on fire. It was odd, he thought, that he had spent just a fraction of his life around rivers – most of his time had been spent on Chicago's arrogant lake – but these muddy waters beside him affected him in ways that it did not. He suspected that the spell rivers cast on him went even deeper than boyhood memories, though exactly what that magic was he could not tell.

Arriving in Grafton he found a small shop that was

part used bookstore, part coffee house, and part barber shop. Entering he was overcome by the smell of mildewing books and brewing coffee. A young Goth couple looked up from their books, appeared to deem him unworthy of notice, and went back to their reading, coffees steaming in front of them. In the back was a woman with platinum hair, sitting behind a counter, watching an old television that had been placed on a shelf in the corner.

"Good evening, handsome. What can I do for you? This time of night a decaf might be in order, but the customer's always right so I'll give you a dark Colombian roast if you want it." She smiled and he noticed she had lipstick on her teeth.

"No coffee – thanks. I was wondering what you had by way of vittles?" To his knowledge, he had never said the word "vittles" in his entire life.

"Well," she said, "we've got all kinds of deli meats and homemade potato salad. And there should be a little pasta salad left as well. That's about it though. Kind of late, you know."

"Sounds perfect. Fix me up two big sandwiches – you decide what you want to put on them – and I'll take the potato salad and what's left of the pasta salad. What about for dessert?"

"Well, I baked some cookies a couple of days ago but they're probably getting a little stale. If you cross the street and walk down a little bit, you'll find the best fudge in the world. They're only open another fifteen minutes, so you better run down there now while I fix you up here."

Edward left and walked across the street. Looking up he saw a sign that read "Grafton: Home of Wintering Bald Eagles Dec.1 – Mar. 1." He wondered why the bald eagles would choose to winter there of all places, where temperatures could be horribly cold, but he figured the eagles were as charmed by the river as he was and never wanted to be too far from it. He found the fudge shop, got a half pound of peanut-butter chocolate and a half pound of chocolate cheesecake from a bored teenage girl, and returned to the cafe.

Entering he noticed that the Goth couple had left, and the blond woman was no longer sitting behind the counter. "Be out in a flash – just finishing up in here!" he heard her yell from a back room, so he went into the book room to look around. Most of the books were paperbacks of the Louis L'Amour and Jackie Collins types, but he was surprised to see – nestled between a Sidney Sheldon and a Judith Krantz – a hardback copy of *The Wind in the Willows*. It was not the same edition that he had, but the drawings were the same, and seeing Mr. Mole and Mr. Rat frolicking on the pages…

"OK, we're all set," announced the woman, now back behind the counter. "You want that book too?" she asked, noting it under his arm.

"Yes. Oh, and also: you wouldn't happen to have any wine, would you?"

She looked around conspiratorially. "I don't have a liquor license. But since you're a friend, I could maybe share some that I made myself – not sell it of course! – just give it, like from one friend to another."

"Sounds good, friend," Edward said and the woman blushed. He still could work his magic, he thought. She bundled everything up, added the two bottles of wine, and he paid and left.

It was dark outside by the time he returned to find Hank sitting in an overstuffed chair, looking at what appeared to be a photo album. He barely looked up when Edward entered.

"What's that?" Edward set the bags on the bed.

"It's a guest book. I'm just reading what others who have stayed here had to say. It's a bit sickening, to tell the truth, but I can't put it down."

"Why's it sickening?" Edward extracted the wine bottles and opened one.

"Oh, everyone is like 'This is the most romantic spot in the world' and 'We come here every year on our anniversary' and – my absolute favorite: 'As the river washes over the ground below, so our love keeps washing over each other.' Who *writes* such things? Jesus, thank God I don't have anything in my stomach, or I'd have ralphed all over this pastel palace!"

"Oh, come on," Edward said, handing him a glass of wine, "don't be so harsh. I think it's cute."

"Jesus, here we go. It's the attack of the smiley-faces all over again."

"This wine's not half bad," said Edward, desperate to change the subject. He was just coming out of his funk and didn't feel like defending happiness again. "A tad on the sweet side for my tastes, but not bad all the same."

Hank closed the book and set in on a table. "Edward," he said, "earlier I was talking about regret – living with regret. And your face got all cloudy like you were remembering something. But you didn't say a peep. What were you thinking about? You know, maybe I'd have an easier time dealing with the smiley-faces if I thought you could also – on occasion – be more like me. So what gives? What great regret were you talking about? I was very honest with you; why don't you do the same?"

Edward got up and looked out the window; darkness greeted him. Darkness, he had once thought, was like an animal: if you just stopped feeding it, stopped inviting it into your home, it would wander away in search of a new master.

And – for the most part – Edward had been able to do just that. He could make reference to the darkness, to that time when he was young and "got in a little trouble," could speak about it as dispassionately as one could a childhood friend long moved away. But he had never allowed himself to really visit it, to talk about it for what it was, not to dismiss or undervalue it, but to go back there in his mind and heart.

"I've been in love once in my life," Edward said, still looking out the window. "That sounds kind of tragic coming from a forty-six-year-old man – and I guess it kind of is – but it's the truth. He was a boy from Bradington named Jeff, and I thought he was the most fascinating and beautiful person in the world. We met the summer I was sixteen and we just clicked. We carried on that whole summer, and during the school year, when we were separated, we wrote each other every day. It's hard to imagine in this day and age, piles and piles of letters going back and forth through the mail. I've still got them all, you know; could never make myself throw them away.

"Anyway, my Grams figured out what was going on and wasn't too happy about it. It's weird, she was born into a dirt-poor family, whose only claim to social fame is that her daughter had married very well indeed, and yet she was the biggest snob I think I've ever known. She didn't seem too upset about the gay thing – although I'm sure she was. It was probably so far out of her experience that she just didn't really understand or even believe it. No, what seemed more distressing for her was Jeff's – for a lack of a better word – *class*. She said he was white trash, that he was out to trap me in some kind of blackmail scheme which could ruin me, that I was going to throw my life and future away on someone not worthy of me. She even convinced my father of it all and – in a *real* coup – got my stepmother on the bandwagon, a woman who had always referred to Grams as 'that horrible old woman.' I was outnumbered. My father – who had, I'm pretty sure had an affair with a housemaid and quite possibly also a gardener when he was a teenager – didn't think it was anything to worry about and allowed me to return to the Bay the next summer, but I was basically on lockdown. It was so … I don't know … I guess I'd have to say *disorienting.* I mean, here was this place that for as long as I could remember was a place which offered so much freedom from the rest of my world, a place where I didn't have to act and talk and be a certain way. And then all of a sudden that was all gone. Everything *looked* the same, but it wasn't the same. And I began thinking that all the freedom to be who I was had just been an illusion."

"It has a little bit of everything, doesn't it?" said Hank, "the poor boy, the rich boy, the difficult family, impossible love? Chains which bind?" His tone was sincere, not mocking.

"Yeah. My father said I was living a cliché. I also think he thought it was just a hormonal thing – you know: two horny teenagers in a summertime romance. But it wasn't. It really wasn't. There was a whole lot more there."

Edward turned around.

"So the next summer comes and we continue meeting on the sly and eventually we decide that I will tell my father that I won't go to Harvard or Columbia but I'll stay in Illinois and go to the University of Illinois. Then Jeff would graduate and – if he could get in – he'd go to the U of I as well. But even if he couldn't, he could go to a nearby junior college. He laughed. I was going to be a writer."

"Really?" said Hank. "I can see it – I can totally see it. You with your deep thoughts and symbols and signs and all that crap. You would be a great writer!"

"Yeah, well, my father didn't seem to think so when I told him. I got the usual spiel: he would not allow me to throw my life away, people like Jeff and me were doomed to live a life of tragedy but if this thing was real it would last until after college, if I had any harebrained ideas about running off and doing it anyway I would soon discover how difficult life was without money."

"He was going to disinherit you?"

"I don't know if he would have gone through with it, but I'm sure his bitch of a wife was goading him on in that direction and he has always been powerless to stand up to her. Anyway, things got even worse because at Christmas-time – I was at my Aunt Margaret's house in Boston – I called Jeff and he tells me that his father, who knew Jeff was gay and this wasn't just a phase, beat the shit out of him and he didn't know what to do."

Hank poured two more glasses of wine for them. "How awful. So what did you do?" he asked.

"Well, the next day I hopped on a plane and flew to Illinois. I was too young to rent a car, so I had to take a bus to get to him. It was all kind of romantic, I have to admit. I'd never been on a bus in my life, and I remember feeling all Bruce Springsteen-y, riding on a Greyhound, making my way to my working-class boyfriend."

"Fucking snob."

"I know, but I'm just trying to accurately portray what I was feeling, and I have to admit that some rebellion mixed with a little blue-collar romanticism was going on."

"Like *An Officer and a Gentleman*," Hank said smiling.

"Exactly like in *An Officer and a Gentleman*. Anyway, my father found out about it because – get this – my weird-ass Uncle Bill recorded every telephone conversation that came in and went out of his house and he told my Aunt Margaret about it who couldn't wait to tell my father about it. Dad – and in a real shocker – the *stepmonster* beat me to the Bay and confronted me in the presence of Grams and Gramps. Dad said the usual things about this being some sort of phase, that I would grow out of it and do the right thing for my family. I kept looking at Gramps to stand up for me – we had always been so close, and all my father's talk about destiny and heritage and honor and all of that was bullshit to him – but he just looked away while Dad and the stepmonster just wailed on me. But more than the gay thing – which I don't think my father really believed, I still think he thought it was a phase – what seemed to upset everyone was that I was cavorting with the wrong sort of person. I was given an ultimatum: I was to end things immediately. After that, my father would assure that "the boy in question" – how I fucking hated him, that he kept calling Jeff that – would no longer be a problem. He would take care of things from there. But I had to man-up and do the right thing for a Bradington and an Allerton, which was *not* throwing away my life."

"Edward, I'm so sorry." Hank exhaled slowly, seemingly searching for the right words to say when the right words probably didn't even exist. "What did you do?"

"Well obviously I would like to say that I told them all to go to hell and left everything to be with the boy I loved. But I think you know that didn't happen. I wasn't courageous enough at the time. Hell – I'm not sure I'd be courageous enough now. Eventually my father paid for a private school out west for Jeff's last year of high school and then he got a full ride from one of my family's foundations to study political science at UCLA. We never saw each other again."

"O God, Edward. I don't know what to say."

"Yeah, and then – to add insult to injury – my bitch of a stepmother decided she just couldn't deal with the 'gay thing' and wouldn't have me in her home, which was the home I had grown up in, learned to read in, cried my eyes out every night missing my mother in. The Bay was out of the question – I was pretty much banished from there which meant I no longer got to see Grams and Gramps. I was pretty pissed off at them anyway, but I know if I had been able to see them more, I would have forgiven them; they were the only real family I had. So I travelled, stayed with friends, and then eventually I went to Columbia for both undergrad and law school. I settled in New York and tried to become one of those guys who sees the smiley-faces. And I was doing OK with it all, until you started talking about regret."

Hank came to him and wrapped his arms around him, swaying lightly back and forth. "I shouldn't have pried. I'm sorry for being such a dick."

"You weren't a dick," Edward said, kissing the top of his head. "It's the road trip, you know? Remember? We're *supposed* to have these big discoveries. And I guess I've allowed myself just now to feel the regret that I couldn't seem to muster when it all happened."

"What do you mean? You were obviously upset from the beginning. I don't buy that this regret thing is new." Hank's voice was challenging but not unkind.

"I think you're presuming I was as deep and complicated a person as I am now back then," Edward laughed. "Back then ... I don't know ... I just sort of shut down. The whole ugly ordeal didn't really matter to me, I'm ashamed to say. I told myself that I had tried to do the right thing, but I knew I was lying. I didn't care enough – it's that simple – not about Jeff, anyway. I can see now that I just didn't quite have the maturity *not* to be selfish, to think about it from Jeff's perspective. And later, when I really owned up to what I had done, what had happened, it was too late."

"Do you know what happened to him?"

"No," he said, shaking his head. "I eventually made some half-hearted attempts to get in touch, but by then the damage had already been done. And I'm not sure why I even tried, to be honest. I was so lost in my own pity party that I couldn't see beyond my own shit. But there's probably not a day that's gone by that I haven't thought about him, wondered about him." He wanted to cry, but tears would not come. "I'm damaged goods," was all he managed to say.

"Join the fucking club," Hank said in response. "But I'm just wondering: we're tracking down long-lost daughters and nuns from the past on this trip of ours. Maybe we're looking to the wrong people. Maybe there's someone else you should be looking for." His voice was calm, even.

"No no no," said Edward. "Really, that ship has sailed. Besides, why would I want to dredge up some summer fling from the past when I've got me a real live hot man in the present?"

Hank just nodded as if he believed him. And Edward, looking at the yellow walls, tried to believe himself.

They didn't have sex that night, both perhaps knowing that the intimacy that had been shared during the day would have made sex seem anti-climactic. They finished both bottles of wine and, drunk, crawled into bed and slept immediately.

Around four in the morning, Edward awoke with a horrible headache. He grabbed the book he had bought at the cafe and began reading it, allowing thoughts of his mother to calm him. He could almost feel her there as he read of Mr. Mole thinking of what had been his home before the wonders of the river tempted him away. There, buried somewhere deep in the earth, was the place who had made Mr. Mole who he was. And even if he didn't want to live there anymore, even if the chuckling and swirling of the river above had become his life, he wanted to go back – just for a time.

And he did go back, taking Mr. Rat with him. And he did not see his old home with eyes misted over by romanticism and nostalgia; instead he saw it for what it was: dirty, cramped, limited. But it was his home.

Edward read on:

He saw clearly how plain and simple—how narrow, even—it all was; but clearly, too, how much it all meant to him, and the special value of some such anchorage in one's existence. He did not at all want to abandon the new life and its splendid spaces, to turn his back on sun and air and all they offered him and creep home and stay there; the upper world was all too strong, it called to him still, even down there, and he knew he must return to the larger stage. But it was good to think he had this to come back to; this place which was all his own, these things which were so glad to see him again and could always be counted upon for the same simple welcome.

Edward closed the book and crawled back into bed beside Hank. Maybe his journey was not so complicated, the insights he hoped to receive not so byzantine. Maybe he wanted a home again. And leaning over he kissed Hank lightly on the cheek and wondered if his home could be a person: all his own, glad to see him, and who could always be counted upon.

And for the second time that day, Edward said a little prayer, a prayer that asked a God he wasn't sure existed to help him find a home that maybe didn't exist either.

Chapter Ten: 1983

I'm thinking about Jeff, and actively, too. A lot of times I think about things passively – something will enter into my brain unwanted and I can't stop myself from thinking about whatever it is that has entered. And when I think about things passively it's true I can zone out and not pay too close attention to anything or anyone ("EJ? EJ? Where the hell are you? Mars?" my father asks me a lot) but when I am thinking about something *actively* all bets are off, as Gramps would say. I could walk in front of a bus and be killed because it's almost like I'm not even awake, it's like I'm a sleepwalker. But it's summer and I'm at the Bay, so I'm obviously not going to get hit by a bus, because there aren't any buses around for miles and miles. But how funny would it be if it actually happened? If some Greyhound driver got wasted on cheap wine and just kept driving around and around central Illinois, ending up somehow on the private road that leads up to the house, smashing through the gate and plowing right down the road, not paying any attention as I am walking down the lane listening to *Hi Infidelity* by REO Speedwagon on my Walkman (even if my classmates make fun of me, still listening to that same album over and over again). It wouldn't be funny like ha-ha funny because – of course – Grams would fucking *wail* if I got run over by a drunk Greyhound driver right there at the Bay – but it would be funny like unusual or interesting if it happened.

That's *exactly* how thinking passively works. It's not

like I asked for that image of the drunk Greyhound driver to come into my head, but it just did.

But I'm thinking about Jeff actively, I know, because I can get lost in my thoughts and before I know it something like an hour has passed, not just the usual few minutes involved in passive thinking.

It's sheer wonderment I can think clearly at all after what happened at the end of the previous summer, when Grams caught me and Jeff going at it in the boathouse. She'd probably been in that boathouse twice in her life, but for whatever reason she just *had* to stroll down there right at the moment when I was rounding home plate with Jeff, all bases having previously been touched that summer. Gramps stood up for us – said we were probably just wrestling – but for Grams it was less about maybe catching her grandson fucking another boy and more about the other boy, as she just kept talking about "white trash" people who were out to mess with me in some way because they knew I was rich. And in a move even rarer than her going to the boathouse, she actually called my father, completely ratting me out – not only to Dad but also to Morticia. That was right up my father's alley, as he didn't want me getting involved with the "wrong type of people" – whatever in the hell that meant – and the stepmonster preached at me about the evils of being a homo – the only one of the whole lousy group that even mentioned that part of things. And the stepmonster suggested that maybe I should spend the summer in Boston next year (where she knew a doctor who could help me). But my father – for once – grew a pair and allowed me to come back to the Bay. So now Grams is watching me like a hawk. And Gramps – maybe tired of Grams' bitching or maybe not completely able to ignore that his grandson might be a homo – doesn't seem to be as much on my side as he used to be.

And though I know I have to be on my best behavior, I can't help it: I'm actively thinking about Jeff. And I'm naturally thinking about stroking and sucking and fucking and getting stroked and sucked and fucked until I can't think of anything else.

But I'm not just thinking about that – not even by a long shot. I'm thinking about the way Jeff's hair smells all coconut-y and the way he turns his head and rubs his neck a lot like he has a pain there even though he always says he doesn't and the way he sometimes gives a short little hiccup – but just one – for no reason and doesn't even seem to notice that he's done it, and even looks confused if someone tells him "You just hiccupped."

And I'm thinking about how we talked and talked and talked about the future; how I want to be a writer even if I know that my father would never stand for such a thing and how Jeff wants to work in politics and how he could maybe become a big lobbyist and keep me as his love slave, giving me time to write a novel that will win all kinds of prizes and then be made into a film that will win an Oscar out in Hollywood where homos seem to do OK, or at least where they seem to do better than they do in Illinois. And I'm thinking about how I'm ready to read to Jeff the horror story about a haunted coal mine that I've written – even if I'm not sure it's ready yet – because I know Jeff won't laugh at me or think it's stupid because he loves me and I love him and people who love each other can talk about anything without that love being harmed in any way.

And I'm thinking about how I'll inherit the Bay – probably with Annabel, if she even wants it – and just move there full-time, writing on the front porch, and inviting back my other cousins who have all but stopped coming now. And there will be card games and drinking and fishing and barbecues and burgoo and all the things that I remember from when my mother was still alive, even if I can't always remember her there. And me and Jeff can sit on the porch just watching my cousin's kids play out in the yard and splash around in the muddy waters of Bradington Bay.

I'm actively imagining it all because it's fun, but also because Gramps always says that if you dream about something hard enough it'll come true. And I so want it all to be true that I don't want to just dream about it at night but during the day as well, during every waking moment that I can spare.

I know that it's all a bit far-fetched, that my cousins probably wouldn't even want to bring their kids around if they knew what me and Jeff got up to and that we'd probably have to pretty much lock ourselves in the big house because people in the town wouldn't accept us either. And I know that I can't even turn to my closest family for support, that my father, stepmonster and Grams don't share the dream, and they're trying everything they can do to get in its way. And even Gramps – the big dreamer himself – sure as hell isn't helping me too much, and this is the thing that gets me upset the most. I can understand it and even take it from the others, but Gramps? Gramps is supposed to be on my side; I'm supposed to be Gramps' Spark Plug. And the fact that Gramps isn't standing up for me, can barely look me in the eye, hurts a lot. I'm not entirely sure what a broken heart feels like, but I think it must be something like this.

It's Saturday and I'm in my father's rooms, which are basically my rooms now that my father has stopped coming to the Bay. I'm typing a story on my mother's old typewriter, but the F key keeps sticking and I have to reach up and pull it back every time it happens, which is a real pain in the ass, and I'm amazed at how many words have "f" in them. So when you combine the fact that I'm both passively and actively thinking about Jeff with the pain-in-the-ass stuck key, as well as the fact that I'm having a hard time getting inspired, the end result is putting me in a bad mood.

Gramps yells up the stairs that he and Grams are heading into town because Grams has to get her hair done. Do I to want to ride along? And although I usually do like to ride along because while Grams gets her hair done me and Gramps always go to Buck's Tavern which is just our secret because Grams would tie a knot in Gramps' tail if she knew that I was drinking beer inside Buck's, and I imagine my father wouldn't be too happy about it either – not so much for the beer drinking part, but just for the fact that Bradingtons and Allertons don't drink beer in riverside taverns. But today I'm not in the best of moods so I say that no, I'm busy writing and want to just stay in today, and maybe go for a swim later.

And Grams yells up not to swim any further than the part of the bay in front of the house and I'm pretty pissed off at Grams because she's treating me like I'm a baby and I'm seventeen fucking years old. And for a fraction of a second I think about yelling down the stairs, "Hey, Grams: I'm seventeen fucking years old!" but I know that she'd probably have a heart attack or something if I ever talked to her like that so I just say, "I know" real smart-ass like and she says "Don't you sass me! You're not too big to get a whipping," even though Grams has never in her entire life whipped me and I doubt that she would begin now, since I'm seventeen fucking years old and have to shave every other day and have more muscles than even Gramps.

"OK Grams," I say, again with a kind of smart-ass tone and I hear Grams say "I don't know what's got into him," and Gramps say, "Oh Lucille, get off his ass," which makes me a little less pissed off at Gramps.

As soon as I hear their car leave, I get on the phone and call Jeff and tell him Grams is at the Klip and Kurl and I'm going for a swim and maybe we could meet at the usual place. Jeff says "Cool!" and just the way he says "Cool" makes me happier right then and there, and I all but forget the stuck F key and the lack of inspiration and that Grams is treating me like a baby.

I strip out of my clothes and look at myself naked in the mirror and have to admit that I look pretty damned foxy, even if I say so myself. And even though people swimming in dirty bays off the Illinois River usually don't wear Speedos I put on a pair because I know I look good in them and that you can clearly see my wang and that maybe if Jeff sees my wang he'll offer me a quick hand job or even more. I love just being with Jeff even when we don't do anything, but I obviously love it more when we *do* do things, so trying to draw attention to my wang by wearing my Speedos can't hurt.

I run across the lawn and wade into the bay, waiting for that moment when the small stones that my father had put down by the dock so that Annabel and people like her could wade into the water more comfortably end and I can feel the sweet mud between my toes. It's always so exciting: walking, walking, walking, walking and not knowing exactly how far I have to walk and then SPLOOGE one foot finds the beautiful mud and the other foot rushes to catch up to it. And both feet are happy and it's always an exquisitely enchanting.

As I begin swimming, I think that it's weird how often, while I'm thinking about Jeff, I'm thinking about my mother, too. Obviously not in a pervy-oedipal way – I don't think about my mother when I'm thinking about Jeff's mouth around my wang – but more in a way that Jeff and my mother seem connected somehow. I talk a lot about my mother to Jeff, who also has some stories of his own to share, since his mother often made cakes for Bradington parties and said that my mother was the nicest, most down to earth person she had ever met. And Jeff's Aunt Tiggy called my mother a "living saint" and said she was better than the whole rest of my father's family combined. And Jeff also works part-time in the Bradington Public Library, which my mother founded. And the librarian there, Mrs. Denby, tells lots of stories about my mother, a portrait of whom hangs above the circulation desk like she was the beautiful queen of Bradington, which – to hear people in the town talk – she practically was. So I swim and swim, and each time I look up at the sky to take a breath I think of my mother there looking down and smiling like in that portrait.

I arrive at the clearing and am a little disappointed to find that I have beaten Jeff there, because Jeff says that I always look like some kind of god coming out of the water and I always flex and pose a bit because I know he's thinking that. And I think about just swimming in circles until Jeff arrives and can see me coming out of the water like a god, but the water is a little cold and I'm worried that if I stay in it too much longer my wang will shrink to the size of a mushroom and since I'm wearing my Speedos it would be very obvious that my wang was now the size of a mushroom and that would significantly lessen the impact of the god coming out of the water. So I get out of the water and lay on the hard ground and adjust my wang so that it's a little fluffed up and hope that the sight of me glistening in the sun with a slightly fluffed wang will make Jeff think I still look like a god even if I'm not coming out of the water.

And I'm lying there, feeling the sun shine warm upon me and I'm thinking that even if the F key sticks and I'm having difficulty with inspiration and my Grams treats me like a baby and my Gramps has not been as Gramps-like as in the past and my father has been all-too-father-like and my stepmonster is a bitch and I'm locked in a boarding school most of the year that there, lying in the sun in my Speedos, waiting for my boy, life's not as bad as sometimes I make it out to be. And I'm pretty damned happy.

And I think about the people in my life and wonder how many of them can say they're pretty damned happy. Certainly not my father and the stepmonster. Gramps, maybe. And maybe Grams but she so often gets her panties in a wad, as Gramps says, that I think her moments of happiness must be short-lived. (Which my teacher, Mr. Alberforth, says is correctly pronounced like the noun "life" with a long *i* and not like the verb "live" with a short *i*, even though everyone else in the whole goddamned world says it with a short *i* like the verb "live.") And I'm wondering just what the secret might be to being happy and remaining that way, when I sense a shadow before my eyes, like someone is blocking the sun. It could be some axe-murderer towering over me, of course, but I'm going to go with it probably being Jeff so I don't open my eyes because I've been told that I look like an angel when I sleep and so even if he didn't see me coming out of the water like a god maybe being an angel will be good enough. And then I feel soft lips on mine (I hope they're lips, anyway) but I still don't open my eyes. (I hope it's Jeff kissing me and not some axe-murderer).

"Wake up Edward James Allerton Bradington the Fourth," I hear Jeff say and I open my eyes and put my arms around him and pull him down on the ground next to me.

"Were you really asleep?" Jeff asks.

"Nah," I say, "I was just resting my eyes and thinking."

"Oh yeah? What were you thinking about?"

"I'm thinking about what the key to happiness is – you know, deep shit like that." I smile and sniff Jeff's hair and think that coconut shampoo just might be a part of the key.

"Well? Any ideas?"

"Nope," I say, opening my eyes and looking up at the sky. "But I think I'm close."

"Well, let me know when you find out."

"I don't know if I can. You see, I think maybe everybody has a different key. Mine may not be the same as yours."

"Well that sucks." Jeff's rubbing my chest and I'm nervous that I'm going to get a stiffy right then and there, which would be way too early.

"Maybe so. Maybe not. Because even though I haven't found *my* key, I can report that I *have* found *yours*." I sniff Jeff's hair once again.

"Oh really? And what would that be?"

"You're lying in his arms right now!"

"Is that right? *You're* the key to my happiness?" I'm not looking at Jeff, but I can tell he's smiling.

"Yep," I say, pulling him closer. "Some people go their whole lives never finding the key, and I have already found yours for you. You should thank me."

"Is that right?" he says. "How should I do that?"

"Well," I say, turning to look at him, "you can start by giving me a kiss. Then we'll just play it by ear from there."

Jeff kisses me, but just a little peck like married people give each other.

"That's it?" I say. "I give you the key to happiness and all you give me is a peck? Why I'm sure there are millions of people out there who would give a lot more than that."

"Yeah," Jeff says, "but since everybody's key is different, you can't be anybody else's key. So I really doubt you'd get more than that from anyone else."

"When I said that everybody had a different key, I didn't mean *everybody* – I was using poetic license. I am probably the key to hundreds – if not thousands – of men out there. Probably some women too. And they would most certainly give me more than a quick peck."

"I doubt that. But just in case, here's something better." And Jeff kisses me long, and I immediately get a stiffy. But this time it's OK because you're *supposed* to get a stiffy when you're making out with someone.

I pull Jeff on top and start rubbing against him. He seems so light on top of me, like an fall quilt.

"Hey, calm down, buddy!" Jeff says, breaking away from me. "The boathouse is one thing – and that didn't turn out so good anyway. But we're just asking for trouble doing anything out here. We need to find somewhere else so that we can do things right."

I think about this for a few seconds. "What does doing it right mean? I think we've been doing OK."

Jeff thinks about this for a few seconds. "I don't know. Maybe something more romantic. With candles. Maybe Lionel Ritchie."

"You want to fuck in front of Lionel Ritchie?"

Jeff pulls away. "I mean his music, you asshole. Can't you ever be serious for one goddamned minute?"

I think I know every one of Jeff's looks, but suddenly I'm seeing a new one – major annoyance (eyes scrunched up and eyebrows raised at the same time). So I give what I think it one of my best looks (head down a bit, eyes looking up so they look big and deer-like) and say, "I'm sorry. Go on. Really – go on."

Jeff gets over things pretty easily, which is one massive thing in his favor. Jeff continues. "You go to all these fancy parties and get to wear tuxedoes and drink champagne but

I don't. So I just think it would be nice to do that together, you know. Maybe at some fancy place up in Chicago. And we have a whole evening where we don't give a fuck about what anyone else thinks, we just think about how *we* want to live. You and me in black tuxedoes with white shirts and yellow ties and ... what's that thing you wear around your waist with a tuxedo called?"

"A cummerbund."

"Yeah – a cummerbund. We've got on yellow cummerbunds too."

"Well, you don't really wear a yellow cummerbund with a tuxedo. It's not acceptable evening wear."

Jeff rolls away from me, frowning. "Of course you would know that. OK. Fine. We don't have to wear yellow cummerbunds. We don't want the fucking high society police on our backs."

"They can be just awful – trust me. You've made the right decision by not putting us in yellow cummerbunds. So, go on. We're in tuxes. But they're pretty fucking complicated what with all those buttons and cufflinks. Wouldn't it save time if you were already naked in a hotel room and I came in wearing a tux?"

Jeff hits me and I realize that it's not playful, like usual, but that he is hitting for real. "Ouch!" I yell. "What the hell did I say?"

"I was trying to be romantic and talk about something besides just getting off. I guess you wouldn't understand that." His voice seems small, like a child's.

"Jesus, I was just kidding. Can't you take a joke?" As soon as the words come out of my mouth, I know that I shouldn't have said them, but there's nothing I can do now but hope that Jeff *can* take a joke, which seems pretty unlikely at this point.

Jeff gets up, brushing imaginary dirt from his clothes.

"Fuck you, Edward! You know I've put up with a lot of shit from you. My whole fucking life revolves around you, and you only live here three months out of the year and when you are here we have to sneak around like criminals because you can't even consider for a minute being openly gay. Plus your fucking snoborific family thinks I'm too trashy for you. I'm too trashy for you? My Mom and Dad are two hard-working people who fell in love and got married and have remained faithful to each other. And your daddy was just born rich and thinks his shit don't stink . How *dare* you look down on us!"

I'm thinking that "snoborific" is a great word, but I can't really say that, so I say, "*I* don't look down on anybody. And don't forget I've got Grams and Gramps who aren't exactly amateurs in the faithfulness department. I was kidding. I'm sorry. Come on – don't make this a big deal."

"Jesus – you don't get it, do you? It's not the kidding and joking. It's that I love you and you don't love me. Not enough to be open about us, anyway." Jeff's begun crying now and I step towards him, but Jeff backs away from me and for the first time I really have no idea what to do. And I'm beginning to think that I could really lose this person, and this realization is hitting me so hard that I can feel it in my chest, like someone has punched me there and I can't breathe right.

"I *do* love you," I say, and I feel bad that this is the first time I have said it when I know I have felt it for a year. "Really. I'm not just saying that. It's just…complicated."

"Let's just leave things be, Edward. You'll go back to school in September and then you'll graduate and go to college out in Boston or New York. I'll go to a junior college here. We're nuts if we think this is going to work."

I feel as if I'm suffocating, seeing Jeff like this but not

really knowing what to do or say. "It can work, I promise!" I say but Jeff has already disappeared into the woods and I am alone. I really think I am suffocating now – I literally can't breathe – and I lie back down on the hard ground and look up at the sky, thinking that any minute the clouds are going to part and someone – Jesus? my mother? – is going to swoop down and take me to heaven. The thought that the earth may open up and someone (I'm thinking briefly about Hitler) may drag me down into hell also enters my mind, but I try to ignore it. And I'm crying and suffocating and waiting for my mother, and the clouds are watching me, just watching me, in a way that might be harsh or might just be accepting – I'm not sure which, but obviously hope for accepting. And I close my eyes which are bathed in tears and I think that "bathed in tears" sounds pretty cool but it only *sounds* cool; it feels horrible.

I wake up and see Linda standing above me. "Where's Jeff?" she asks, looking around.

I have no idea how long I've been lying there – it could be minutes, or it could be hours – and I'm a little embarrassed that I've just got my Speedos on, especially in front of Linda.

"Uh, he went home," I say, because I'm afraid that if I get into it I'll start crying, and crying in front of Linda in my Speedos is *not* something I want to do.

"Now listen," Linda says, stern as a librarian demanding silence, "Jeff is like a little brother to me. I don't want to stick my nose in your business but ..." She pauses, like I'm supposed to know what comes after the "but." And I think that Linda is full of shit, and that she *completely* wants to stick her nose in his business, but right now I'd welcome that nose because my own isn't smelling anything.

"Hey, it's cool, Linda," I say, "say what you need to say."

"Well, it's just that Jeff really loves you – he knows who he is. And – I'm sorry – you don't seem to. And I swear to God if you hurt him I'll kill you. You got that?"

I nod.

"OK. That's all I have to say." She starts to walk away, but I know I have to get more information from her.

"Linda?"

"Yeah?"

"Listen ... I want to make things right with Jeff. Want to do something nice for him. Any ideas?"

"Well, you can start by not being an asshole. And by maybe coming out of the closet? For Christ's sake it's 1983. The world is changing."

"Yeah, I get that." I'm thinking it's a little easier in her world of cosmetology than it is in my world of fucking centuries of tradition, but I don't say anything.

"And, I don't know, who doesn't love a big gesture? His folks are leaving for a weekend in St. Louis after his dad finishes work. They'll be gone by six. Maybe you could drop by and surprise him with something. *Not* just getting off."

I'm embarrassed because it seems that Jeff's been talking a whole lot more about our private life than I would like, but I ignore how uncomfortable that makes me feel. I can deal with that later, so I just say to Linda, "Thanks," and turn and jump in the bay, swimming as fast as I can, lungs aching because they've gone from not having enough air to having too much – it's like the air is cutting my lungs to strips like little knives. But I keep going because I know I need to get home, grab the keys to Gramps' old work truck, rush into Havana and then be back with the truck before Grams and Gramps get back. Then I'll sneak out after supper like I have a million times before and I will make things better with Jeff.

And each knife-breath seems to be saying that to me now: bet-ter, bet-ter, bet-ter.

It's seven-thirty, and I'm not entirely comfortable walking through Bradington in broad daylight. Of course, it would be better if it were dark, but there's nothing I can do about the sun setting, so it's better not to think about it. It's hot and I'm worried that I'm sweating too much, but I can't do anything about the heat either, so it's better not to think about it.

I find Jeff's house and for the first time have some real doubts about what I'm doing. Maybe his parents didn't go away. Maybe he's so pissed off that he decided to go with them. Maybe he'll open the door holding one of his daddy's shotguns. As I open the front gate and walk closer to the house, each step seems to bring up in my mind another scenario, each more horrible than the last.

But I've got to do it. "No guts, no glory," I say to myself as I ring the doorbell.

The door opens and Jeff is there, blank stare on his face, eyes somewhat red. I look at those eyes and knows that I am responsible for them and my own eyes fill up with tears, too. Jeff says nothing, just stands there, staring at me.

"I'm an asshole. I'm a gay asshole." I hold out the flowers that I bought in Havana. Jeff doesn't take them, but he doesn't slam the door in my face either, so I continue: "I love you – I really do. And I know I haven't always shown that, but things are going to be different from now on – I swear. I'll talk to my father, make him understand. I'm not a child anymore – he'll have to listen to me. I just know I love you and – if you'll forgive my assholishness – we can work something out and stay together. I could go to college in Chicago or even at the U of I. I swear. That means we only have to put up with another school year and then we'll live in the same state year-round. And I'll have more freedom."

Jeff still says nothing.

"Please, Jeff. Say something!"

"Where in the hell did you get that tux?" Jeff is not smiling, but his voice seems soft, so I figure I've got a chance.

"It's mine."

"You keep a tux here in Bradington?" he asks and I wish I had lied and said it was a rental but I'm all about the honesty now.

"Yes – I keep a tux in all my homes because you never know when you might need one." I realize this makes me sound like a rich dick, but I kind of am a rich dick and I'm all about the honesty now so I won't hide it, can only hope to become less dick-like in time. "But I had to go to Havana to get the cummerbund," I continue. "Did you know there is only one tuxedo rental place in Havana? And that they won't just rent you a tie and cummerbund, that you've got to rent the whole nine yards? And I said, 'I've already *got* a tux – I don't need to rent one!' but that damned lady said, 'Them's our policies, junior' and I said 'Alright give me the whole goddamned tux' and she said she was a good Christian woman and didn't appreciate that kind of talk. But then she wants to take my measurements and I have to practically *scream* at her that it doesn't matter because I have my own goddamned tux and so finally she brings the yellow cummerbund and tie out from the back room and I pay the deposit for the whole tux rental, grab the tie and cummerbund and rush out the door. And – this lady *really* doesn't get it – she shouts after me, 'You left the tuxedo here!' but I don't really care because I know I've got to get on the road so that I can get here to you."

I know I'm rambling. But I feel like this moment could either make or ruin my entire life, so a little nervous rambling has to be tolerated, right?

"I don't have a tux," Jeff says in a way that seems both sad and happy at the same time. And I'm ready to say that I'll drive to Chicago if I have to, that I'll fly to London itself if he wants me to, because I love him, and would do anything for him.

But before I have a chance to say anything Jeff steps out on the porch and wraps his arms around me. And I know that we're right in the middle of the town named for my family and that it's still daylight and someone might see us, but I don't care. I know that beyond passively thinking about Jeff and actively thinking about Jeff there lies this. And I know I never want to be away from this ever again. And I think that not only am I Jeff's key but Jeff is mine as well.

And later, when Jeff puts *Endless Love* on the stereo, I even find myself thinking that Lionel Ritchie isn't that bad either.

Chapter Eleven: 2012

"We're on the wrong side of the river," said Edward, looking in the rearview mirror as if being followed.

"You mean we're in Missouri?"

"No. This isn't the Mississippi anymore."

"When did we lose the Mississippi?" asked Hank.

"We didn't *lose* the Mississippi," said Edward. "Don't you remember a little way back when I said, 'And this is where the Illinois comes into the Mississippi'?"

"Vaguely. How the hell was I supposed to know that we were going to follow the Illinois and not the Mississippi? Let's turn the navigator on."

"No," Edward shouted more forcefully than he intended. "We don't need the navigator! The river goes north, we should hit Kampsville up here in a bit and we'll take the ferry back over to the right side of the river."

"Right as in the opposite of left, or right as in correct?" Hank asked teasingly.

"Both," Edward said smiling.

"I didn't know there was a right and wrong side of the river," Hank said.

"Lot you know about these things – and you coming from a river town. Thank God you've got me to show you the way." Edward touched the side of Hank's face, a gesture that seemed suddenly too intimate somehow.

"Just because I grew up in a river town doesn't mean I grew up literally *on* the river," Hank said, "our house was about ten miles away. I'm not as comfortable around water as you are, obviously."

"I'd forgotten you can't swim."

"Exactly," responded Hank, voice small. "So maybe since I've got issues about this, we should take a bridge instead of a ferry."

"Hank, we'd have to either backtrack quite a way or go way out of our way to find a bridge. The Kampsville ferry has been shuttling cars back and forth for ages without any problems. We'll be fine."

Hank furrowed his brow. "You're right, I'm being silly," he said.

"How is it that you never learned how to swim?" asked Edward, who couldn't remember a time when he *couldn't* swim.

"Well, we didn't own swimming pools and bays and rivers like you did," he said, "so perhaps it wasn't urgent. But there was a time when I was about seven or so that Stella enrolled me in lessons at the local community pool, but by then I had seen *The Sound of Music* and I was already terrified of water."

"*The Sound of Music*?" asked Edward, smiling. "You are afraid of water because of *The Sound of Music*?."

"That's right – laugh at my insecurities," Hank said, looking with suspicion at the river snaking alongside them. "Stella *loved The Sound of Music*. She had seen it in the theater when it came out and she rushed out and bought the album. I grew up listening to it nearly every day of my life. I know all of the lyrics by heart."

"Right," Edward responded. "Leaving aside the sheer overwhelming gayness of that statement I still feel a need to comment that, to the best of my knowledge, there's nothing in the lyrics about drowning or being eaten by a sea beast."

"Smart ass. Anyway," Hank continued, "when I was a

little kid it came on TV for the first time. Stella was beside herself. For weeks all she could do was talk about it. She even planned a special menu for the big event, although I remember it being fried chicken, which doesn't sound too Austrian to me. Anyway, it came on and Stella and I sat down to watch it. She literally cried when the title came on the screen."

"How sweet," said Edward.

"Right," Hank responded dismissively; this was clearly *his* story, and he didn't enjoy being interrupted. "Anyway, my friend Todd had a birthday on Leap Day – which was the day the movie came on – and I had been over at his house – he had a big party because it was *actually* the 29th – and I was just plum tuckered. So when I got home and we started watching it I fell asleep right near the beginning."

"OK," Edward said hesitantly.

"So at one point I wake up and there's Maria and all the kids in a boat on the river – was it a river or a lake? I don't remember – behind the house and they all fall in the river or lake. *That's* what I see as soon as I wake up, and it terrified me. I screamed and jumped and kicked Stella and sent her cup of coffee flying across the room, staining the good guest chair."

"But the water was so shallow," said Edward, "that the kids could stand up. They were in no danger. Even the little one –"

"– Gretl."

"– Gretl was in no danger. They walked out of the water without any problem."

"I know that *now*," he said with exasperation, "but I didn't at the time. And it's terrifying – the thought of it – being trapped under water, not being able to breathe. And for whatever reason – and I'm sure you will make all things clear for me, Dr. Freud – this image stayed with me and I developed this horrible fear of drowning. So, no, I can't swim and, yes, I know it's crazy but that's the way it is. So the idea of getting on some ferry with a car this size makes me feel a little woozy. But if there's no other way ..."

"Well, of course there's another way. We can prolong this part of the trip and drive north and find a bridge and drive back down south on the other side. Or we could face our fears and take the ferry, realizing that a classic journey throws all kinds of obstacles in our paths for us to bravely get beyond. Beyond which to bravely get, I mean. Or I guess it really should be beyond which to get bravely?"

"Easy for you to say," snorted Hank, "it's not your fucking obstacle."

"Fair enough," Edward said, "but I promise if – *when*, more likely – one of my obstacles comes up I'll face it with the same force. Here's Kampsville now. What do you say?"

"Fine. Whatever. I'll close my eyes and you tell me when we're on the other side of the river. The *right* side of the river."

Edward thought about saying that one didn't bravely face obstacles without looking them square in the face, but then thought about Perseus and the Medusa. Maybe the importance was facing the fear – putting yourself in its path; whether eyes remained opened or closed was irrelevant.

He positioned the Range Rover behind two other cars waiting for the ferry, which was returning from the other side. Here the Illinois was calm and not too wide; he wished Hank would open his eyes and see that it wasn't a threat, that it was smooth, graceful, the cherished companion of Mr. Rat and Mr. Mole.

But he knew that fears were not always rational, that the things that the eye could see did not always register the entirety of a situation. And so, as the ferry arrived and he positioned the car on it; as Hank tensed, sensing the swaying motion of the water, Edward reached out and grabbed his hand. And Hank seemed glad of it, clutching it gratefully.

"Raindrops on roses and whiskers on kittens," Edward sang softly, feeling every bit the gentle protector.

"Fuck you," responded Hank, eyes closed tightly.

It was afternoon when they reached Springfield, and the rays of the sun seemed to hover over the surrounding prairies in horizontal waves. Sunlight and clear skies usually made places sparkle, but Edward was shocked at how dull it looked, how things that as a child he had remembered being grand and exciting now seemed sagging and tired. Had it always been that way, or had his child's memory added magic to something that was ordinary? When Hank suggested maybe staying there for the night, taking in the Lincoln sights, Edward said no. There was something melancholy and even deathlike about the city that he didn't want to be a part of. This, he thought, was an obstacle better left avoided than battled.

While the city itself seemed to have shrunk, the hospital complex had grown enormous. Edward remembered it as a couple of buildings surrounded by houses; now it was sprawling, labyrinthine, comprised of so many new looking buildings that Edward was disoriented, uncertain where to go. Walking around the main building he couldn't find the large waiting room where he had often waited while his father and grandparents went up to visit his mother. Had he invented it?

They found what appeared to be the main entrance of the largest building and saw an information desk with a young woman talking quietly on her cell phone. "Gotta go," she said as they approached.

"Can I help you?" Her smile seemed tired for someone so young.

"Well, I hope so. I spent a lot of time here nearly forty years ago now. And there was a nun here then. I guess I'd just like to know if she's still around."

"Forty years ago?" asked the woman. "My *parents* were just children forty years ago!" She smiled insincerely.

"Yeah, well, I wasn't suggesting that you, personally, knew her," said Edward, returning a smile that he was pretty sure was as tired and insincere as hers had been. "I thought maybe you could give me some information about her, that's all." He pointed to the plaque which read "information" on the desk; Hank gave him a little punch in the back.

"Yeah, sure, of course. What's her name?"

"I don't really remember. I just called her 'Sister.'"

"Well, that's going to be a little difficult. Oh wait – here's Nancy. She'd know more than I would about the nuns."

Nancy turned and looked at them through sparkly eyes framed by red rectangular glasses. "What can I do you for?" she asked warmly.

"He's looking for a nun," said the woman behind the desk.

"Not many of those left, I'm afraid," said Nancy with a laugh. "Which nun are you looking for?"

"Well," said Edward, embarrassed, "I don't exactly remember her name. She used to kind of take care of me when the adults would go up to visit my mother. I wasn't allowed up at the time."

"Ridiculous rule, that," Nancy said, shaking her head. "But you must be talking about quite a while ago."

"Well, my mother died in 1973, so it would have been that year and the couple leading up to it."

"What a coincidence – I started work here in January of 1973. Of course, I was just a child myself!"

"That goes without saying," said Edward. "You must have worked as a baby model for hospital publicity."

"This one's fab," she said to Hank.

"*This* one is full of shit," responded Hank with a laugh.

"Aren't they all?" laughed Nancy. "But some make it seem nicer than others."

"OK," said Edward, "enough with the flattery. Any idea who my mystery nun may have been?"

"I'm not sure," she said, putting her glasses on top of her head. "There used to be a lot more nuns running around here – there used to be a lot more in general. Many have died, of course, quite a few left, and not many have come to take their places. If she was looking after you, she may have been what we call pastoral care now, or she may have been a nurse who was on your mother's floor who came down when you were there."

"Is there anyone we can ask? I mean are there any nuns who still work here? Maybe they would know."

"Well, let me see if Sister Frances Mary is in her office. She's the hospital administrator – the big boss – and she has been here in one capacity or another for nearly fifty years. She might know something. But I have to say: without a name it's probably going to be a little difficult." She reached across the desk and dialed a number.

"I don't think we're going to find her," said Edward quietly to Hank. He was surprised at how disappointed he felt.

"OK," said Nancy hanging up the phone and turning to face them, "Sister is intrigued. Her office is on the fourth floor. Just take those elevators there and turn right when you get off. The hallway ends at the offices, so you can't miss it. Hope you find who you're looking for!"

*

"Surfer Jesus," said Hank, pointing to a painting on the wall in the receptionist's office where they were waiting.

"What?" said Edward. The receptionist shot a stern look.

"When I was growing up, that picture was in some of the classrooms at our school. Look at him: hair that looks feathered – and even some sun highlights in it. Tan, smiling. We used to call him 'Surfer Jesus.' We always thought he was such a fox!"

"Hank!"

"I'm just saying. All the cool nuns – there weren't many of them – had Surfer Jesus on their classroom walls. Most of the others all had Jesus' graduation picture."

"Jesus' graduation picture?" asked Edward. "Do I even want to know what that is?"

"Well it's that one where he's sitting formally with perfect long hair in like a burgundy and white robe, with his head turned at a three-quarter angle. So, naturally, we called it Jesus' graduation picture."

"So you had the cool nuns with Surfer Jesus and most of the others with Jesus' graduation picture. Was that it?" asked Edward.

"No," answered Hank, "I remember Sister Claire had Jesus-Locked-Out-Of-The-House. You know: he's standing outside, he's left his keys inside, and he's knocking so the Blessed Virgin will let him in. But she's gossiping with her cousin Elizabeth and she doesn't hear him."

"I missed out on a lot not being a Catholic," said Edward. "I never knew there were so many different Jesuses."

"You don't know the half of it," responded Hank .

Edward was just ready to ask what he meant when the

intercom buzzed and a voice on the other end said, "Ask them to come in, Gloria."

They crossed the receptionist's office and headed towards a large door. Edward wasn't sure what to expect, and images of Maria Von Trapp entering the Reverend Mother's office entered in his mind. He opened the door and was somewhat disappointed to find a modern, spacious office not unlike his own.

"Be right out," a voice yelled from a small room off the main office. "Just getting some coffee. Have a seat."

One part of the office had been set up like a little sitting room with two modern sofas, an armchair, and a coffee table. They sat on one of the sofas. Looking around Edward noted that there were diplomas and certificates peppering the walls, as well as some picture of a saint whom he presumed to be Francis, but no pictures of Jesus anywhere.

"There's no Jesus," he said under his breath.

"This doesn't strike me as a Jesus type of office," Hank responded. "This is one high-rolling nun."

A woman walked in holding a tray with a thermos and coffee cups. She was wearing a very nice gray suit with a navy-blue blouse. Her short white hair was artfully spiked. Except for a small cross around her neck, there was nothing to suggest that this woman was religious at all, let alone a nun. She had a young, fresh demeanor and Edward found it difficult to believe she had worked *anywhere* for fifty years.

"Hello there," she said offering her hand as Edward stood up to greet her. "My name is Sister Frances Mary Steckler, the hospital administrator. I hear you're looking for some lost nun." Her easy smile was as familiar as an old afghan.

"It's you," said Edward. "It's you." He felt dizzy, frightfully old and ridiculously young at the same time.

"Me?" asked Sister Frances Mary suspiciously, "*I'm* the nun you're looking for?"

Edward studied her carefully. She was, of course, nearly forty years older, and she wasn't wearing a tablecloth on her head. But her smile, the way she tilted her head, the way her hands moved as she poured the coffee: all combined to instill in him a sense of familiarity that was as strong and pervading as the smell of the dark coffee.

"Can I ask your name?" said Sister Frances Mary, tilting her eyes and squinting as if she, too, recognized him.

"Edward James Allerton Bradington the Fourth."

"Einstein? Wowzy wow!" she replied and reached over to grab his hands in her own.

And Edward, he who was usually controlled and shallow and light, began to cry. They were not the quiet tears that come to the eyes and then gently spill over down the face when one finds something beautiful, and then gently; they were not the tears of pain that come unbidden and angrily stay; they were not the tears of regret or anger that bathe the eye but will go no further. Edward's tears were those tears which come from deep within, felt in the stomach and in the chest and throat. There were the tears of beauty and pain and regret all combined and, although he knew he was probably shocking and possibly even frightening the two people in the room, he was powerless to stop them.

He had found someone. Though everyone else from the past was long gone, this woman was not. She was there, and she was holding his hands like she did all those years ago when as a boy he had to battle with beauty and pain and regret. She was alive and breathing and filled with memories which were somehow connected to his memories as well. She was proof that the naysayers were wrong: you *could* go back again, even if what you went back for was changed, grayed, stooped, uncovered.

And so he continued to weep, in the end, tears of revelation. And Sister Frances Mary would not let him go, continued clinging to his hands as tightly as his father had once done, as tightly as even Gramps. Hank seemed confused, embarrassed, a little frightened even, and although Edward didn't hate him for it, he knew somehow that he couldn't love him in that moment either. But the nun was there, a bridge between past and present, strong enough to bear it all.

They fell into easy conversation after the initial intense impact of their meeting had faded. Sister remembered Edward's mother, had spent quite a bit of time with her keeping her company during chemo rounds, and her memories comforted Edward. His own memories of his mother were vague, informed much by photographs and family legends; hearing someone else speak of her made her seem more real than she had seemed in years. He knew he couldn't expect his father to break his silence of decades, so the nun's words were perhaps the most he could hope for. They spoke about her for some minutes before Edward said they had to be getting on the road. Information was exchanged and promises were made to keep in touch.

Sister Frances Mary accompanied them to the main entrance. "I'm so glad you looked me up. Life used to be so much simpler, and it's nice to have a reminder from those days every now and then, know what I mean?"

"I certainly do," replied Edward, "thank you for your time, Sister." Hank shook her hand and Edward gave her a little hug and they turned to leave.

"Einstein?" Sister Frances Mary cried out after him.

"Yes?" replied Edward, turning towards her.

"A quick game," she said conspiratorially. "Look at

those two women walking down the hall there. They're seventy years old if they're a day, but both of them are dressed in matching mini skirts. What's their story?"

"Gee, Sister, I don't know if I can make up stories anymore. Real life has jammed my head with so much that I worry there's just no more room."

"You're full of crap," replied the nun.

"You're probably right. OK, let's see: they're from England and once, many years ago, they came over to the US because they used to be models – worked with Twiggy in the Sixties, both of them. They always kept in touch with one of the other girls at the fashion shows – Marjory was her name – and they've been pen pals and now email pals ever since. They were informed that Marjory's had a stroke and they offer to come see her even though her son – a nasty piece of work named Burt – says that his mother is basically a vegetable, don't bother. But they know that this connection that they've had for all these years is still strong; they know that Marjory will know them in the present because they shared something so strong in the past. So they say to each other, 'Screw Burt!' and get all dressed up like in the old, swinging-sixties days and are making their way to Marjory, who will remember them and love them for coming, even if she is unable to tell them. But the mini skirt grandmas will know that Marjory knows, and that's all that matters."

"Wowzy wow!" replied Sister Frances Mary, clapping her hands. "But, Einstein, you really shouldn't say 'Screw Burt.'"

"And you shouldn't say 'crap,' Sister," Edward replied.

"You've got me there, Einstein," she replied laughing. "God bless you."

And he walked out the door into a city that suddenly seemed a little less tired.

*

"You're awfully quiet." They had been driving through the country for an hour, and the silence that was accompanying them didn't seem intimate or harmless as silence can seem, but rather foreboding, the powerful absence of things that should be said.

"Don't really know what to say," he responded.

"Well, what did you think about Sister Frances Mary?"

"She was really nice."

"Really nice? That's it?"

Hank turned to look at him, face illuminated by the dashboard lights. "I'm not sure what you want from me, Edward. I came on this trip because a hot guy who I fell for asked me and I figured what the hell. But we've known each other like ten minutes and this whole trip has been one heavy thing after another. It's not exactly what I signed up for, that's all. And I guess there, in the nun's office, when you had your breakdown – or whatever you want to call it – I just got to thinking that it *is* possible to enjoy each other's company without digging deep into others' souls. That it's possible to just see some of the country, have a few drinks and good meals, and have sex without making it into some Greek drama. *That's* what I signed up for."

"I'm not so sure it was a break*down* so much as a break*through*," said Edward, hurt.

"That's exactly my point!" he shouted. "Not everything has earth-shattering significance, not everything has to *mean* something. Sometimes, as they say, a cigar is just a cigar. Jesus is this why Ben wanted out?"

"I don't know," Edward responded softly, looking at the darkened road ahead of him. "But I think it's probably because I never cared enough to even *try* to find meaning in things or have breakthroughs or breakdowns or whatever the fuck they are. I didn't care enough and now I seem to be caring too much. I can't win."

"It's not about winning, Edward," Hank said, voice softer. "It's just that not everyone's in the same place, you know. It's like Charlton Heston in *The Ten Commandments*."

"What?"

"*The Ten Commandments*. It was another of those movies that Stella watched every time it came on TV. Charlton Heston was a person who had these big encounters, who got to go up on the mountain and stand right there smack dab in front of God while everyone else was OK with just staying down below. That's me, Edward: I'm happy to just stay below. I don't need the big revelations – I'm not even looking for them, to be honest."

"You're probably right," Edward said. "I'm just tired and a little over-emotional these days. Let's just relax a little bit now. I promise – no more revelations." He reached over and rubbed Hank's leg.

"Sounds good," Hank said, placing his hand on top of Edward's.

But as they rode on in silence, as the epicenter of Edward's boyhood drew nearer, he thought how difficult it is to stop revelation once it gets you in its sights. Charlton Heston tried to get away from it – kept saying how unworthy he was – but it didn't seem to matter; he still ended up there on the mountain, face ablaze and hair whitened. Charlton probably would have liked to have had someone up there with him – and Edward would have, too – but in the end there was no other way. The mountain was just too damned strong, and it seemed to call people whether they liked it or not.

And then he saw a green sign in the distance, white letters reflecting his own name. He lowered the window slightly, breathing in the air that his father said was the sweetest on earth. And then, quietly, so as not to wake the sleeping Hank, he recited as a monologue that which had once been performed by two people: "What's that sign say? Bradington! What's your name? Edward James Allerton Bradington the Fourth. Welcome to your town, my boy!"

The house was far bigger than he remembered. Having spent so much of his life in New York, his point of reference had become the spaces one found there. Some were grand, but nothing, of course, could approach the size of this house with its verandas and enormous screened-in porch that looked out over the dark water. He wandered through sitting rooms and parlors and the formal dining room and the informal dining room and the breakfast room and the kitchen and upstairs, through every suite of rooms.

Leo had done a fantastic job preparing the house for occupancy once again; everything was clean and ordered. But no one had bought anything new for the house in decades, and the furniture seemed outdated. Pausing to plunk out a tune on the piano in the main parlor, he thought how the heavily brocaded and sturdy furniture had been sitting there, waiting to be of use, while the world outside had passed it by.

The only rooms where the old things seemed to fit in were his father's rooms, which had been *his* father's rooms, and which had been *his* father's rooms before him. Here Edward thought things were as they should be. If he ever renovated the house, these rooms would remain untouched.

Hank had asked for a room of his own, which Edward had not expected, but neither was he surprised. He showed him to the Governor's Suite and lightheartedly regaled him with the legends of the crooked and shady men who had slept there, even – according to his father – Al Capone. But the lightheartedness was forced, insincere. He kissed him lightly on the forehead and said that they would explore the whole house together the next day.

He retired to his rooms and, perusing the lines of shelves in the sitting room, came across the familiar green book of his childhood. He took it down, reverently, and opened its yellowed pages, smiling at the small grimy fingerprints that marked the pages here and there, touching them and marveling at how small his fingers had once been. Charlton Heston had his golden tablets; he had this. He took the book to bed with him and fell asleep mindful of rhythm and the feeling of beating on his chest, dreaming of skull-faced witch doctors taunting poor, unfortunate Casey who – even though he had been the hope of all his team – disastrously struck out anyway.

The days passed pleasantly enough. Hank, though never moving from his own rooms, visited him from time to time, but the sex lacked the urgency and passion of before. Edward knew that the hesitancy was coming from Hank and Hank alone, and he couldn't shake the sense that he was deciding whether to stay or go. A few times, resting with a book on the screened-in porch as the waters of the bay lapped below them, Edward thought about confronting him, broaching the subject, poking the elephant that was clearly in the room. But he did not. He didn't want to face the mountain alone, and Hank had been spooked when things got too heavy; Edward refused to scare him off.

But as October trudged on, unseasonably warm and thus unnerving somehow, Edward could no longer deny something was not right, and he was beginning to see Hank's refusal to talk about it as counterproductive. Maybe

Hank was waiting for him to bring it up, longed to talk about things but was unable to get the ball rolling himself.

And so, one Saturday evening, having eaten fried cat-fish at a new restaurant in Bradington town, Edward decided to talk seriously for the first time since that night in the car. Drinking after-dinner bourbons, being serenaded by country music on the jukebox, he said, "I think we need to talk." The words were difficult, dark, seemed inappropriate among the pool-players and revelers. But they had been said.

"Here we go again," said Hank.

"Yep, here we go again," said Edward. "I know you don't want to get all heavy, or however you would refer to it, and I know we're supposed to be on vacation where – by its very nature – one is specifically *forbidden* from getting too heavy, but I've got some things I need to say."

Hank nodded. Tammy Wynette and George Jones began singing about a pawn shop in Chicago on a sunny summer's day.

"OK," continued Edward. "I've come to a couple of conclusions over these past few days. First of all, Ben left me – and I think I can say now that that is, in fact, what he's done – because I wanted him to. Oh, maybe not, you know, *willfully*, but I think I wanted him to, nonetheless. It's kind of like a plant that you see day after day in your living room, and you've forgotten to water it, and every day you say 'I need to give that some water' but you don't because it's already a little wilted at that point and you're not even sure *why* you got the plant in the first place so you just keep on *not* giving it water but not throwing it out in the hopes that someday you'll come home and see that it's really dead and so you might as well just give up on it – it's too late."

"Don't really have a green thumb, do you?" said Hank teasingly.

"You get my point, right?"

"Yes. You and Ben have been dying for some time and you've just accepted it. I'm not Ivy League but I'm not a moron." He sipped his drink, looking at Edward the whole time.

"Right. So that's the first thought. The second thing is that – amazingly and just by chance – I met someone who came along at just the right second who made me feel something for the first time in a long time. And I don't want to do anything to fuck it up with this one – with you – because I want things to grow and be living. And so I want to say – because I kind of feel like I *have* to say it – that I care a great deal about you Hank. And I think that what I feel for you could grow into something beautiful and living. And I guess I'm just asking you if it's possible – could you be with a guy like me, who – at least in this period of his life – can go all Charlton Heston-y on your ass from one moment to the next?"

"Edward James Allerton Bradington the Fourth," Hank said. "You are one of the most beautiful men I've ever met. You're hot and sexy and funny and kind. Oh yeah – and you're a billionaire who has a whole fucking town, for Christ's sake. You're smart and pretty much what most people have in mind when they think of Prince Charming."

"Why do I feel like I hear a 'but' coming?" asked Edward, voice barely audible over the music.

"And it's not that we come from different worlds," Hank continued, "that's not a problem. Things like that work out all the time, as you can see in so many Richard Gere movies. And it's not that I have my life and my business in Ohio and don't want to leave, because I think you're probably crazy enough to say you'd move there for me. And it's not that we don't have fun and laugh a lot, because we do. And the sex, of course, is fantastic."

"Then what is it?" Edward asked, finding the simple words cumbersome.

"I'm not in love with you Edward. It's harsh putting it that way and I know it sounds even harsher hearing it, but that's the way it is. And I know that you think you could be in love with me, but I don't think you really are, not really. And because life with you would be pretty damned sweet, I could continue – I know that – but here's the thing, Edward: As much as I try to hide it, I'm a fucking romantic at heart, I'm ashamed to say, and I still believe that there is someone out there I could fall in love with. I know I'm probably full of shit, and I know the odds are pretty slim that *another* Mr. Wonderful is going to stroll into my bar in Bumfuck, Ohio, but I can't help it – I've got to keep looking for him. And I just know, somehow, that you're not him. Jesus, you have no idea how much I wish you *were* him, but you're not. And I think if you look inside yourself, you'll have to admit that I'm not the one for you either."

"Don't tell me what I feel," said Edward more forcefully than he had intended.

"You're right – I can't tell you that. I'm sorry. But there ain't no good way to say this Edward, so I'm trying to go at it from all angles to make it a little easier to swallow."

Someone else had gotten a hold of the jukebox, and the classics had now given way to Shania Twain. Edward felt angry and foolish, and the music seemed to be taunting him.

"I guess there's nothing left to say," Edward said, feeling foolish while Shania sang *Looks Like We Made It*.

"Nothing," said Hank, "except thanks for the best few weeks of my life – really. I have had such a great time and done so many things that I never would have done had I not met you. The biggest of which, of course, was meeting

Ellie-short-for-Eleanor. I *am* going to see her again, going to invite her out to stay with me for a few days. *You* did that, Edward, by forcing me to shit or get off the pot. I'd have never done it without you. I owe you so much for that. And thanks for giants and princesses and rivers and ferries and your beautiful house. I'm probably out of my fucking mind to throw this all away, but I've just got to. Please don't hate me."

"I don't hate you," he said. "I couldn't. But I'd be a liar if I said I agreed with you. I think we could have something real, make it work. But it takes two to tango, obviously, so I've just got to accept it. So much for my amazing fucking journey."

"What in the hell are you talking about?" Hank asked, voice rising. "Jesus Christ, Edward – the things we've seen, the experiences we've had! If this wasn't a classic journey, then I don't know what would be!"

But Edward was no longer listening, trapped in that place where his mind knew that something was right but was waiting for his heart to catch up. And it would, he knew – it was all part of the journey – but at that moment it wasn't there yet, *he* wasn't there yet. And the jukebox returned to an oldie, a my-woman-done-me-wrong kind of song and he slowly drank his bourbon, looking at the man sitting in the chair in front of him, knowing that that chair would soon be empty, but hoping that the journey hadn't ended, but rather that he was moving forward forward forward.

Chapter Twelve: 1983, 1984, 1985

1983

I'm trying to read *The Hotel New Hampshire* by the little light that is above my seat, but the bus driver is hitting every pothole in the road and I'm starting to feel like I'm going to throw up, so I put it down and close my eyes, hoping to sleep. There is a couple in the seat in front of me just talking away – they don't seem to care too much that everyone else on the bus wants to sleep – and although I want to ignore them I just *can't* ignore them. It's not like their conversation is interesting – they're talking about taking a dress back to Sears that the woman bought but doesn't want now – but I've been listening to them for more than an hour so I'm beginning to feel invested somehow. And so I close my eyes and begin imagining the scene in Sears and I guess I sleep a little because in my mind there is a bear present and so I'm pretty sure that I'm conflating – a word that I had to learn when I was studying for my SATs – I'm conflating the couple's story and that of *The Hotel New Hampshire*. But then *that* becomes the story and I can't sleep because now I'm all charged up coming up with a story about a bear being turned loose in Sears. It's not a nasty, maul-everything-in-sight bear, it's a gentle bear whom I've named Burt because every Burt I've ever met is just lovely and real gentle.

I hear the couple say that they're going to Havana like me, so there is something about knowing that we are ending up in the same place that kind of puts us in the same category, even if I'm only on the bus because I'm too young to rent a car and I'm pretty sure they're on the bus because … well … they shop at Sears.

A year ago I would have chastised myself for being such a snob about people who shop at Sears because I know that Grams and Gramps shop there and a year ago I would have told you they were the fucking cat's pajamas. But now I'm not so sure. Last summer Grams could barely look me in the eye. On the surface things seemed OK with Gramps, but I got the feeling that they weren't really OK. Gramps used to look at me and not say anything, but the way he looked at me just made me feel like everything was alright – like *I* was alright – and that they would always be alright with us. But last summer I noticed that Gramps looked at me less and I'm not sure what that's all about. Gramps has always been my rock and it's weirding me out that there seems to be something strange between us.

The guy of the couple mentions something about Bradington and my ears perk up for obvious reasons. I'm eavesdropping – which I know is wrong – but I think it's probably not as wrong on a bus, where the camaraderie factor is higher than, say, on an airplane. I've been able to piece together that they had an overnight with their daughter Mary Jane in Chicago and they left their car near the courthouse in Havana. The woman is saying that Havana is not what it used to be – she's talking like it's a massive metropolis and not a hick town of fewer than 3000 people – and she's hoping that hooligans didn't mess with their car. I think to myself because that is exactly something that Grams would say but that thought becomes oddly painful because I wonder if I even know Grams well enough to make such a connection. And – I'm just thinking this for the first time – Grams doesn't seem to know me. I'm not sure anyone does except Jeff. Maybe Jeff does, maybe he doesn't – I don't know for sure, but I know I want to find out.

The woman starts gathering her things up and I look out and see that we are in Havana. I don't think I've ever seen a taxi in Havana – not that I've ever looked – and it dawns on me that I didn't think about how to get from Havana to the Bay. I could hitchhike – I like the way that feels when I imagine it – but it would be my fucking luck that I'd get picked up by the next John Wayne Gacy so I decide that's not a good thing. So I decide to turn on the full force of my charm on the couple, drop my own big-ass name, and see if they would give me a lift to Bradington town and from there I can hoof it to the Bay.

They get off the bus before me and I kind of run after them but not freakish-like because I don't want the lady to think I'm one of those Havana hooligans that she apparently thinks roam the town wreaking havoc on good people like themselves.

"Excuse me, ma'am, sir," I say with a smile. Ordinary people eat ma'am-and-sir shit up with a fucking spoon. They turn around; the woman looks a little worried.

"I'm sorry to inconvenience you," I say, "but I over-heard you talking and heard that you are from Bradington. I'm going there myself … well not to Bradington town proper but to my family's home just outside the town. I'm Edward Bradington and my grandparents are the McCul-loghs who take care of the big house for my family. I'm going to surprise them, so I don't want to call my Gramps to pick me up. Could I inconvenience you for a ride to the town? I'll be happy to give you something for the gas."

Their faces break forth in massive smiles. "Of course you can have a ride," the woman says. "A Bradington in our car!" She acts like Elvis just asked her for a smoke.

"We'll take you up to the big house," the man says, "it

will be our honor."

We walk from the bus stop over to the courthouse. I discover their names are Les and Francine Dennis, and that Les retired from the post office two years before. They know Grams and Gramps well and they know of my father. Les points to a green Chevy Caprice and says, "This is us. Sorry – it's probably not what you're used to."

"It's a noble chariot," I say and Francine sighs like she's swooning.

"Francine, you get in the back seat," Les says because it's obvious he wants to give me the place of importance when I naturally think the place of importance would be in the back with the driver up front.

The ride to the big house is only twenty-five minutes, but the Dennises are obviously nervous talkers, and I get a whole lot of information in that twenty-five minutes, including that daughter Mary Jane was living in sin with a Mexican who was nevertheless the salt of the earth. By the end of our journey I kind of just want to stay with them, go to their home and let Francine spoil me like Grams used to (or maybe like Grams still does – I'm not real sure). I imagine it for a moment: me being adopted by the Dennises. Christmases with them and Mary Jane and that Mexican whose name they never say – it's always just "The Mexican" – where they're happy for me to be me and I'm happy for me to be me. I imagine Christmas dinner with red thick paper napkins and sweet wine and cherry-scented candles bought from the Kroger burning unevenly on the table. I imagine drinking beer and playing cards after dinner while a football game blares from the TV in the living room (do they play football at Christmas?) and Francine says "Anyone want some coffee" and we all look sheepish, like we don't want to put her out, and she says "I'm making some for myself" and so we all say, "Sure, I'll have a cup" -

except the Mexican, who doesn't drink coffee. And I imagine that no one talks about money or business or Harvard or Columbia or Brown or Yale or how crowded the Hamptons are becoming or how common Hawaii is becoming or how a proper housekeeper is worth her weight in gold or whether polo will ever really take off or what Nancy Reagan wore to the last year's Meridian Ball.

But the moment ends as soon as I see the gates of the big house and I know that I'll never be permitted to be like the Dennises and that I'll forever be talking about the Hamptons and housekeepers and polo because I'll never be free. As I wave goodbye to the family-I'll-never-have I see for the first time how the gates in front of me resemble either the front of a cage or the gates of one of those abandoned insane asylums in the movies where some psychopath is killing kids who are just wanting to drink a few beers and fuck a little. I stand and watch that green Chevy Caprice drive away and I feel like I've been punched in the gut.

As I press the code to open the gate (my birthday, the day of the arrival of everyone's Golden Boy!) another thought comes to me as if from deep in my punched gut: in all the imagining of my future, not once did Jeff enter into any of it at all. I know this should be significant, but I figure I've only got so much imagining I can do at any given time and there's not room for everyone. But there will be room for Jeff. I'm sure there will be.

I'm sitting in one of the formal sitting rooms looking down at my shoes: white leather Nikes with a red swooshes that suddenly seem less like they're showing swift movement and more like they're the after effects of a knife fight. Everything seems foggy, in part because my father is there and he hasn't been there in forever but more so because there –

right there where my mother entertained the wife of the Governor – is sitting the stepmonster, who has *never* been there. For the first time I notice how much she resembles my mother and yet how different they are. She is pretty – there is no doubt about it – but it's a cool beauty, like she's a statue and not a real person. I notice that she is wearing some earrings that my mother loved, and this makes me angry, even if I know the earrings didn't belong to my mother anyway. Grams is looking at me with concern, Dad with disappointment, Gramps with something very much like pain, but the stepmonster is looking at me in a way that makes me think she is finding this whole intervention thing eminently entertaining (which is assonance, but she sure as fuck wouldn't know that).

The stepmonster talks first and I think what fucking gall. There she is sitting in a room with three people who have known me my whole fucking life and she thinks what she has to say about me is so important that she needs to set the tone for all of them. I kind of have to admire her cojones; I think she suffers from high self-esteem. She's bringing God and Jesus into this whole mess and I could not be less interested. If God gets his panties in a wad over two boys who love each other well ... who needs him? She's telling me that she won't have me in any of her homes – she will not "reward deplorable behavior" – and although I know I'll be sad not to see my father (I'll forgive him some-day – I know I will) I don't really give a rat's ass about not being able to be around her. I half feel like jumping up and kissing her and saying, "Thank you thank you thank you that I don't have to be around your sorry ass ever again!"

My father goes next and is talking and talking and talking and he must use the word *legacy* like a hundred fucking times. He's talking like he needs to explain the con-cept to me, but I think I'm pretty hip to it, so I'm not really listening too much; this man has nothing to teach me about legacy. He refuses to use Jeff's name, and each time he mentions *the boy in question* my lips mouth the name *Jeff* but my I don't have the strength to produce the breath to make the name heard. It's like Jeff is just a skeleton and I have the power to put flesh on him but I just can't. I feel both weak and apathetic, and after a while I don't even have the strength to mouth the name. The bones are turning to dust; there's nothing left of the boy in question except an empty place inside of me which has been hollowed out by my own cowardice.

Because although I can imagine a life like that of the Dennises, can romantically envision those red paper napkins, can almost taste that sweet wine and smell those cherry-scented Kroger candles, I know it takes a shitload more courage to live their life than it does to live mine, and I just don't have it. Back when Jeff was flesh and blood and a part of me I felt it – the courage – but now that he's dust I know I don't have anything except my fucking illustrious names and money and more privilege than anyone realistically needs. And I know I don't want to be without my fucking illustrious names and money and more privilege than anyone realistically needs. So I just bow my head and give up the ghost. I am defeated, but with some pretty fucking awesome consolation prizes. I've competed in a game where the loser ends up with a lot more than the winner and, hey, that's just how my life is. That's how my life will always be. Not fucking bad for a coward.

Maybe for people like me strength doesn't come from courage, but rather from not giving a fuck about anything.

*

1984

I'm waiting for the fireworks and I know they'll be thrilling. I probably should be laid back and cool and just relax until they happen. But I can't; I'm like a kid. They can be simple, little more than firecrackers, and I get all jittery. I remember running around the lawn at the Bay, sparklers in each hand, writing my name in the air, smoke and sparks telling everyone who I was. I remember Uncle Jerry shooting off bottle rockets right from his hand – *not* out of the RC Cola bottles that had been set there expressively for that purpose. I remember Grams yelling, "Jerry you damn fool you're going to blow your hand off!" before running – rather quickly for a woman of her girth – to hide behind the gazebo, laughing and scared at the same time. I remember one of my cousins – but I can't remember which one – daring me to do the same thing, to light one off right there from my small hand. And I wouldn't be a chicken – I just wouldn't – so I snuck a bottle rocket from the pile, stole a lighter from the cook's purse and, when everyone was eating, went down to where the waters met the lawn and showed Jimmy that I wasn't afraid. And with hands that were shaking like a shitting dog (as Uncle Stan used to say) I lit it. Jimmy yelled, "Close your eyes – you could hurt yourself!" but I wouldn't. That was all a part of it: watching the red glow move closer and closer to the rocket, wondering when it would go off, worrying that I probably could lose a hand and maybe even an eye, but being too caught up in the thrill of it all to throw it in the bay. I heard the sound before I felt anything – something between a whoosh and a pop, or maybe a whoosh *then* a pop – and then I felt a warmth on my hand that wasn't exactly painful but didn't feel good either. And it was almost like in slow motion, I saw it arc up over the bay and explode over the water, sound echoing loud enough to make everyone turn. I liked the sound more than the sight of it, I think. I liked being able to do something that would make heads turn. People could miss all kinds of things with their eyes, but give them a big POP and they'll look, every last one of them. And they did. And I was hooked on fireworks, even more than before.

And it's August now, but I'm not waiting for fireworks at the Bay – haven't been there since last December – but I'm at Monroe Harbor on Lake Michigan for Venetian Night. And I'm with my buddies PJ and Todd and – even though the three of us were in the *real* Venice the month before – we decide it would be cool to go down to the lakefront and check out the scene. And it's not bad – we've been sneaking beers and flirting with girls and acting all high-and-mighty because we're going off to Columbia, Harvard and Brown in a week's time – but for me it's just like a Peanuts band aid on a bee sting: it's not bad looking down and seeing Snoopy caught in the middle of his dance, but it can't entirely cover the fact that there's a big honking sting underneath that won't go away and won't be forgotten.

Last year I would have certainly written that in my notebook, tried to use it in some story or another I was writing. I was constantly writing then, story after story – most of which I didn't finish but I didn't care, I just loved writing. But I'm not writing now, not a word. It was probably stupid thinking I could be a writer, anyway. But it sure was nice, while drinking a cold Miller and staring out at the blackened skies above the lake, waiting, waiting, waiting for the light and the explosion. It sure was nice thinking about sitting on that large porch at the Bay, using my mother's typewriter, listening to the locusts and loons and the water below lapping up against the boathouse dock. I won't allow myself to think of Jeff there – all of my most recent letters have gone unanswered, and they've even changed their damn phone number – but it's not a bad thought without him, all the same. It's not complete, of course, but maybe what the whole terrible experience has taught me is that life is very rarely complete, that you just have to be happy with what you can get. I need to face facts: I'm rich, I'm good-looking, I'm getting ready to go to a great university and live in an apartment that my father has bought for me right in Manhattan. There are probably a billion people who would trade places with me.

Todd and PJ are chatting up a bunch of high school girls and they're trying to involve me, but I don't want to look at them, don't want to miss even a second of the fire-works. One of the girls is saying that she doesn't think Co-lumbia is Ivy League – probably just to goad me into stand-ing up and joining in on the conversation – but I couldn't fucking care less whether Columbia is Ivy League or not (though everyone knows it is); I just want to sit and drink my beer and watch the black skies. I feel like if I miss even one flash, one pop, that the evening will be a total bust.

And besides, I'm not really interested in girls. I know I like men, but still can't bring myself to talk about it, and I'm still allowing everyone who knows about Jeff and me to think it's some kind of phase. But I know it's not. Since I'm staying in a room on my own at the Drake and not at my own house with my father and cunt of a wife, I have begun buying more pornography than probably the perviest of pervs. Those boys – flat, silent, spreading and arching – are really the only thing I am interested in now. I can look at them, get off, and forget about them. They don't care about me, and I don't really care about them.

Just then a streak of white light goes up over the lake, and everyone stops talking and turns to watch. It starts tiny – it always does – and at first there are only small slivers of silver, icicles slicing through black gauze. They don't have much of a sound – the first ones – but they're beautiful, calming. They don't make any demands. But then the lights get bigger and brighter – mushrooming blues and reds and yellows and greens filling up the sky and making the lake look like a skating rink surrounded by Christmas trees. And the more insistent pops begin and then become more rapid, like someone's mowing down the skaters at the rink with an Uzi. And then eventually comes the point where it's nothing but color and rat-a-tat and I know that the finale is seconds away, when the big sounds will make their appearance. And because the lights are less important to me, I close my eyes and wait for the sounds.

And they come. Huge booming bazooka shots that I'm sure people in Indiana and maybe even Michigan can hear. And the crowd around me is going "ooh" and "ahh" but I refuse to open my eyes. I imagine it – this sound – sailing over the surface of the dark waters, dipping under it even, animating the bones of sailors buried deep within. I imagine it snaking through the city behind me, sliding through and avoiding the big steel and glass guardians to hover over the air in the western suburbs. I imagine it heading south, finding a river, and following it until it comes to a chute and then to a bay, and I imagine it resting on that bay, that water. And then, because I've got my eyes closed, I can see how the sound booms on that water and somehow animates it, giving life to all that is within it. And if the sound can do that to everything in the water, surely it can do it to that which surrounds the water, and I imagine the house itself, bursting with life and laughter. I imagine barren woods becoming lush, fertile, steamy.

And certainly, if the waters can be reborn and the house can burst with life and the very woods grow into a vibrant forest, then the sound can animate people as well, can make dust turn to bones which become flesh and blood. And just for the briefest of seconds I see him. And his face is not gray and hurt, but truly alive and happy and filled with love. The sound wouldn't let what I did have the final say. There's life inside of us both, intertwined, luscious.

My friends are calling to me, their voices straining above the sound, but I won't open my eyes, because I knows that if I do all of that life which the sound brought about will disappear. So I wave them off, eyes closed, say I'm not feeling well, I'll catch up with them in two days' time when we have our proper going away party, dripping in excess like the night before princes go to war. "Go," I say, eyes closed, still hearing the echoes of the sound. And they do – I hear them walk away.

And the echoes become fainter and fainter, the memories and the life begin to fade until nothing remains, just the shuffling feet of people walking. And when I can no longer hear the echoes, no longer see the memories and life, I open my eyes.

My first impulse is to be sad, for what was so vibrant before is now nothing, as dark and shapeless as the skies above the lake. But I know I shouldn't be sad, because as long as I can train myself to hear the sound, as long as I can surf along with the echoes over time and space, I can remember. And I've known my whole life: if you can remember something, someone, they're never really dead. Boomlay Boomlay Boomlay Boom!

1985

I've come back from class and I see that my answering machine is blinking, red and insistent. No one ever calls me here except my father and I just don't have the energy to speak to him now, to act like everything is all hunky-dory between us and that things are as they always have been. I have, for more than a year, been meeting my father in restaurants and bars like that's the most normal thing in the world, like it's perfectly OK for me not to be able to ever go home. And I love my father and so I put up with it, play along. But it takes strength, and today I have none. I open the fridge, grab a beer, and sit in the living room, watching the light blink, not caring.

I have no strength because I've just come from an intense meeting with Dr. Seubert, one of my English professors. And Dr. Seubert is cool in her own way – campus legend says there's a picture of her somewhere dancing topless at Woodstock – but she can be like a dog with a bone when she gets something in her mind, and lately it's like I'm the bone.

We've been writing journals for English class, working on observing the world and putting it down on paper – standard college freshman stuff – and she wants to collect some of my journal entries and try to have them published. But I know I will never be – *can't* be – any kind of a writer. I'm pre-law and my father might tolerate me doing something else for a while, but I've got responsibilities to the family business and will eventually end up there.

And it's exhausting talking to Dr. Seubert because she is just saying, "Look it's just a series of essays; it doesn't mean that you have to shuck everything and become a writer" but she doesn't get it. She doesn't get that doing even a piddly-ass part of a dream makes the dream come at you with full force. And I just can't do it – can't look back. I've got to move forward. Happy people move forward. Forward, forward, forward.

But trying to make Dr. Seubert see this without the aid

of a bong and six-pack proved futile and tiring. And now the light is blinking on my answering machine, red and insistent, and I'm pretty sure I can't even talk to my father right now without the aid of a bong and a six pack. So I grab my keys and run downstairs.

Naveed's sitting behind the counter, reading a *People* magazine. I always give Naveed shit about his reading material, tell him he'll never be more than a convenience store clerk if he just reads *People* and *The National Enquirer,* but Naveed always just says "Fuck you very much" really rapidly so it sounds like one word, and ignores me. Or at least I *think* Naveed says "fuck you very much;" Naveed talks so fast that I only catch about half of what he says. Maybe the reason we're such good friends – Naveed is, basically, my only friend in New York – is that I only understand about half of what Naveed says. We get together, we smoke pot, we drink beer and Naveed starts talking about conspiracies and crap like that, and I can only make out half of it, and what I can make out is fucking nuts. But I like hanging out with Naveed, like the rhythm and clipping and clucking of his speech even if I don't get it all. And Naveed doesn't seem too pissed off if I don't appear to be a good listener; he's content to just talk without expecting anything in return. We're fucking *made* for each other. It's a fucking shame that Naveed's not into guys or I'd probably ask him to move in with me.

So Naveed is saying that he'll be off in twenty minutes and so I know I need to go to my dealer and get some weed. But since my dealer is up by school, and Naveed lives up near there as well, it makes sense that we get together at Naveed's place.

I take the subway and get off at 103rd, deciding to walk for a bit. The air is cool and damp, but not too terribly cold for February, or so everyone keeps telling me. I think that

New Yorkers talk more about the weather than any other group of people I've ever met, but I think that's kind of cool, especially since it usually lets one avoid talking about other things that are probably best left unsaid anyway. New Yorkers have this bad rap for being rude – people in Chicago talk about it all the time – but I don't think they're rude at all. New Yorkers, I've decided, just don't have time to take shit from anybody. And I like that. I wish I were more like that.

My dealer's name is Bob and so *not* what I expected from a dealer. I got Bob's name from a guy I hooked up with for a few weeks at the beginning of my first semester and was expecting some big bruiser whom no one would ever dare to fuck with, mainly because I had never met a big-city drug dealer before. But Bob turned out to be a pudgy, prematurely bald guy with glasses so thick that they made his eyes look like raisins. But Bob can get anything you need, so I love Bob. I would like to think that Bob is my friend too, even if I know he probably isn't. But I sure would *like* to be Bob's friend, as there is something behind the twitching and piggy eyes and even occasional stuttering that makes me think Bob just might have a story to tell, might have figured out some things that remain mysteries to most other people.

I buy the pot from Bob and go to wait for Naveed, only to find that he has beat me there. We enter Naveed's apartment – empty except for a television with an Atari, a dining chair with caning that will certainly go at any minute (it's like the chair version of that Don't Break the Camel's Back game that my cousin Pam used to bring to the Bay) and a sofa that smells like onions and always transmits that smell to whomever sits on it. So each time I go to Naveed's I have to choose between the chair and possibly falling on my ass and doing myself harm, or the sofa and reeking all the way home on the subway. Which has become kind of a game in and of itself.

I choose the sofa and Naveed pulls up the chair and sits in it, placing the bong and the beer in between us. In between bong hits, Naveed is talking about some sort of Jewish conspiracy and I just sort of let him go on and on, meaning that I take about ten times more bong hits than Naveed does. Every now and then Naveed pauses and says, "Well?" like he wants at least some demonstration that I have been listening and I usually just answer, "You're full of shit," which is enough to get Naveed to continue.

Bob has given me some particularly powerful stuff and it's affecting me a lot more than usual.

I think I have just had a long blink but realize that I must have fallen asleep, because the chair is empty as is the bong and the twelve-pack box next to it. I stumble into the bathroom, take a leak and leave.

The subway is the best place to *not* think, so I enjoy the ride back to my place. The lights, the rhythm, the other passengers, the smells, the sounds: all of them combine to form this barrier to thought that I find comforting. Enough to just ride and listen, blinking slowly and trying to be happy.

The damn light is still blinking on my phone when I get home, red and insistent, and I'm so annoyed at it that I turn it off completely and take the phone off the hook. That'll teach him! I grab a beer from the fridge to take the edge off and fall asleep after one sip.

The doorbell is ringing ringing ringing, red and insistent. Wait, how can a doorbell be red? I get up to answer it and feel like my jaws have been pried open and clamped; what the hell was that stuff that Bob gave me? On my way to the door I look at the clock: 3:39 p.m. So much for classes.

I answer the door and the doorman Stuart is standing there, judging the fuck out of me. Stuart is some kind of holy-roller, and almost lost his job once because he was proselytizing to too many of the people in the co-op. He promised to stop, but he still gives the hairy eye to some of the people there: Tom and Larry, the old gay couple in 11B, Mrs. Sternstein in 9A, Dr. Nayad in 12B and me.

"Yes?" I say, jaw aching.

"Your father called very worried. He left you several messages yesterday and he has been trying to call you for over twenty-four hours." Stuart hisses slightly on "hours."

"OK. Thanks, Stuart. I'll give him a call."

"Didn't you have class today?" Stuart asks.

My first impulse is to say "None of your fucking business!" but I remember a line that Gramps used to say whenever he would come to Chicago and take me out of school for a day of fun: "I gave the teachers a day to catch up with me." I shut the door in Stuart's face.

I plug the phone in and call my father. Damn the luck – the witch answers.

"Let me talk to Dad," I say.

"Where have you been?"

My first impulse is to say "None of your fucking business!" but instead I say, "Just let me talk to Dad, OK?"

"EJ?" says my father, "where in the hell have you been?"

"Study group. And I just discovered that I knocked the phone off the hook. What's up? You coming to town?"

"It's your grandma. She's had a stroke. Things are very serious. Your Gramps is asking for you."

I can't quite wrap my head around it. Grams was fine when I last saw her. But then it dawns on me that I haven't seen her in well over a year.

"Get on a flight to Springfield as soon as you can, EJ.

I'll arrange a car for you there and I'll book you a room at the Hilton. I've got to go to Boston, but we'll touch base later tonight."

"Boston? You mean you're *leaving*?"

"Edward," he says, "She's not my mother. We haven't been close in years. And you have no right judging me. For more than a year that poor woman has been saying nothing but that she missed you and wanted to see you. And you couldn't be bothered. So, little man, don't put this on my plate. She is my ex-mother-in-law who has not always been very kind to me, who told me about ten years ago that I was nothing more to her than her husband's employer. But you are her grandson, her favorite. Don't try and throw shit at me because you couldn't be bothered to visit her. I've got to go now. Just get on the plane. I hope it's not too late." The line goes dead.

I take a beer into the shower with me. I wonder what I should pack. I decide that packing a suit would be jinxing things; I'm not going to need a suit to wear to a funeral because Grams is going to be just fine. I throw some t-shirts, jeans and underwear into a bag and call a taxi. On the way to the airport I just keep thinking Thank God she's in Springfield, because I don't think I can go back to the Bay.

I finally land in Springfield late that night and call the hospital. They put me through to the family lounge and Aunt Louise answers the phone.

"Hey Aunt Louise, it's Edward. How's Grams?"

"She's hanging in there." Her voice is tired and cold.

"Can I still get in even this late if I come over now? Do visiting hours apply to ... such situations?"

"'Such situations!' Jesus, how you talk, Eddie. No, I suppose visiting hours don't apply to such situations."

"Sorry, Aunt Louise. I'm a little thrown for a loop by the whole thing. I'm not thinking clearly. I'll be there in ten minutes.

I arrive and by then there's Aunt Melinda, Uncle Jerry and just one of my horde of cousins, my cousin Pam.

"'Bout fucking time," Uncle Jerry says. "What's wrong: couldn't get away from the pep rally, Joe College?"

"Jerry!" says Aunt Melinda. "Good to see you Eddie."

"Where's Gramps?" I ask.

"Louise took him over to the motel. Mom is stabilized, so we thought he should get some rest. Everyone will be back in the morning."

"Can I see her?" I ask.

"She won't know you're here," says Uncle Jerry. "You should have thought about this earlier, like maybe every day for fucking years when she was saying that she never heard from you."

"Yeah, OK, Uncle Jerry – I get it: I'm a dick. I'm an asshole. I fuck up everything I touch. We all know that. But just answer my fucking question: can I see my Grams?"

"Everyone's a little tired and emotional – let's just calm down and remember we're family," says Aunt Melinda. "They told us that she is resting peacefully now and that – unless there's some big change – it would be better that we don't disturb her. Eddie why don't you just go and get a good night's sleep, and you can see her first thing in the morning."

"I'll stay here," I say, looking at Uncle Jerry, feeling more alone than I have in a long, long time.

"Suit yourself," says Uncle Jerry, who walks out of the room, followed by Aunt Melinda. Pam stays as still as shadows, big eyes glued to an old *Newsweek*.

I sit down and rifle through the magazines that are on the table. Nothing grabs my interest, so I stare at the picture on the wall, a horrible oil painting of a covered bridge in autumn that looks vaguely familiar. It's really frightful, the painting, what a cliché would look like if you could paint a cliché. Who would choose such a thing? Then it dawns on me: it's very similar to a painting that hangs on the wall of Grams' living room. *Grams* would choose such a thing – that's who. This realization makes me acutely feel something that all my imaginings and happy thoughts and beer and pot have been trying to cover: I am alone.

A nurse shakes me awake. I am alone in the room. Where is Pam?

"Excuse me? Are you here for Lucille McCullough?"

"Yes, I'm her grandson. There were some others here earlier. I fell asleep. I don't know where they've gone."

She seemed nervous. "I'm really sorry Mr. ..."

"Bradington."

"Mr. Bradington. I'm Selene, the charge nurse in ICU. I'm sorry to have to be the one to tell you that your grandmother has passed. She went peacefully. In her sleep. She was in no pain. I'm so sorry."

"Can I see her?" I ask, although it's the last thing I really want to do. But it seems like the thing I'm expected to say. Even in such a circumstance Edward James Allerton Bradington IV must do and say the right thing.

"Of course. Come with me."

We walk down the hallway, unnervingly quiet and bright. We pass the nurse's station, and a kind-faced nurse looks at me and mouths the words "I'm sorry."

We stop at a doorway. "Mr. Bradington," Selene says, touching his arm. "I don't know if you are a person of faith or not – I suppose it doesn't really matter. I've worked in ICU for twelve years now, and I've seen a lot of people leave this earth. And many of us who work here know – we just *know* – that souls sometimes stay around a while after death. Now you might think that's a bunch of baloney, and it may be. But I just want to say: I was just in there, and I don't think your grandmother's soul has left yet. So if you've got anything to say – maybe even on behalf of the whole family – maybe you want to say it. I think she'll hear you. At any rate, it can't hurt."

"You're right," I say, but I do think it very well may just be a bunch of baloney. I enter the room.

Grams is in bed, eyes closed. Her mouth is drooping a little to one side, but besides that there is nothing really different about her. She could be sleeping, except for the fact that she's as still as death itself. I reach up and touch her face; it's still warm. I realize that the last time I touched someone's dead body was this woman's daughter, and this thought makes me feel both connected and utterly isolated at the same time.

I'm thinking of all the things that I should say, just in case Grams' soul is still in the room, hovering like the smoke clouds after fireworks. I'm thinking that I should say how sorry I am that I stopped coming to see her, stopped coming to the Bay. But I know if I get into it I'll have to say that I stopped coming because I was pissed off, because she and everyone else were dead wrong about Jeff, that there was something real and living between us and in us and everyone made us kill it and now a part of me is dead as well. And I know that if I say that I'll have to say that there's a part of me that will never forgive her or Gramps for not going to bat for me. My father? I could almost understand. But Grams and Gramps? How could they not know that they were helping to kill something real?

But I can't say these things, especially if Grams' soul is still there. Because I know that Grams loved me and I loved Grams, and that we both hurt each other but that somehow it doesn't take away the love. And I begin to cry, less for the loss of Grams, and more for how awful it is that hurt and love are so frequently intertwined.

And finally, after the tears have stopped, I say, "I had to move on, Grams; it was the only way. But I'll always remember all the love you gave me, and it will always be with me. I'll take it forward with me." And I lean over and kiss her forehead.

Chapter Thirteen: 2012

Hank's gone and I wonder if I should be devastated, wonder if I should be wandering around the house in my underwear, despondent and unshaven. And for a day or two, I basically decide to do just that: sleep late, stay inside with the heavy curtains closing out the revealing sun. I figure it's a sort of sacrifice demanded of me by the relationship gods.

But even though I am sad, a kind of sadness that rests like the hint of perspiration on my upper lip even in the cool night air, I know it's not a despair that consumes. I don't, in the end, even feel related to this despair, it's more like we are disconnected strangers rather than intimate and connected. It will pass, brushing past me and exiting into the world to find someone who will cling to it, maybe even need it. I am not that person.

After two days I've had enough, feel the gods have been sufficiently propitiated, and I leave the tomb-like quiet of the house and venture outside where even at dawn there is still enough of the unseasonable heat in the air to hit me like a sandbox bully. And although it's almost shocking, the presence of this heat in October, it's alive. There's even humidity, so thick that at first I feel I can barely breathe, as if the air is too filled with living matter for me to be able to get it in through my nose, my gasping mouth. But I like it – like the struggle. It's alive.

I walk to the water's edge and strip, aware for the first time of how white I look surrounded by the colors of autumn. Dad said a few weeks ago that he'd been told that the stones which had been placed there to protect delicate feet have been washed away or – more likely – stolen by industrious thieves who have been able to get around the barrier in the water or the gate on the road. I step in the water and my feet sink into the mud, the bay does not – cannot – lie and the water is piercing in its frigidity. I dive in and feel actual pain. I open my eyes to slits. All is dirt and moss, and I can see very little but shifting shapes and colors, and I struggle to make out anything discernible in the swirling darkness and pain.

I come up, breaking through the water's barrier to the surface. And now the air above is easier, and I breathe it in in greedy gulps. My body has become accustomed to the cold, so I know where I want to swim. I allow myself a moment of doubt – I am naked and should stay in the private part of the bay lest someone sees me or in case I develop hypothermia – but the doubt is washed away by the bay, burned off by the single ray of the rising sun, just beginning to lift its hand like a hesitant schoolboy.

I begin swimming in slow, measured strokes. A voice in my head calls for caution: I haven't swum this far in a long time; I'm not a teenager anymore; there will be no one around at this time of the morning; if I must do it for God's sake go slowly and stay near the shore. It's annoying, this voice, and I find I can drown it out by going faster, by making more noise in the water than a leisurely stroke can achieve. And so I swim, faster and faster, mocking the voice. And as I approach the divider that blocks off my part of the bay from intruders, the voice starts in on me again: climb over it if you must continue; you have no idea what kind of tentacles have enclosed it below in all these years. But the voice is powerless now, so I dare to dive down down down in the murky water and go under it, feeling somehow that if I should get tangled down below I will be able to breathe, take in the even colder water there like Aquaman or the Man from Atlantis.

I emerge on the other side, victorious, and slow my pace. The voice has been silenced; there is no need to prove anything. I swim slowly, cautiously, using the breath-intaking turn of my head not only to drink in the warmer air but also to look at the sky, pink with the possibility of a new day. The alternating rhythm of face-in-dark-water and the sky above is thrilling. Each time I look up it's as if the sky has changed color once again. It's slight – this difference in color – but I see it, am aware of it in ways that I think the people in the nearby town somehow are not. Because if this is my bay (and it is, she embraced me like a long-lost mother the second I was immersed once again in her waters) then somehow this is my sky, too.

I arrive at the clearing, leave my mother's arms, and collapse with a thud on the hard ground, shivering. I lay there, breathing heavily, eyes focused on the brightening sky above, feeling a part of the earth. It's not only my bay and my sky but my earth as well, and I imagine myself sinking into it, becoming indistinguishable from the gray-brown dirt around me.

An opossum ending its nightshift and heading home to sleep, pokes its head around a nearby log, startled. We look at each other for a few seconds – the opossum's red eyes seeming to register recognition – before the curious animal judges me either benevolent or unworthy of attention and scurries off.

I sit up and look around the clearing which is at the same time familiar and alien. There are still logs arranged in a semicircle around the bones of a campfire; the simplicity of gathering, fire, stories, dares, conspiracy still going strong. But the area is now littered with beer cans and food wrappers. The presence of comforting, simple images from my youth and the excesses of modernity thrown together is jarring. I cannot fully embrace my present reality, not with the logs and campfire there like pews and an altar, but neither can I be completely enveloped by the romance of the simple past, not with recently crushed and crumpled Keystone Light cans and Doritos bags strewn about like a wilted garland. It's a struggle, putting it all together, making sense of both past and present and maybe future. But I like it – the struggle. It's alive.

For a few moments I manage to overlook the rubbish and see the past, shimmering like the water in front of me, finally fully kissed by the sun. I see it all – I *feel* it all: timid glances, shared laughter, soft kisses, wet skin, forbidden touches, release. And the sadness that did not consume me earlier makes its presence known, seems to say that if I keep this up – this draping myself in the past – it will over-power me. And part of me doesn't care, part of me wants to be entrenched if not buried by sadness; I deserve to feel *something*, don't I? But the other part, the part which makes me remember to breathe while swimming, knows I can't allow that. It's a struggle, this battling between the enticing danger of emotion and the caution of self-preservation. But I like it – the struggle. It's alive.

Suddenly I hear the sound of faint voices and crunch-ing twigs. And though I'm not ready to leave, though I want to stay in the past for just a few moments more, I know I must be prudent and leave, know on a rational level that someone finding me, of all people, there naked would be at least awkward and possibly even scandalous. I get up off the ground and take a final look at the logs and camp-fire-bones, ignoring the trash, and rush once again into the cold embrace of the bay, whose muddy waters seem to accept both past and present without any struggle at all.

*

I'm sitting on the screened-in porch with my mother's old typewriter sitting in front of me, challenging me. It works – I've typed my name on it three times: once all in capitals, once all small and once the correct way – but I am just staring at the page, at my name, and can't decide what to do, how to go on. I'll eventually need to write a few words to say at the Collection, when I am to receive the symbolic offerings of the tenants, but I can't help but feel I don't really know these people who live in this town with my name, was never allowed to be a part of their lives. So I decide to go to the tavern, where Friday evening will most certainly have gathered people around her like courtiers. I will just walk into the tavern and sit at the bar and drink in their words and glances and scents along with beer. They will accept me immediately, will embrace me as one of their own. I type my name again. It's my name and it's somehow theirs as well. We are brothers. I am going to find my brothers.

I decide to walk because I want to go by the cemetery first, and it was always a thing that was done on foot, a pilgrimage undertaken hand in hand with my Gramps. Gramps is gone now, and in another cemetery, but I imagine him there, walking beside me, firm hand gripped around my own like a protective giant. I walk and as the light grows dimmer the dusk song swells. I walk over holy ground and I'm beginning to think that the crickets are not just chanting some monotonous hum, but a melismatic chorus with words. I'm not sure what the words are – I can't seem to understand their language – but I know they are somehow connected to my pilgrimage, to my destination.

I arrive at the gate and step inside. It is getting dark but not so dark that I cannot clearly see the grand mausoleums. The trees above are blocking out the stars but not the light which seems to come from all around. I approach the first mausoleum and see my grandfather's name, which is my name as well. I peer inside the stone house, hoping that I will find a memory, a vision, of the man whom I barely remember. I close my eyes and images flash before me like buckshot: leather, white hair, a tuxedo, a spittoon, an unremarkable face which seems neither kind nor malevolent. I feel I should say a prayer, but words do not come to me. Either this unknown old man is in paradise or hell or he's nothing at all; what good are prayers? So I slowly say the name etched above the doorway.

I move on to the next mausoleum and again look inside. And here the memories are stronger, and I am overcome, not only by images (thin arms, an open book, delicate hands pouring water over my head, a tear-covering embrace) but also words (darlink, where did I find you, can you feel the rhythm, boomlay boomlay boomlay boom, bewitched, entranced, fascinated, love, love, love, love). And now that the crickets have stopped, I think that that is what they may have been saying all along: love, love, love, love.

I look back into the mausoleum, but the images have changed (cold, white hand, anguished faces, a coffin, defeat) as have the words (no, not fair, why, be strong). And just when I think that the words have finished, they start up again, the crickets (love, love, love, love).

My whole life has been marked by death. But I'm surprised to find that acknowledging that, vocalizing it, is far from depressing. It was born with me – this death – grew alongside me in my mother's womb, was a constant guest even before it came to stay. I have become the man I am due to this unwelcome guest, this dark brother.

I lean over and kiss the cold stone and caresses the iron gating like a child would an aged parent. "Mommy," I say. I repeat "Mommy" again. The crickets begin again, stronger than before: love, love, love, love.

I can't remember the last time I was in Buck's Tavern, but it would have to be more than twenty years, when Gramps and I would sneak in during Grams' hair appointments. It has changed somewhat – a pool table has been added in the back and there seem to be more small tables than I remembered, all but four booths disappeared. But the most fascinating part – a giant brick wall covered with neon beer signs from floor to ceiling – has remained. Gramps always let me choose where to sit at the bar and I always chose that point where the bar curved around like a country lane, where the waitresses would come to drop off their orders and I could smell their perfume. They would flirt with me, tousle my hair and call me "darlin'" and "cutie" and I would revel in their attention, their touch, witnessed by the multi-colored wall nearby which bathed us all in its glow. "It's just like Christmas," I would say to Gramps, squinting my eyes and allowing the colors to blur and go gauzy. "Why Spark Plug, it's better than Christmas," Gramps would say, "because we've got beer and beautiful gals to boot. That sure beats the hell out of Christmas any day!" And then, to give me communion with that manly fraternity of racy words and secrets, he would offer a sip of his beer and I drank and watched the lights reflect off the beads on the bottle, making the blue ribbon on the label seem like a jewel. Then, when I was older – maybe thirteen or so – Buck himself would get a small glass from the mirrored shelf behind the bar and Gramps would pour me my very own glass. "I'll skin you alive if you tell your grandma or daddy," Gramps would say and I promised never to do so, sealed in that colorful conspiracy with my Gramps.

Although the tavern is crowded, there is a bar stool empty on the corner – my corner. Buck is no longer behind the bar. In his place there is a young man and an older woman (it took two people to replace someone so grand, I think). The man is young and has a shaved head and a neck tattoo, some vine-y looking thing that could either be an actual vine or some sort of calligraphy. It curls up to just behind his right ear, where it disappears into his hairline. He has three earrings. Neck tattoos and earrings! Bradington is not the same as it once was.

The woman is older – she could be the younger man's mother – and used to be quite pretty, I think. She is large and dressed in a way that makes the most out of her curves without them seeming lumpy. Her hair – died the color of straw in a children's coloring book – is tied up with a silver hairband that reflects the lights nearby, sparkling to be noticed. Her face is pretty but pinched; she doesn't seem entirely happy.

Next to me, on my corner, the very young waitresses are coming and dropping off orders. They notice me – I've still got it! – but they don't tousle my hair or call me sweet names. I smile at them – the half open-mouthed smile that I used to practice in the mirror – and they smile back. I see one point me out to the other as if to ask who I am.

The tattooed man with the earrings announces to his bar partner that he has to go change the Bud Light keg – she's on her own. She sighs heavily enough to be heard over the music playing and shouts "Hurry up – I've only got two hands!" She approaches the corner of the bar, looks at me and says, "What can I ... holy fuck!"

I look at her, trying to recognize her, but I don't. She obviously recognizes me.

"You don't know who I am?" she asks with a smile

that isn't really a smile but isn't *not* a smile at the same time. There's something in it that is familiar.

"I have a shit memory," I say lamely.

"Yeah, well, I don't exactly look like I did the last time I saw you. You – you stupid motherfucker – *do*. You haven't changed a bit." She leans on the bar in front of me, trying, it seems to be challenging and provocative. "No bells?" she asks.

"Sorry," I say.

"It's Linda Shamansky. You know: Jeff's friend? Do you remember Jeff?" She smiles again.

"Of course I do," I say half-smiling. "And now I remember you as well. My God – it's been such a long time. Wow. So you work here?"

"Buck was my granddaddy – I own this place."

"Sorry, yes," I say quietly. "I had forgotten. Sometimes I don't think I have too many functioning brain cells left."

"I can't get over how young you look," she says, "you're a little wrinkled around the eyes but that's it. What's your secret?"

"Well, up in the big house there's a portrait of me where I look like shit," I say smiling.

"Right," she says, confused. "Why the visit? Are you staying here through Thanksgiving? Founders Day? Doesn't your father usually take care of these things?"

"Yeah, usually," I say, "but he's had a little fall. Nothing serious – but just enough to make the festivities too much for him this year. So I'm stepping in. I've opened up the house and been staying there for a little bit. It's nice to be back."

"Right," she says, as if she doesn't believe me. I'm not sure whether I believe myself or not. "Well, what can I get you? I can't really chat right now. I'm temporarily alone back here and I can't ask any of these young bimbos –

237

that's right, I'm talking to *you* Lisa! – to help out because they'll just lean here and flirt with you, especially when word gets out who you are."

"Do you still have Pabst Blue Ribbon?"

"Does the pope shit in the woods? Fucking ay, we've got it. These young people all want microbrews and fucking cosmopolitans, but there are still enough of us around who were raised on PBR. I'd have never pegged you for a Blue Ribbon man." She shakes her head, like she doesn't entirely believe me.

"I first sipped it sitting right here," I say, "on this very stool, with my Gramps one Saturday afternoon. And your grandpa eventually started giving me my own glass. Right here," I repeat, emotion palpable in my voice.

"PBR coming up," she says, voice softening, a smile dusting her lips. And then, looking at one of the waitresses hovering nearby, watching them, she says, "Don't just stand there drooling, Lisa, hop behind the bar and get my old friend a PBR. I'm going to take a break now and catch up." She lifts the counter and brings a stool from behind the bar and wedges it next to mine. Lisa brings over two beers and sets them down, lingering longer than necessary.

"Oh, for Christ's sake, Lisa: keep it in your pants!" says Linda, shaking her head. Then, to me: "We don't get too many good-looking strangers in here."

"Well," I say, "I'm not exactly a stranger, am I?"

"Guess not," Linda says smiling. "You know who this is?" she says to Lisa, wiping down the bar in front of them. "Edward Bradington. Like in *those* Bradingtons. Like in this fucking town. And I was spying on him getting hand jobs in Bradington Woods before you were even a twinkle in your daddy's eye. We're old friends, ain't we, Eddie?"

"That we are," I say, even if I'm not sure about it at first. But sitting there, drinking that beer, the colors winking at me, I think that she's probably one of the closest things I've got to an old friend.

"So, Eddie," she says, pronouncing my name almost like a challenge, "we've heard a bit about you here and there. Fancy college. Law school. Big New York City boy. No boyfriend?"

"No, not really."

"Girlfriend?" she asks.

"Not really into girls," I say smiling.

"Well, a girl can hope, can't she? By the way, you're not alone here in Bradington now. My nephew there – the one behind the bar with all that shit on his neck – says he's bisexual. We've come a long way from when you and Jeff were the only boys who dabbled in that sort of thing."

"I highly doubt we were the only boys dabbling."

"You're right – I stand corrected. So you've never met the right boy?" asks Linda.

"Something like that," I respond. "Or I met the right one and things got fucked up. A long time ago."

"I was wondering how long it was going to take to get into that!" she says, clapping her hands in front of her. "Do you want the scoop?" She scoots her barstool closer to me; she is enthusiastic and conspiratorial.

"Of course," I say. "You two still in touch?"

"Well we weren't," she says, looking towards the wall of lights. "After everything happened, he really just sort of disappeared. I heard from his cousin every now and then who said he was doing well in school and all that, but then … I don't know … I just stopped caring. I stayed here, got married, was unhappy, got divorced, and I guess at the end of the day I didn't really want to know about someone who had got out of Bradington."

"Was it so bad living here?" I ask. "The place has its charms."

"I don't know," she says. "It's just, I don't know, not like you see people on TV living. Jeff was in California and then he got a good job up in Chicago and I think I imagined he was living like people live on TV. You know: nice clean homes, problems that get solved in an hour, great hair, no weight problems. That doesn't describe life in Bradington, that's for sure."

I think I should ask her more about her own life, ask if she is happier now, if she has children. But just thinking about Jeff, talking about him as if he is a real live person and not a ghost from the past, makes me *only* want to think and talk about Jeff.

"So, when did you get back in touch, then?"

"Three or four years ago. Facebook, of course. We wrote each other really long messages and caught each other up on our lives – like you do – and then we've been in contact here and there ever since. He has his own lobby firm – I have no clue what that actually means – and comes to Springfield a lot when the politicians are there. Oh, and he's not Jeff anymore, he goes by his given name, which was Geoffrey with a G. I'm not sure how Jeff with a J became Geoffrey with a G but there you have it."

"Have you seen him? Is he dating someone now?"

Linda smiles. "Slow down, partner! Don't tell me you're still carrying a torch after all these years? No, I haven't seen him. His family moved away from here years ago – after *it* all happened. We were supposed to meet up one day over in Springfield last year but there was a damned blizzard and so we had to cancel. I think he dates on and off, but nothing serious. He's really into his work, I think."

I take my iPhone from my pocket. "Here: get on Facebook so I can see his picture." I feel like a child.

"I can't believe the great Edward Fucking Bradington is acting like this!" she says, taking my phone with a smile.

Then, looking it, says, "I have no idea how to work this. Login with shamanchick@westerncoop.com. My password is 'buckstavern62.'"

"You really shouldn't give out that information," I say, typing on my phone.

"What are you going to do – rob me for all I got?"

"Could do," I say. We both laugh.

I click on her Friends page and scroll down to the J's. I don't find him and begin to panic, until I remember he's a G now. I find his name and click on it, and then click on his photo.

He is smiling, gently. Some people, I have noticed, put up very serious photos, as if to say that the world is not an easy place, but I'm doing my best. Some put up manic photos with exaggerated smiles as if to force the idea – true or not – that life is fun, and their lives – in particular – are to be envied. Some put up artistic shots of paintings or photographs or scenes from films as if to say that their lives aren't interesting or beautiful, but there are interesting or beautiful things to be found.

Jeff's – Geoffrey's – photo shows a beautiful gently smiling man. It is a smile that is sincere and tinged with just enough sadness to make it all the more attractive. His face is serene and interesting. If on my own face one can still see the presence of the boy I once was, on Geoffrey's I think I can somehow see the face of the man he has become. I know on a rational level that I am observing a still, flat image, but the more I look at it I can detect subtle movement, change. It is the simple face of one who is moving forward, mindful of the past but not mired in it. It is the face that I want to have as well.

"He looks good," is all I say to Linda, because I think – perhaps unfairly – that she wouldn't understand the epiphany of the photo, would probably tease and laugh at me as she used to do so many years ago. And then, because even though I want to be strong, sitting in that spot, drinking that beer, being colored by those lights, I know I cannot be strong, that in moving forward I have somehow magically moved back as well, which naturally weakens someone, makes them smaller. And so I ask, "Has he ever asked about me?" I hear my own voice as if from outside of myself. It is childlike.

"What are we – in high school?" asks Linda. She is teasing me again, but it's not so bad.

"I know – pretty lame."

"Nah," she says tousling my hair (finally, someone!), "it's cute. Yeah, he asked about you, but I didn't really know what to say to him. But maybe you can ask him yourself."

"What?" The lights are less gauzy, more brilliant.

"He's coming back for Thanksgiving and Founders Day. He's staying at the B&B on the square. He'll be here on the Wednesday afternoon. I'm sure he'd love to see you."

"Are you?" I ask, shocked by my own neediness.

"Beats me, really," she says, rising and dragging her barstool behind the bar. "But if he is glad to see you, and you're glad to see him, wouldn't that be cool? I'm not talking about you getting back together and getting married and all that, I'm just talking about two people who went through a lot in the past somehow coming out on the other side of it, like friends." She looks over to the wall of lights. Her face looks softer now.

"That would be pretty damned cool," I say, throwing some money on the bar and getting up to walk back home. I walk through the tavern feeling young, or, if not young, ridiculously filled with possibility, which is one of the best things about being young.

*

I'm not sure when the idea for the party came to me, but it won't let me go now, is constantly tugging at me like a beggar who will not be ignored. It is always a bit of a downer on Sunday when the Founders Day festival has ended; so I think why not invite everyone to continue up at the big house. If it's still like in years past most people in Bradington take that Monday off anyway; we could continue until all hours.

My father is not supportive of the idea. "What's got into you?" he asks incredulously on the phone when the subject is broached. "Do like I do. Make arrangements with the beer distributor and buy beer for everyone at the end on Sunday. I don't like the idea of complete strangers poking their noses in our business. Besides, if you really want to show the place off it needs to be renovated. It's an embarrassment the way it is now. If you want to have it redone, by all means, do so and then after the work is done you could have a proper open house, invite people down from Chicago, call the governor. But a last-minute thing thrown together for a bunch of hayseeds? It's just not right."

"Are you telling me that I am not allowed to have a few people over to a house which – correct me if I'm wrong – is really mine anyway?"

"A few people? You said you would invite the town, EJ. That's not a few people. I really don't know what's got into you. First you decide to spend your hard-earned vacation in that white elephant and then Leo tells me you brought some man with you who then quickly disappeared. Now you want to have a party for a bunch of people you don't even know. It's strange. What the hell has happened to you?"

"Well, Dad," I say, as always trying to imagine the father of my childhood on the other end of the phone, not the man he has become "I don't really know that anything has happened to me. It's just something I want to do. I wasn't asking for your permission or even opinion so much as informing you, making conversation. Remember when we used to talk?"

There is a silence on the line. I think that either my father is uncomfortable by my being what he would refer to as "all emotional," or he *is* remembering when we used to talk, when there was a connection of blood and story and love that flowed within and between us. Either way – uncomfortableness or memory – I figure it's good, it's something.

"You'll not find a reputable caterer for Thanksgiving weekend now," says my father.

I smile at the thought that in my father's world caterers can be classified into reputable and non-reputable. "I'll deal with that. Sure you don't want to come?"

"Eddie, my boy, that ship has sailed." There is defeat in his voice, it infects the phone line like a crackly virus.

"Maybe so. But it'll be great if I can pull it off, won't it? Just think, Dad: that place, *our* place, alive again, if only for a day." As I say it, I can imagine it: dark drapery pulled back, light streaming in like happiness itself, the great lawn adorned with a quilt of people and tents. The dead themselves brought back, joining in the revelry. "It'll be great, won't it Dad?" I say again, surprised to find I am weeping.

"That it will, my boy," comes the response, weak but happy, "that it will."

"Dad?"

"Yes EJ?"

"I love you."

There is a silence on the other end of the line, but not

the disappointing silence of apathy or the tragic silence of regret, rather the silence of revelation.

"I love you, Dad," I repeat because I do love him. And he needs to hear it, this audible manifestation of moving forward.

"I love you too," he says, and hearing him say that after so many years I think that going back ain't half bad either.

I am standing out front (which is really the back since the front sits on the bay) greeting guests. People are arriving stiff and formal, as if for a funeral. They seem unsure, hesitant, worried that they will make a mistake. They walk through the house with the detachment usually reserved for a museum, looking but not entering most rooms as if they were sectioned off by invisible red ropes. The formality, while understandable, saddens me.

I am not prepared for how alone I feel. Linda and Sister Frances Mary – the only people invited whom I personally know – have yet to show up. Some of the older people talk about my Grandfather Bradington, a few more about Grams and Gramps, but they are few, and so I am left standing there, shaking hands with strangers, while all the while looking around and trying to imagine the ghosts of my youth arriving. If I let my eyes go lazy and unfocused I can see them all, arriving in the golf carts that I've hired to bring people from the town: Grams, Gramps, Lorraine, Snickers, even that cross old maid of Grandfather Bradington's, Elsie, she with the Chiclet teeth. The living walking up to greet me don't seem to have that much life; maybe the dead will show them what they need to do.

Sister Frances Mary finally arrives, accompanied by a stern-faced younger sister who emanates disapproval. "Einstein!" she says, and we embrace. She smells like cedar. "Wowzy wow," she says looking up at the facade of the house, "this is one big place. Thanks for the invite. We're – this is Sister Patricia – as happy as clams to have been asked. Never hurts to have a little getaway, does it Pat?"

"No, sister," Sister Patricia says like she's reciting a multiplication table answer. "Where shall I put our bags?"

"Up the stairs to the second floor. First left and then all the way to the end. I've put you in the Governor's Suite. Al Capone stayed there."

"Interesting," says Sister Patricia, although the tone of her voice suggests she doesn't find it interesting at all. She walks into the house.

"A little tightly strung, that one," says Sister Frances Mary, shaking her head and taking my hand. I love the touch. "I brought her with me in hopes that she'll loosen up a bit. These young ones seem to be afraid to have fun. It's not like it used to be."

"Is it ever?" I ask, squeezing her hand.

"Probably not, Einstein, probably not. But we can always try, can't we? There's enough crap in the modern world as it is; doesn't hurt to try and bring back a little glory from the past, I say."

"You bet your ass, Sister," I say with a smile.

"You really shouldn't say ass, Einstein."

"And you really shouldn't say crap, Sister."

Hours pass and the initial formality has worn off; the house is alive as I had hoped it would be. In the main parlor some man named Butch has begun pounding out tunes on the piano while several people sing along, their voices a symphony of drunken joy. Francine Dennis comes up to me and gives me a big hug like an old friend and not just someone who gave me a lift in her car once. In the breakfast room a poker game has broken out, and I am not surprised in the least to see Sister Frances Mary among the players. In the main dining room foursomes are arranged along the long table playing euchre – some for money and some for apparent pride. The great lawn is filled with children playing soccer and teenagers are smoking and sneaking beers down at the boat dock. I stroll around and feel very much like Toad of Toad Hall, filled with satisfaction at the glittering gathering I have called into being.

I am sitting in the screened-in porch when I see him, illuminated by a string of lamps hung above one of the drink stations. I can see immediately that he is clearly now a Geoffrey with a G and not a Jeff with a J. His hair is much shorter than when they were young – maybe a bit receding – and he is not quite as thin as he was all those years ago, but he still looks good.

His face has changed very little. He is looking around the great lawn (for me?) and I can still clearly see the inquisitive look in his eyes, as if the world and all in it have been presented to him as strange gifts and he's trying to figure out whether they're precious or not. It is this visible gratitude mixed with curiosity that I have imagined all of these years, that I have frequently brought to mind (or that have been brought to my mind without my willing it, cropping up like wildflowers on the side of a country road).

I realize – perhaps for the first time since so long ago – that I have never left this Geoffrey, not really. Seeing him on the lawn (he is now talking to someone) I understand that I am not revisiting a face and a presence that has long been far away, but rather reveling in something that has always been quite near to me. I can't tell him – I won't frighten him off with my intensity – but I feel it nonetheless, this familiarity, this comfort. Is this the reason why I have not already rushed out to meet him, to speak to him?

Is it not perhaps more fulfilling for me to stand there, to tap into this connection I have always felt, rather than approach him and risk disappointment? Am I afraid of discovering, after all these years, that there is no real connection, that I have been fooling himself? That Jeff-now-Geoffrey is really just another of the ghosts that surround me?

I am afraid. I am also encouraged.

I leave the anonymous darkness of the screened-in porch and walk to meet him. I know you can't go back again, but I also know that I don't want to go back – not really. I want to move forward, forward, forward. And forward – in this moment – is directly in the path in front of me. I know that moving forward means encountering him and accepting the possibility that he has already, indeed, moved on. I think I'll know in an instant if this is the case, if he is like the ghosts who are now gathering around me, watching and listening, holding their breaths as they (and I) wait for Geoffrey's response.

With each step towards him the crowd of ghosts increases, and I am strengthened by their presence. "Come what may," they seem to whisper on the air, faint above the sounds of the living, "we are with you." And I know that I will survive – come what may – because of them, for they have always been with me, and they will not let me down.

Acknowledgements

The journey between Ithaca and Troy is about five hundred miles by land, meaning that if Odysseus had just walked, he'd have got there in maybe two weeks and not the decade (and thousands of nautical miles) that his trip would eventually require. A story – like a journey – is all about time, place, and the people one meets along the way, so I'm glad that Odysseus took the path he did so that we ended up with *The Odyssey* and not a travel pamphlet.

Though there have been some pretty awful battles along the way, I'm also glad I've taken the path I have. My journey with this book took longer (some eleven years) and the writing of it saw me move from Rome to the Costa del Sol to Norwich. I couldn't have made that journey without the love of my life Maurizio Farina, whose constant presence and support helped me hear stories in the midst of our own. He also patiently listened to me read aloud each chapter as it was completed (in a language that is not his own) which is pretty amazing (as he is pretty amazing).

Because I just sense that he would be most vexed to be excluded, I also need to say that I am grateful for my canine companion Linus who is constantly by my side and seems equally as enchanted with exquisite Norwich and its stories than I am.

I am thankful to my dear departed sister Kathy (to whom this book is dedicated) and friends Brittan Bolin and Mia van den Broeke who read the first version of this book and helped me believe that there was a story to be told.

I am most grateful for the support of editor and publisher Sam Ruddock who helped me make this story more authentic with his wisdom, patience, and diligence, and also for teaching this (somewhat) old dog new tricks so that I can be a better storyteller.

I am humbled by the love and support of my three wondrous church communities – St George Colegate, St George Tombland, and St Giles-on-the-Hill – and count myself fortunate indeed to be a part of them.

And finally, as I believe that we're all connected even after death, I would like to thank: my Gramps Lester Blankenship for teaching me the story's the thing and showing me how it's done; my Grams Mary Blankenship for showing me constant and intense love; my mother Shirley Lewis for sharing her love of books and words with me and teaching me how important it is to write things down; and my father George Lewis, for a lifetime of letting me know I was his pride and joy.

Thank you for supporting planet-positive, carbon positive
publishing

Story Machine seeks to have a net positive social and
environmental impact. That means the environment and people's
lives are actually better off for every book we print. Story
Machine offsets our entire carbon footprint plus 10% through a
www.ClimateCare.org programme. We are now investing in
converting to use only 100% renewable energies and seeking out
the most planet-positive means of shipping books to our readers.

The printing industry is a huge polluter, requiring the use of huge
amounts of water, toxic chemicals, and energy. Even FSC
certified mix paper sources drive deforestation. That's why we are
proud to be working with www.Seacort.net, a global leader in
planet positive printing. Not only have they developed a waterless
and chemical-free process, they use only 100% renewable
energies, FSC certified recycled paper, and direct absolutely no
waste to landfill. That's why they were crowned Europe's most
sustainable SME in 2017, and have been recognised as one of the
top three environmental printers in the world.

Planet-positive printing costs us a little more. But we think this is
a small price to pay for a better world, today and in the future. If
you agree, please share our message, and encourage other publishers and authors to commit to planet-positive printing. Stories can
change the world. They deserve publishers that want to make sure
they do.

Together, we can make publishing more sustainable.